War of the Lost Song

The Ruach Saga Companion Volume

Mark A. Cornelius

ISBN
978-1-959314-36-3 (Paperback)
978-1-959314-37-0 (eBook)

WAR OF THE LOST SONG

THE RUACH SAGA
Companion Volume

With Illustrations by
Shay Cavender

Dedication

Disclaimer: All of the characters in this book are fictional although their descriptions are influenced by real people.

"ONCE MORE THE LIGHTS QUIVER,
THEN DARKNESS RULES US ALL."

After the cataclysmic *Blanking,* what remains of the population of the former United States enters a chaotic struggle of survival. Elements of the remnants migrate to a hostile wilderness area which offers scant resources. Social order has broken down and every individual must fend for their own existence. Will humankind rise to the occasion and overcome their adversity, or is a darker scenario more likely?

As with any work of fiction I've attempted, I began with one concept in mind and by the end, discovered that the story had written itself quite differently. Still, the results are based on one of my "What If" explorations. The journey led down a path which has taught, and continues to teach me about the nature of our existence and the consequences of our choices.

What will society be like for those who survive the purported "rapture" suggested by some spiritual groups? Will our culture be radically altered by the circumstances? Will humankind rise to the occasion and overcome their adversity, or is a darker scenario more likely?

Any mass extinction event of the past suggests a period of upheaval where natural order is suspended, where the rules and the rulers change without regard to previous convention. Those who struggle to adapt must quickly choose how to exist and whom, or what, to follow.

In War of the Last Song, Two separate camps are highlighted. Each are shaped by their different heritages and their perceptions of the new reality. They ultimately confront one another, struggling through and adjusting to the complete shifting of social and physical norms.

This book is one that I did not set out to, nor desired to write—God had to convict me (a LOT) to see it through. My fear still is that my efforts do not match His desire, so I'll ask if you see any spiritual inspiration evident in the results?

Or, if you prefer, read this work from a non-spiritual perception, and consider the potential outcome presented. Either way, I hope you are challenged by the read, and just as do the characters in the book; discover a new way of perceiving the world and its occupants.

Enjoy,

The end of the matter; all has been heard. Fear God and keep his commandments, for this is the whole duty of man. For God will bring every deed into judgment, with every secret thing, whether good or evil.

—Ecclesiastes 12:12-14

PRELUDE

"CLACK, CLACK, CLACK…" echoes the gavel continuously as the cacophony refuses to subside. Moments earlier, I had wondered in a vacuum of muted voices. *What can any of us do?*

So unusual, this magnitude of meeting: The entire Congress of the United States, the Joint Chiefs of Staff, the executive branch, and a number of dignitaries, domestic and foreign; sitting in silence, watching three giant view-screens hoisted and rigged at the front of the congressional chambers. On the center screen, the Draggon-One, Darius Mede's dream-rocket telegraphs a report, through its myopic camera view, of its approach to V4641, known now colloquially as The Singularity. To the left, a shot of the *Dome of the Rock*—Al Aqsa Mosque—in Jerusalem, an iconic and familiar backdrop to most in the room. On the right, a very unfamiliar picture, nine people gathered around a long table, eating, and chatting as if this is some holiday gathering.

Occasionally, a muted voice is heard, someone questioning the purpose and protocol for all to be gathered, but for the most part, the anticipation and curiosity of the moment holds all of us speechless. No pomp, no circumstance, just waiting. To add tension, the doors to the chambers are guarded by numerous uniformed and armed bodies. I know they are there to keep threats out, but I wonder if perhaps there is an alternate purpose—to keep watch for any internal threat and restrain its escape from the confines of this place?

Below the screens sit the Speaker of the House and Senate, the Secretary of State and, in a break of tradition, the President, Gregory Bluewater substituting for the absent Vice-President who typically presides over any such an event as this. All of these but for the President, scan the room or fidget nervously, seeming ill equipped to the task at hand.

What is the task at hand? I only know that we have all been summoned here into what was described as an emergency session. There were and remain, rumors about a potential action designed to stop, even reverse the effects of the mini-quasar that has strangely encroached and parked on the edge of our solar system.

A handwritten note had been delivered to me earlier in the week, penned by Bob Cornet, the Senate Commerce, Science and Transportation Committee Chair. Its warning rattled me then as it does now:

Teagan,

> *This may be my last chance to talk to you. Be careful, lad, I'm afraid these will be our last days as a nation, much less as a civilization. Make your plans and make them well. Find a safe place to dwell and be ready to flee.*
>
> *As my intern, I have found your integrity is far and above that of the leaders you have served. I wish you well and am honored to have known you.*
>
> *Best,*
> *Bob.*

Bob is not at this gathering, but he should be! I can only hope he has found his own safe place. Constant seismic activity, cataclysmic weather events and volcanic confluence are now our norm. The planet is seeming to come apart, yet it survives. The one constant of it all is this common understanding—We are not in control of anything—the room is humbled and collectively unnerved at the revelation.

As if cued by my thoughts, a rumble from deep beneath us shakes the room, then subsides into spooked stasis. The rear section of the chambers abruptly erupts with commotion and frenzied movement. An all too familiar metallic clattering, like the sound of someone trying to crush nuts and bolts in a kitchen blender, permeates the room and grates in every ear.

It is a lone *Ripper*, so named for the damage the queer flying menaces do to the body and the brain. The moniker hardly does justice to the pain and chaos of the bites and stings the creatures are able to inflict and we have all had to adapt to their threat. Immediately, I pull the hood and protective mask of my bulky leather coveralls, over my head. It is a communal synchronized response performed instinctively by everyone in the space. We have all known the agony of facing the creatures without coverings and so all wear their *sting-suits*, as they have become known, at all times. We dare not risk even one poisonous incision from the evil creatures' fangs or tails.

The Capital Police manage to nab the flyer in a net after some effort. There is only one casualty, who is also carried out screaming incoherently. The reminder of the times does not help calm the charged atmosphere and tense circumstances. The distinctive scent of human perspiration, now ever familiar because of our smothering costumes, pervades more so in the anxiety of the moment.

Again, only one man seems at peace in the place. Gregory Blueroad, Commander and Chief of the country's armies and people, sits with hands clasped and eyes closed. He seems to be humming to himself. The tune is undistinguishable, but his whispered purr somehow comforts me, at least in part.

I glance at Secretary of State, Thomas Langard, whose increasing anxiety is palpable—a flame held too close to brittle leaves. He surveys the room with anxious eyes, sweeping right, left, right again, and then stands.

Removing his mask to be heard clearly, he states, "Alright. If no-one else has anything to offer, I'll do it. We can't just wait around, placing our hopes on a science project or hoping for some promised miracle by religious fanatics. We have got to take action!"

"And what action exactly do you have in mind?" asks a congresswoman toward the back of the chambers. "Hasn't everything you people suggested been tried? I wonder now if our predicament hasn't suffered by too much testosterone being released into the atmosphere. Perhaps if we had been more attentive to the motherly attributes of Gaia, our beloved home, then…"

"What in the hell are you talking about," explodes a four-star general now rising to his feet from the gallery. "After we have tried everything, now you claim offence by gender?"

"Wait," yells a voice from the balcony. "As a transgender, I insist on inclusion in this debate. For too long we've taken sides on what man or which woman is qualified to lead us and this is the direct result. We need to all come together by abandoning our physical distinctions…"

"—I object," joins in another.

Now the chambers are flooded with frustrations and pent-up animosities. The Speaker of the House's hammering on his wooden tool continues to impotently insist on order.

"CLACK, CLACK, CLACK, CLACK…"

"— People, please," a calm solitary voice somehow rises above din of the others. "I would like to offer you more." It is President Blueroad who is now standing next to the Speaker of the House. He has gently placed his right hand on that of other man to restrain the ineffective gavel-pounding. Blueroad's respected position and temperament does what nothing else can, slowly subsiding the clamor until the attention of all in the chambers is focused on his words.

"Cannot we stop for one moment? Cannot we pursue together, an understanding of our differences, to see what is happening, to peer at the larger mirror before us to consider what we? Cannot we strive to change into what we might be?" His tenor is fatherly-kind, imploring somehow yet encouraging. There are one or two in the room who try to polish the points they had been expressing to their nearby colleagues, but they are shushed to silence. Quickly, Blueroad is the center of our universe.

"Once, there was a dream. We fashioned a place built on a theory. We agreed that each and every one of us, not some or one of us, had an equal chance to better ourselves.

"We agreed that each and every one of us, not some or one of us, had the right to pursue life freely with a hope we might find individual satisfaction.

"We agreed that each and every one of us, not some or one of us, would honor the freedoms we held precious and that we would respect, not over-rule those freedoms when pursued by others who shared the dream.

"Though our individual beliefs and desires differed, in our agreement of our ideals, we were…united.

"Can we return to that place, even for a moment? Can we want together before there is no time left for our wanting?

"Join me, please, in that pursuit. Let us look passed the mirror to the horizon, where we abandon our selfish positions and instead walk together with encouragement for all we call our brothers and sister…"

"—I am neither your brother nor your sister, old man," yells another voice from somewhere unseen. "Why do you insist on labels that limit. I am freed from the gender prison and am offended by your terminology!..."

"—Yet you voted against my bill for abolishing the words, 'person of color' from being used in this room," rancors another from across the aisle. "If you are so offended, think how I feel being considered inferior because of my ancestry!..."

"—I'm sick of your class-warfare rhetoric, we just need to let each person live as they want and not worry about what others want…"

The conversations become a verbal brawl, the mirror of focused potential Blueroad pictured for us is shattered, his hoped-for horizon wiped away by the flurry of expressed opinions. I watch him watch us and then, he does something no-one is prepared to accept. He lowers one knee to the ground, then the other. His hands rise toward the gilded ceiling over the fracas and he shouts, "Father forgive us, for we know not what we do!"

Again, for a brief haunting moment, the room is silenced. Then a final anonymous attack is hurled from the middle of the mass, "Don't you dare spew your self-righteous spiritual quotes as if your god somehow has command over all, I…"

It is at this moment that the screens at the front of the chambers go static, the lights flicker and an indescribably piercing noise blares throughout the room, driving the rest of us to our knees, all cupping hands over ears to stop the deafening. Once more the lights quiver, then darkness rules us all.

Verse I

Then the LORD God made the man fall into a deep sleep, and while he was sleeping, he took out one of the man's ribs and closed up the flesh.
He formed a woman out of the rib and brought her to him.

Then the man said, "At last, here is one of my own kind—
Bone taken from my bone, and flesh from my flesh.
'Woman' is her name because she was taken out of man."

That is why a man leaves his father and mother and is united with his wife, and they become one.

—Gen 2:21-24

Ga'al:

THE SMOKE THAT SHROUDS THE CAVE entrance invites only the brave to breach its mysteries. I once considered myself courageous and strong enough. But now, I am finally who I once fought never to be: Finally, a mother, finally a wife—things I was called before, but they were titles only.

I desired greater things, now, I crave something simpler, something deeper. And on cue, my thoughts trigger emotions I have fought all my life to push away. I had declared them my enemies, and now they consume me in revenge. Moisture clouds my vision. *Stop it!* I command, but tears do not obey the weeping woman. They are both friend and foe wetting and working away the locks of the prison gates that hold back sadness or joy, grief, or gladness, setting free the rushing flow of my memories and emotions.

The tears tell only truth: I am not now who I once desired to be. But I am who I have always been meant to be. And that is not a fearless one. Instead, I am one who has hidden behind the guise of false bravado. I am not the one who should enter this place. I shiver in my newfound wrap of cowardice. No, I am not the one who should enter, but I am the only one available, the only one capable. I am compelled to cross the threshold and fearfully, my feet obey.

The muted light from the early day struggles to reveal the story of what has happened within these walls. A strange blue glow emanates from the two bodies lying on pallets. They give off more light than the ebbing fire, but their condition is evident, they have both been seriously injured. My weeping begins again. I have missed them. This place, and they who are here, need a mother's touch. Their injuries require immediate attention. But first; better light.

As I repair the hideaway and restoke the fire, much of their tragedy is illuminated. This had been both hiding place and sanctuary. Such distinctions are important. How long have they been hidden within? What drew them together and what kept them close?

I could blame myself for their condition, but it matters not. This is no longer about me. It is about them. Their wounds so deep, the story told by their broken lair, breaks me.

What or whom were they trying to avoid by camping within these confines? Strewn implements also speak symbolically. An old wooden spoon, and two pewter goblets placed carefully on a chipped clay dinner plate—primitive, but important to them. And curiously, a number of crayons, carefully wrapped in a piece of tattered burlap.

The burning wood of the fire nearly masks other embedded aromas— nearly: A faint odor of echinacea, goldenseal root and leaves of feverfew, also carefully wrapped; with them, a mortar and pestle. Healing agents I am very familiar with. Garlic and ginger root too, tint the air—I'm sure they are both for cooking and remedy. A small hide pouch lays beside the herbs. It contains a bitter clear jelly-like substance that smells of tar or licorice.

The victims had to have been treated by an apothecary of sorts. I examine the wound-care of the two that lay together on the straw bed, breathing shallow in their deep resting states. I know that another, not present now, must have administered to their needs before exiting the place. Will the one who fled return? The evident skills, the healing craftwork bears a familiar signature from remembrance past. I can't, I won't mention his name—even the memory of him rips at the scabs of my own inner wounds. But I do wonder whom he has passed his gifts on to?

Firelight dances on the cave walls and a new page turns of the occupants' tale. Images painted of events. Three circles intertwined with symbols etched within the intersections. An image of a ram's horn chills my spine; a stream of water by a cliff face; flocks of doves, and many others decorate this dwelling—all reminders of a recent past with which I'm all too familiar. And one other depiction—two armadillos, the prehistoric relics that in their own way deserve reverence, having served to save us as unique protectors.

Coincidentally my senses are brought to full alert by a rustling in a dimly lit portion of the cave. The sound registers in my brain and I'm put at ease, realizing that two of the unique shelled creatures roam freely and welcomed, in these confines.

I approach the noise to see if the armadillos have found prey, but if they have, the victim is long since consumed. At my approach, the guards scurry deeper into the recesses. My eyes adjust to the dim light in the cranny, and I catch sight of another object, an old square steel canister tipped over on the dirt floor in the same dark alcove. Also, there is a leather satchel, some sort of self-fashioned carrying case strapped for placement on one's shoulder. The contraption is slightly smaller than a compact suitcase. It might have once been used as what had been called a "carry-on" in the days when we breezed so casually over highways and rails and through the upper atmosphere in our amazing vehicles.

There is bulk to the case and on testing, I detect the weight of something within. Hidden treasure? Two other short straps buckle the portfolio's lip, and when undone, the satchel unfolds.

Inside, two sections; pouches holding paper. One side reveals a few pieces of unused paper. The other side, volumes of notes.

A shiver travels my spine. This is blasphemy within any tribe or clan. Words on paper, *parch,* have been forbidden to protect our future from our past. I am of the remaining few capable of reading such stuff. If these documents were tucked away in the dark, not to be easily detected by intruders, these victims knew their danger. The risk of scripting and hiding the pages alludes to their great importance. The disarray of the cave suggests that a quest to discover them may have possibly been the cause of a struggle which at least contributed to the wounds of the inhabitants.

Outside of the cave the wind rustles. I pause to discern if a draft of it will enter to challenge the fire or bring with it some other trespasser besides myself. This place is well hidden, and I am soon convinced it would take another strange voice or encounter such as the one that brought me here, to beckon another. Such a chance is remote. I remain wary, but after a sip from my canteen, turn back to my examinations.

I pull the written sheaves from the satchel and discover two distinct sets. One is in a more delicate hand and full of common language, raw, earthy as from one who has adapted new ways in the time after the *Blanking.* That term, now so common, still feels foreign to me. But to those I know who have survived, it best describes the mysterious disappearing of people, and radical changes in the planet's condition.

The other set of script is educated, from high schooling, with extravagant wording from another time I have tried to put behind me. The phrasing by the author brings history back, unwanted memories in a flash. Writing history and memories down had been forbidden. Reading it now reminds me why. I should end their lives without another thought based on what I see, but my commitment to that action is outweighed by…so much…not the least of which is my desperate desire to know their shared story, regardless of its rendering in forbidden calligraphy.

I can't stop myself. Glancing through, I do not read any dates or seasons—little wonder, the tribes and clans want little to do with the old ways of tracking, preferring now, a day-to-day measuring. Most folk have little hope in more than that.

But on further inspection, the pages from both sets of parch spell out similar tales, though of different minds and approaches. Sometimes they each seem to tell from the individual, sometimes in the later pages, they speak of same events: Communal, interlaced with impossible passion and intimacy. I decide that, to understand them properly, I must conjoin the tales as best possible. My cause will be to learn how these two, and the missing healer, came to be occupying this hideaway all together.

Stoking the fire once more I recheck each patient's wounds. Huddling close to the flames, I keep my ear tuned for unlikely intrusion from the outside. My focus, my interest, becomes the pages before me.

Ilona:

Red-Sacrifice is everywhere, on her jersey, sticky syrup on her arms and legs, dug into her fingernails, woven to her hair. Even from a distance, I can see the taint of it causing her nostrils to flair, firing her to hungry madness as she clubs the body before her.

"Is that what you wanted?" She screams at the carcass. "Was that worth it to you, *teso cur*? Where is your kingdom now, where have you gone?" Are you with the *Blanked Ones?*

No one else stands to stop her mania as she pummels the remains on the ground—her focus. The action seems good-right to all. Eventually there is a flatness to the job. The baseball bat, an efficient method for her duty, is no longer required and is tossed by her onto the pile of pulp at her feet. She does not respond to the clanging pots and hurrahs of the other she-dames. They sound their noise-flag in her honor, but she seems not tuned in to it. Turning, she makes her way straight through the door of the arena, to the oppressing world outside. I follow, knowing I will be needed in the aftermath. The warrior leans into the ever-howling wind, catching several long breaths of the dusty night air. It is not good-right refreshment; it is just an unhappy need. At least the atmosphere outside is less black than that inside the confines of the *Law House*.

Our Law House is an old pig killing plant. Part of its interior includes a large dirt oval surrounded by platforms we now use for gathering such as the warrior's most recent slaughtering moment. Our tribe is all about sport and judging of *wrecks* we capture. All men—any with parts 'tween their legs—are named this by Law House rules. Wrecks are what my mom-dame says they are to be called and so it is.

For wrecks who wander or hunt our direction, from their clans of the Black Mountain caves, this is their doom-place. It would be good-right for them if they had taken their own knives to themselves rather than to be brought here. When Aella the warrior demands a trial, this is the place of it. We camp near it, not by or in it because it stinks of death.

"Too many sacrifices", she mumbles as she gathers her calm. I think it with her. *Too much pain in the pleasure of ending the lives of those others. Why do we enjoy the rush of ending another, so much?*

What is to come of all this? I can see the question in her distant gaze of fatigue. It shows in her slouched shoulders. There is no victory in her stance as she pulls her battle-tatters over her head and tosses them thoughtlessly to the ground. There is scant water to cleanse herself, the precious river liquid is guarded good-right for food cleaning and drinking. Washing after a sacrifice is lawed as a poor use by the warrior herself. 'Stead, she squats, grabs handfuls of dirt and scrubs it into her skin, making her look like some old pics from the afore-time that I remember from a book—pics of hunters in distant mud-lands, all covered in white dust, looking like ghosts.

Aella is our head warrior-dame, and she is my mom-dame. My mom-dame is a force, standing taller and straighter than any other dame or wreck I have ever seen. She has focused whatever spare time she can manage on working with and lifting heavy things and body-martialing, so that she is muscled-up. Now she turns her head in my direction, grins in her sad way at me and motions me to her. I carry her ways by name. I also carry a fresh pair of wears—leggings and her safe-leathers to replace her battle-tatters. I think myself to be as ravaged as the rags which she now swaps out. We all are ravaged; we have lived so much, too much. We are the tatters of a once pretty place. This is the last time I will see her, so I must burn her to my memory. She knows nothing of my intent, or of the dark things I have done. If she knew of it, I would be the next in the Law House to taste her sacrificing. There is no longer good-right in our history together, only what we each do to live a day more.

I will walk away as my mom-dame walked from the old way. Mine will be a new trudge, in search of a new destination. She and I are really no different—neither of us willing to re-think our purpose in this place.

There are surprises in all walk-aways; in all of breathing,: mine is yet to be told. Re-clothed, my mom-dame pulls me to her, into a hard embrace, then puts me at arms-length to examine me and my full growth, looking me up and down and then telling, "Seven and ten years. How can it be so?" She for the first time I remember, tugs my head by the hair, close to hers, kisses my forehead gently (nothing ever she has done has been gentle) and whispers in my ear, "Go do what you must."

For a breath's time, I am not sure of my plan. What is it I wanted my next walk to be? Is it good-right? Yes, my mind is set. This is the end of us. The new is near.

Teagan:

Where am I? I can tell you that it used to be the western region of what was once called South Dakota in the United States. I learned a great deal about the plains people of this area from the last President of that former union. Gregory Blueroad made it part of his mission to educate his congressional counterparts on the treaty abuses heaped upon his people, since the time of the country's western expansion.

Now however, who once possessed or who owned the land is a pointless argument. The geography itself has been as radically changed as have the politics and society itself. Where millions thrived, now only thousands roam. Vegetation and animals for food are so scarce that their discovery is best kept a precious secret for risk that others will claim, steal, or kill for what was not fairly gained by honest efforts.

With the appearance of *The Dark*; what survivors now call the V4641 mini-quasar, the familiar became unfamiliar. No former natural rules, laws or order can be depended upon, and surviving the unpredictable nature of things has become the biggest challenge.

Do you notice how the changes even show up in my attempts to describe the circumstances? So many "UN" words—UN-familiar, UN-predictable—better describe our new existence. It's like a phrase I recall from past days, NON-dairy creamy, which described more of what wasn't than of what was.

Here's two more for you. The UN-known came at me in a completely UN-expected manner. Upon the disappearance of the masses and the vanishing of electrical current, mine and the plans of the other Washington D.C. leadership became moot. There had been a contingency option in place to move everyone to an isolated region of Virginia, but chaos made a coordinated move UN-doable.

And one more UN from the past—Faith. I've lost mine. Honestly, now I can't accurately explain what the word meant before. Sure, there's the dictionary definition; *belief in the UN-seen*. But if it can't be seen, does it really exist? Now I'm convinced that whatever I had faith in before *The Blanking*, never really "was" at all.

And that's another one. The Blanking? Everyone left calls it that, but what does it mean? Millions, possibly billions of people disappeared in the blink of an eye. Electrical power became an invisible wish. Blanking doesn't explain it, but it certainly describes what happened as well as any words can.

I think my parents were *blanked,* I don't know. There is no way to reach them. But I don't "feel" like they still exist. That's the only way to explain my current perceptions. It is clear that many other relatives and my friends who resided nearby my location in Virginia, were blanked.

I searched, and am certain they would have searched for me, were they still… here.

And weirdly even as I describe these events, I know my emotions are blanked. I have trouble remembering the idea of "happy". "Sad" is just an everyday thing and so describing it is…UN-useful.

I was raised in the Midwest, so it makes sense to make my way back to find any family. There is no other way to establish who still lives in this bizarre reality. One of the caravans of others searching for their own past legacies, allowed me to join up. I am aiming toward the Dakotas where my origins began. I don't know and am UN-caring where the rest of my fellow travelers are aiming. We travel in the same direction together because there seems to be safety in numbers.

In my head I have a well oriented map of the roadways across the continent. What I had not prognosticated is how the map, when now viewed through my eyes in real-time, is radically ripped and torn to shreds. Roads, bridges, landmarks, all literally thrown about and rearranged as if by a toddler's playful hands. Many features and memories have physically disappeared as if never having existed at all.

The topography has been so altered, that it is life threatening just to navigate and negotiate the new landscape. Damaged structures, the constant quakes and shifting, storms, and UN-friendly gangs are all likely to end us. Sinkholes and attacks by wild animals competing with humans for survival have decimated our numbers as we struggle through UN-inhabitable lands hoping for answers that most of us know will turn out UN-favorable.

All of us march, or more accurately trudge in dull-minded fashion, without conversation, without relation other than pursuing some more favorable destination that might support us with food and water. Everyone is weighted down in whatever version of a sting-suit they have fashioned and from an outsider's perspective we must appear as some strange animal herd roaming aimlessly along in hopes of better grazing. The metaphor is not far off. As we roam our erratic path, every mile washes away another piece of human dignity and cooperation. Our sense of community has devolved so much that by the time we reached what remained of Chicago, the rule was no rule at all.

Rather than try to fit in with one of the developing gangs, I have chosen to slide off into seclusion. Somehow, I have made it to the area I once called our homestead. There are only a few remnants of the farm that exist. Yes, my parents, uncles, aunts, cousins, neighbors, are gone. They had not left by conventional means; it's like the terrain itself has swallowed them. It is evident by the way vehicles and farming implements are randomly strewn, that they had been in use, and then they suddenly…were not.

I have come to the rockface-end of my search. Everything, and nothing in this bleak field that once had been my home, is familiar. Every path I see before me leads to more…nothing. I have nowhere and no one with whom to share my despair. And with that hopelessness as my sole companion, I surrender to the darkness of my dreams.

Waking with the miserable dusty-warm morning light, I heard a rustling nearby and thought maybe it was an animal large enough to grab me by the neck and perform its final mercy by consuming me. I had fallen to sleep under a partially collapsed barn wall, half hoping it would crumble the rest of the way and finish me along with it. But I had survived the night, and instead of death, a large boot, then next its match, appeared standing directly before the lean-to.

From my angle, still cocooned in my bedroll, I was not able to peer up to see who was wearing the boots. I could however sniff the increase in body odor from more than just this one human nearby. It warned me that I was outnumbered and to be cautious of making any unexpected action that might cause an offensive action on their part. A carved wooden walking stick took its place alongside the boots. The staff then lifted and struck the side of my shelter, banging loudly and repeatedly. Had I been asleep, it would not have let me stay that way, A man's strong base voice added to the clamor.

"Are ye dead down there?"

An interesting question for certain. I actually had to think about what the voice had asked, and while I thought, two other pairs of boots joined the first.

"Leave him, he's obviously given up."

I wanted to agree with the second voice, which was a little more tenor in tone, but nearly as formidable in sound as the first.

"We need all the bodies we can muster; ye know that. I don't care if he's blind and deaf, long as he can walk and hold an auger," said the bass.

A sigh came from the tenor and the second boots shifted. Two bent knees appeared. Arms came in and grabbed me, pulling me out and back into the world I thought to escape.

I squinted through caked unwashed eyes, to see a group of heavily armed men surrounding me. They laughed easily and joked to one another at the sight of an awkward boy-of-a-man, clutching his sleeping bag about him and trying desperately to keep his balance while his feet were still trapped within the bottom of the bag. I failed, beginning a slow-motion descent ending with a face plant into the dirt. My new companions laughed louder now at my comical prostration.

At first, I thought this gang to be a spinoff from the travelers I had been with. But that perception was quickly corrected. The bass showed himself to be an extremely well-built man. His skin was midnight-gloss and his head was shaved to the quick. His sting-suit was all black as well.

I had to crane my head upwards to meet his stare—he stood at least six and a half feet tall. In return, he considered me with a penetrating stare. Apparently coming to a conclusion, he raised and lowered his staff quickly in one pounding motion, voicing a command which was quickly and efficiently carried out. "Clean him off."

One of the other men picked me back up—one handed—and with his other hand helped dust me off as I wriggled from my wrap. Then I was held stationary by him and another man as I was reviewed by the one I assumed to be their leader.

Next to the black man, stood his slightly shorter comrade. His skin was deeply tanned. His protective clothing was all green camouflage, and he sported a billed cap of the same coloring beneath his hood. The cap shaded a pair of intense grey eyes that never seemed to blink. Everything about him shouted "army" or "marine" and "precise". He could have easily grabbed and tossed me well away as discarded trash. Instead, he commanded another man beside him, "Give him some rations and water, he can eat it along the march, we still have a long way to go."

His was the tenor voice.

I looked around, still in half-stupor, to see thirty or so other men. Some are in similar garb as their leaders, others in leather, flannel, and denim sting-suits; all seemed organized and endowed with energy, unlike me. At his orders, they each began to check backpacks and gear in a routine they obviously had rehearsed. How had they come up on my shelter so silently? This was a trained group, familiar and comfortable with regimen and taking orders.

There was no arguing, no further consideration of their cause or my condition. I was provided food, duty, and direction by several of the other men and it was simply assumed I was now among their ranks.

And that was how I came to be a part of my clan; how began my respect of, Matada, our *Clansmen leader*; and equally, how my fearing of our commander, Zeke the military *Overseer*, commenced.

Before we headed out, another unique individual appeared far out in the field of rocks to our right.

"Matada, Monk's back," said a man with binoculars to the black robed leader. He then took up his own field glasses and scouted the one who approached. The men all waited until the mystery man arrived. He went immediately to Matada and affirmed as they both now stared directly at me, "You were right, this one made it on his own, and there are no others tracking him. He must be worth something to have survived this long."

I had not been asked what I was doing here, or if I wanted anything to do with this group. Several miles into our march, the Monk came up beside me. He was of medium build and his was a smooth flowing silent gate I have not observed stepped-out before or since, by any traveler. *Arrogantly humble.* That's the concept of him that began to form in my mind as I grew to know *Portunus*, the name with which he later introduced himself to me and that I came to call him.

His garb was Arabic in style; a white silk thawb with its accompanying kufiyah head-dress. The robe was tailored with a hood and I watched as he reached within the garb, to extract from one of a number of concealed pockets woven into the lining, a container of water which he offered to me without a word. I gratefully accepted the drink and returned the flask. As he reopened his garment to return it to its proper place, my eye caught site of other pockets which seem to contain various wilderness tools along with vials which he later described to me as medicinals, potions for healing and survival.

The man did not appear middle-eastern by descent. I had experienced much of that culture through the diplomats that frequented the congressional halls of Washington. The way of him was distinctive in these desolate times. He carried himself with confidence and there was a clear demeanor of well-being to him. That was strange enough, but it was his skin coloring that distinguished him from all others I had ever met. The man's complexion was not black, nor white, nor the darkened tinge of an Arab or American plainsman. He literally glowed with a pale, yet unmistakable blue aura. And the reason I could determine this was because he walked about without a sting-suit as if there was no apparent danger in doing so!

Portunus began our conversation, "Don't question anything you see here. What is happening will become clear to you as we journey. If you are asked to do something, do it. If you are told not to do something or be silent, obey. If you survive these simple rules, you and I will have a conversation later."

With that spoken, he walked to the front of the caravan and took his place by the side of Matada with Zeke. They entered into an easy conversation as they ambled together. The black leader seemed intent on the Portunus' words. He kept his head cocked in attention, nodding now and again as if in agreement. Several times the dessert scout apparently threw in something of amusement and both men would erupt in laughter—once, Matada even gave the other man a manly back-pat as they shared communion.

I also watched Zeke's reaction to the friendly banter. His shoulders stiffened at every guffaw, and I began to suspect a rivalry between the military clansman and the monk, regarding the attentions of Matada.

Ilona:

Hurry is not a good-right word for me. It was taught to me under bad circumstances. *Deliberate* is so much more the word for my approach. Slow and silent has become my existence.

But first I learned, "hurry". My mom-dame was a big hurrier, even before the Blanking. I couldn't hurry enough for her. When my brother was newborn, it made her hurry even more.

So, I taught myself to be still. I tried to disappear by stealing away within myself. Slow and silent, that is my domain. And that caused me to prefer watching before doing.

My dad-wreck showed me much of what it was to watch. He and I watched together, lots of times with no words. When we did use words, it was for stories. My dad-wreck was good-right at stories. He made us both laugh and cry and sing and dance. We became others; we became whoever we wanted to be in the moment. But the greatest thing he taught me, even above watching, was smiling. His smile was the best lesson of all. He said, "find your smile in the things that are before you.

I found many things that made me smile, inside and out. I especially liked crayons. Picting with the coloring wax was very good-right to me, and crayons had an *add* to them—they smelled best of all things. Crayons colored my world soft and loving. I used my crayons lots to color the stories my dad-wreck taught me how to speak out for the two of us to share.

I colored and smelled everything through crayons, even my folks. And I colored what I saw, things that my folks tried to hide from me, but failed. They battled. They were not likers or lovers of each other. I drew them, when they were together, mostly in black.

Then came the Blanking. Nothing was good-right after that—not even crayons. It was just after my fourteenth birthday. My mom had hurried to have a party for me and my dad was there watching with a smile. I wanted it to last slower. Now there are no parties anywhere—slow or hurried.

Aella:

There was a different thing then; an archaic concept called the nuclear family. It involved two very opposite characteristics, some confused it by connecting it to physiology and lineage—female and male, parents, and children. Ridiculous. Community does not bear any resemblance to those ancient precepts now, nor should they…

Or should they?

I hate my thoughts— Ying and Yang; reversals that stoke a fire of conflict within. I will not be a victim of nostalgia. But to fight it, I must confront it.

So, there was a time when I was a participant of that old culture. When women and men deeply bonded—when children were shared by both. When sexual and social identities were more clearly agreed upon. My husband and I committed to one another, even as we recognized and tried to respect our differences. We shared much, including the birth of two beautiful children: a girl and a boy. The pain and joy I felt at their arrivals into the world started an interesting chain of thoughts for me personally— *had I been the one that worked harder to bring them forth, because I bore them through the pregnancy and beyond the womb?*

I can even admit now to those being special times of sharing. Nurturing the two siblings, play and school times with them. Caring for them in sickness, feeding them food and ideas. We joined in those pastimes and duties, somehow balancing family time with our work duties. But I believed mine was the superior role, as mother, I thought it my duty to rule supreme over the family. But if that was the case, then why did I yearn more and more for my career outside of the home? How proud I was of my ability to maintain equity. How naïve I was to believe I had achieved parity, not only for myself, but for all of us.

I taught and researched pathogenic medical treatments through the university medical center and my spouse pursued a doctorate in religion. This is the topic that started causing our arguments.

At first, we tried to protect Jessica and Caiden from our disagreements, but as the children grew towards awareness, I felt compelled to outline my beliefs for them. This furthered the rift between their father and me. He felt I was not encouraging them to make up their own minds on the subject of spiritual entities—specifically a superior entity.

And he was not wrong. I felt the idea of being subject to a higher, yet unseen authority arcane and insulting to my sense of science. I did not want our offspring polluted or influenced by such nonsense.

Still, we put up the "good front", frequently taking the children on camping excursions, embracing, and honing our shared love for the natural. We became indeed, quite adept and fancied ourselves survivalists, bringing along fewer and fewer accessories on each excursion. We learned to build our own shelter, fashion cooking tools, and find food in the wild. My mate even became somewhat of an herbalist and medicinal aficionado, treating us for the occasional bug sting, settling upset stomachs and fevers; even setting one broken bone in the wild (my right arm when I took a fall into a sinkhole). He became indeed a better practitioner than I.

We watched and participated actively in our children's growing up. Jessica, the oldest, had always been withdrawn and it took special coaxing to get her to emerge from her private world. John seemed to have no trouble engaging with her and I wondered often if I was the problem, if I had chased her into her self-made cocoon.

Jessica had just reached puberty prior to the Blanking and had an incredible imagination which inspired so many strange questions: *Why do some people seem to care more than others?* And *where does the world go to when I dream and what happens to my dreams when I wake up?*

Interestingly, she seemed drawn more to her father as a mentor than to her mother. She even made-up languages which the two would then drama-speak, to play out imagined fantasy worlds where they would conquer all foes who pursued them.

Since those two seemed so deep into their own dream-world, I became far more enamored with Caiden. I taught him the order of things, encouraging him to consider alternatives to traditional roles of males and females along with our own fantasies of utopia where no one had unaddressed needs or problems of any kind.

All of those things kept John and I committed to our shared universe. But as time progressed, it was our deep seated and diametrically opposed ideologies that frayed us to the splitting of our cosmos. On one occasion I attended a lecture at the school of physics presented by Darius Mede himself. At that time, he was not as well known, having yet to become the world's *Premier,* but his presence and intellect even then were compelling and unmistakably alluring to me.

He consulted at the university for a month which allowed us to share insights and I was quickly won over by his positions on social order. He argued that women had been forced throughout history to be subservient to their male counterparts; human eugenics can and should be chemically altered toward obtaining an improved genome; that there are those genetically destined to lead and those destined to follow. He painted a secular and scientific picture of each human having the right to purge any impurities from their bodies and minds, regardless of the effect on other humans or lesser forms-such as a fetus.

There were many other topical issues on which we resonated, including the right of a governing body to assume protective control over a populace that does not realize its self-destructive tendencies. We even came to the agreement that speech is perhaps the truest pre-indicator of future actions based on individual thoughts and therefore should have strict limitations placed on its dissemination, lest others be misguided into action by harmful positions.

I can now see clearly how his mindset led to his rise in popularity and power. His influence convinced me beyond a doubt that women were victims of a flawed structure. I not only became convinced that I was equal to my husband, but as I watched John's behavior and heard him speak out his beliefs, I began to think myself the more logical *superior* in our relationship.

John continued to encourage our family to attend ritualistic services that recited devotion to a god and that insisted on obedience to a patriarchal order. I endured the exercise for a while but reached a breaking point just after the first disturbances began which were found to be related to the appearance near our solar system, of the Singularity known as V4641.

My husband insisted then that we take more opportunities to attend the dismal church prayer services that encouraged confession of our "fallen state" and a purging of our broken attitudes. I did not consider myself in any way broken, being more convinced than ever that humanity was in charge of its own destiny. John became more and more rigid in his ritual devotions, and I could not convince him that he was sacrificing the opportunity for personal relationship in trade for a strictly legalistic approach to supposed redemption.

Then the terror struck. The physical constructs of our planet unraveled before our eyes. The ground shook more and more, the sky darked daily, the very essence of life became uncontrolled chaos. Friends and colleagues died by plagues, famine, and mayhem and so John and I tried once more to unite to save our family. We had begun to gather foodstuffs and essentials necessary to endure a long-term catastrophe.

Most important of all, we were taught by nature's cruelty, an entirely new medical practice and dress code. If any of us dared venture outside, we were relentlessly attacked by vicious flying monsters, bugs as large as a fist that would bite and sting without mercy. Fortunately, the children never experienced a wound, but John and I both were introduced to the agony. It was by John's wilderness training that we discovered a slow healing cure-of all things, tobacco wetted with saliva and applied directly to the angry welts as quickly as possible.

The dress code de jour? Leather, everywhere, head to toe. Fortunately, we had ample supplies in our wardrobe and I, having some skill with tanning and medical suturing, fashioned protective wraps for all of us.

Meanwhile, I tolerated my husband's monotonous prayers, and I privately hoped on the efforts of Darius Mede to reorder the universe. John, I, and the children huddled in the confines of our reenforced home. Together we watched the strange goings-on: digital images simultaneously broadcast of the El Aqsa Mosque, the Draggon 1 spacecraft traveling through the cosmos, and a room of self-righteous god-worshipers congregating together in a place then known as Texas. I could not fathom how the three scenarios had been selected to be projected together and so I focused on the spacecraft, having much confidence in its designer.

It wasn't until the mosque began to rattle and fall and the room of chanting people began to glow blue that my attentions were altered. And then, in the moment the lights went out and I suddenly stopped hearing the laughter of my seven-year-old son, Caiden, I realized the cruelest reality of all. We had all been doomed to fail.

Verse II

The darkest sin is that which pleases only me.

—Portunus

Ilona:

I REMEMBER LESS of the days afore the Blanking than those after. There were tussleings back then but compared side-by-side to now, it was a good-right dream-like time. My fam lived all together, and I was schooled in a place called St. Mark's. My folks taught me too, sometimes my grand-folks and even my great-grand-mom had important stuff they thought I should ponder. Their stories grew my story, but now much of the story is disappeared, along with all the fam, teachers, and friends who were blanked too quick.

All I have now are brain-pics of things that used to work but work no more: Motorized cars that carried us from one end of a land to its other side, mountain sized boats and winged ships of the air, named *jet planes* that floated us to all points on the planet. And even powerfully loud engines called rockets that let some folks travel in black space. *Sparking,* what my mom-dame still calls electricity, was blanked too. It used to light and power the inside and outside of places for all folks. We used other things we called *conveniences*—washing machines, hair dryers, toasters, and ovens.

Best of the conveniences were the computers—desk-computers, lap-computers, and hand-computers. There were even computers called smart phones that let people all over the world talk to each other. All of this sounds impossible now (even to me as I scratch it out!) but it was true afore. The computers let us open windows on a screen which took us to places where almost any pondering could be answered. Most all folks were able to go places without ever moving. I could view other folk's pics that they had made, just by clicking a button or two on a keyboard or on a dial-pad. There were things called *texting, social-media,* and *email*; mysteries sent secretly through some invisible net. The net caught every mind-pic of anyone who wanted to share with any other folks. It was tough to choose what was the best folk-pondering and pics, but I was free to find and share any of it, and to share my own pondering too.

There were other things, in and out of the net, I was free to grab. There were so many answers to so many ponderings, and I could choose the one I liked best, even if other folk didn't like the same answer. We could all read and hear tales called *history* 'bout old places and old folks, or get new stuff, even food, with something called *money*. The computers made impossible numbering possible and finding almost any want was easy. Some computers even helped make sick folks well.

Another convenience, that I miss now, were screens called televisions and giant screened story houses called movie theaters. These screens pict not-real-stories. These stories moved on the screen and were so good-right that they seemed real. There were some folk, called reporters, that spoke out and scratched what was named *news*. Other folk spoke out and scratched that the news was not-real. Real and not-real news was blasted all over through the computers and smart phones and on parch-sheets call papers. The blasts *carroted*—my word for coaxing—folks toward believing and obeying some power-person's way of believing and ordering things.

I come from *class*. That's what *Shorters*—*we* who weren't old enough to grasp-well what happened in the Blanking—call well-off folks. My fam was book-smart and had no complaining 'till the *Blanking*. One day, we spun around with lazy brains on this blue planet: Next day, the sky-hole or quasar or whatever they were naming it, showed up close by in the dark sky. It had a want. What it wanted was us: Some of us anyway—a big lot of us. And lots took that carrot.

I know my scratching 'bout all of this will confuse other Shorters, 'cause most are trying to forget the old things and ways. Me too, but there are things and ways I can't forget: like the *Pointers*. They were always saying how we all should ponder 'bout their god, always pointing to their book and their ways. Always trying to fix others, trying to fix their own fam and folks too; as if no one was going enough, or hurrying enough; never doing enough; making everyone feel like no one was living enough.

And one day, the Pointers weren't. This part I don't know how to pic good-right. There was already a mess with the throwings-about of the planet. *Sciencers* said gravity was "messed with" by the sky-hole, starting things to shake and rattle and shift all the time. It's the same now, but it wasn't the same afore the sky-hole showed up.

What a good-right place this used to be! By good-right, I mean real good. There were green things everywhere; trees, plants, grass; we had plenty of what are now not plenty at all. There were things to pick too: Berries, tree fruit, and bush meat. All of this eating and the breathing, and smellings; were delicious; not like the choke weed, vipers and scrub bugs we live on now. There used to be other critters, 'sides us—all kinds, not just the tiny stinging crawlers of now. There were big and small, four footed and two. And the water! Oh that. How can I even say the gleam of it, the taste and drip of it: Not like the rough, muddy stuff of the wild rivers or the acid-ooze from the ponds of now which need hard cooking afore it's even touched, much as drank.

The dark blue hole in space blanked all things from afore. Lots of she-dames say we did not fight hard enough to keep things green and that the Pointers somehow took the green stuff with them at the Blanking. It makes no sense; no more sense than how a space hole can *carrot* folks away from a spinning rock, I have no good-right words for it. But I'm scratching it out as real; real as anything I grasp, that is.

After the Blanking, there were no babes and no little-folk. They were blanked with the others. My mom-dame, she has words for it and for all things that survive now; it's her grasping of it all; her rule of it. She says in her strong way, that she grasps answers which we other dames can only guess at. But I've come to doubt her grasping. I can't say such things out loud though; that would be death.

That's why when she touched me tender, I almost fell back away from her; I was fearful it was a carrot-trap. She does that, tricking you into showing your inside thoughts. We dames are all 'bout *folk-pondering*, thinking together as one brain—everybody walking the same walk, heading the same way—following my mom-dame's *self-ponderings* and believing her belief. That's how we live on...so far.

Teagan:

He was more cat than man, I think. Not one to talk, but to observe and then strike when none were watching. What was his purpose, who were his prey? I couldn't tell but admit selfishly, that I feared it was me he might be after at any given moment. I had to watch back, being ready to flee because he was stronger and better suited to this place and time. Fighting would have been futile had he decided to come after me.

But as we made our way through the Dakota badlands toward the *Barrens* (what I overheard Portunus call our ultimate destination), Zeke never did assault me. That was the upside-down of it. He always greeted *his troops,* as he called us, with a cunning smile, like a wizened hunter-animal who could pounce at any time but seemed to be waiting while letting his prey fatten themselves to just the right size; whatever "right" was.

I wondered when the moment of my personal doom might be. As I watched and wondered, I too observed, taking in the behavior of others around me—those who Zeke might choose to consume. Maybe I had less to fret about than those others, maybe not. We were all the "waiting", all a potential meal.

My thoughts were naively allegorical. I reasoned there was no real physical threat. I noted that each clan member had skills: each had drive. Well…most had drive, and Zeke's purpose seemed to make sure no-one shirked their responsibility so that he might feast upon their abilities rather than their failings.

Then a real-time example changed my perspective. It involved a younger man, Justin; just past the age when he was expected to join in work rather than be told to work. He apparently believed himself above the strains of day-to-day toil, tending the land or trapping meat. He did not seem prone to build or to clear for building. He was often seen wandering off to be alone instead of joining in the fixing of the day.

I saw Zeke follow him out of the camp one day. Upon returning, I noted the older man with bloodstains on his arms and legs. Later Justin came limping back. His face was badly bruised, but no other wounds were obvious. He did not wait to be told but found work to be done.

Each place where we stopped to camp, a set of *noise-traps*—old tin cans connected around our perimeter by barbed wire and secured with wooden polls—were hammered into the ground. This was tedious work that no one relished. Justin began *working-the-wire* (as setting up the alarm system was called).

I realized that just by standing idle in my observations, I might be the next example to be made, so I jogged over and immediately began to help Zeke's victim. By the time the sun began to set, we both suffered the typical wire cuts to our hands with quiet anguish.

Obviously, Justin, and I by his example, learned quickly. If someone decided they deserved the luxury of idleness, or if another's value to the tribe became diminished, or worse, if any were injured or infirm from age; those were the ones who needed to worry. Their starving threatened Zeke's well-being. In their deterioration, they became his caca to be discarded. It was a lesson that only had to be learned once— Zeke was a very effective teacher.

Aella:

Darkness is all I know now. Darkness is my comforter. There is nothing to live for, yet I live. It means that the purpose of humanity is exactly what I had perceived it to be...

—*do to others before they do to you.*

That is a twist on something John believed in once and so it is fitting to throw it back at him. If only he could now hear the depth of my despair and resentment.

I groped around in that earliest darkness. What was I to do? My son was taken away; my daughter a stranger who seemed more my husband's prodigy project—both of those who survived, now worthless in my eyes. I retreated into my dark thoughts. I left the dealing of the duties of survival in this dismal new world to them—and if they chose not to bear the burden, so be it. Why bother with them, why bother with making sense of it all. Why bother with breathing at all?

Even slogging through the thick mud of my despair, I sensed a similar opinion in John. It made sense. He was the spiritual practitioner in the family and his idol had abandoned him. But even so, I watched with detached curiosity as he cared for and tried to instill some hope in Jessica.

Fine, that was one less thing I needed to bother with. The problem was that he tried the same tricks with me.

"We need you," he would whisper. "We'll make it through this together," was his daily mantra directed to me. We, we, we. He was wrong of course. We both knew it. There was no longer a "we".

And then one day there was no, "he". There was just Jessica standing by my bed. I awoke to her placid stare, she held an envelope in her extended hand, without words waiting for me to receive the message. No pretending that I still slept or was void of consciousness stopped her standing and staring at me. The demand of her presence seemed a lifetime, though it was probably only minutes before I finally reached out and took the note.

It was another lifetime before I realized she would not leave the bedside before I tore open the envelope and read the inscription. I was sure I already knew what it said. I was only partially right.

> *Sweet Aella, it is obvious that I am not capable of raising you from the dead. I feel dead myself and have done you a disservice, enabling you to forget who you still might become if you will only believe. How can I try to believe for the both of us when my own belief has been shattered into something new?*
>
> *So, I have one last option to heal us both. Jessica needs the care of a mother, not the pretending optimism of a failed father. Without you, I am convinced she too will perish. My efforts have interfered with that reality. I now lay her life in your hands.*
>
> *If I survive in this terrible new place, it will be for another purpose, I must seek a greater Truth, or I too will cease. You now have the right reason to live. Your daughter needs you.*

The cur. If I had had the strength at the time, I would have slapped out at his absent face, the face I once loved to stroke. But instead of slapping with my hand, my eye caught the continuing stare of silent Jessica and I decided to toughen her with the slap of a lie—the face, and the body of the one who had wrecked us, was crushed by one of the many earthquakes visited upon us, I told our daughter. John's cowardice had left her with nothing and so now it was left to me to care for someone I cared not for. "Get me some bread and a can of beans," I slurred to her. It was all I could think of in the moment—feeding our starving stomachs and trying, one pathetic minute at a time, to linger for the futile benefit of what I used to call "family".

Ilona:

Afore the Blanking, a wreck named Darius Mede showed up at my mom-dame's house. I was too little then to ponder what he was, but I grasp now that he was a wreck-ruler. When he once spoke out things to my mom-dame, I was in the same room with them, studying book-stuff for school. They didn't seem to think that my overhearing them mattered. Maybe it still doesn't, or maybe worse, it does.

Ruler Mede spoke that he had a way to fix the problem my mom-dame was most vexed 'bout. She had spoken out that my dad-wreck was weak. I remember this vexing my brain. First, I had lots of good-right strong times with my dad-wreck, so I couldn't pic him as weak of mind or body. Second, my mom-dame frequently complained back then that all wrecks—they were called men back then by folks 'cept her—were too strong. It made no sense. How could someone be too strong and at the same time weak? My mom-dame never untied the puzzle-knot of it for me.

So, when Ruler Mede showed her that he had a plan, my mom-dame was all ears. He spoke out of a soon-coming time when children—what I now call little-folk—would be gone. I became terribly fearful then 'cause I had no understanding of how old a little-folk might be when they would become gone. I still thought of myself as a little-folk. I didn't want to be gone. But when the Blanking happened, and I was still not gone, that meant I must be a Shorter—too old to be little, too little to be old. I figured that it must be those that had not yet grown their private hair that were true little-folk. I was past that time.

Ruler Mede spoke out more. He was close to figuring out a way to create little-folk without wrecks and dames touching. He must have been a Sciencer like my mother for they started speaking out formulas and words I could not grasp. Science words 'bout propagational polymorphing and stem cell ignition. They spoke out that it was doable without the help of machines that needed sparking to work. The two of them babbled with excitement and the look they had for one another, seemed to me, like when wrecks and dames used to touch one another—like when I used to watch my mom-dame and dad-wreck touch each other in friendly ways…afore.

I pretended not to hear them, but I heard it all. My mom-dame was the key. She had skilled in something called genome manipulation. Mede bragged that he had chemist skills, and together they could replicate outside of a human host.

How Ruler Mede seemed to foreknow 'bout the Blanking, which hadn't yet happened, I can't grasp. But his speaking out got my mom-dame all bubbly and ready to do good-right work with him.

In a very short time, they had cooked up their new way for making little folk. I saw them together one last time, laughing 'bout their chemical cooking, clinking, and drinking glasses of an old party liquid called champagne.

During the time that all my hearing and seeing of Mede and my mom-dame was happening, I was just at the age of wanting to know more 'bout men…'bout why they looked and seemed so different from…me. But my mom-dame spoke out for me not to ponder such things. It was six months afore the Blanking. Then hell came to earth.

Teagan:

I can't believe I have penned so much without explaining my two talents. When I began my difficult journey into the wilds, I had to choose carefully what I was able to pack and carry. Some non-perishable food, of course; water, these things though critical, would have to be somehow replenished along the way. My protective suit and extra layered clothing for extreme climate swings, and yes. I even brought along a compass. It no longer pointed to the north as we had known it, but instead the needle insisted that South was the new North. The tool would at least give me a constant bearing to use in comparison to my hoped-for direction.

All of those things were necessities, but two others I considered far more essential to me. One was my notebook and cache of pens and paper for journaling. The other was my flute.

I know others would think me daft for porting such things into such perilous and unknown territory, but I considered them as much my life's blood as the red stuff itself. I could not fathom their absence or an existence without the elemental notes each produced when held in my hands. My writings and my melodies had already taken me to exotic places and so had prepared me for this next venture. They must continue with me if I were to continue at all.

And speaking of tools and instruments, I should explain our clan's preferred instrument of death. I'm familiar with the device because of my upbringing on the farm. An auger might be a large metal drilling device attached to the back of a tractor in order to break ground for fence posts. It may also be, more commonly, a smaller bit that was used to drill holes in wood to fit two pieces of timber together with a peg or specially carved dowel. Augers of all sizes are available throughout the area, found in the ruins of barns and tool sheds that still memorialize the farmers' former role in the midwestern plains.

Zeke was apparently of the same background as me (though he was far different in character) and made a point of scavenging long and far for tools and implements we could make use of as we progressed on the trip where the clan discovered me. He expressed that such ventures were of great importance and one of his reasons was to seek materials to design weapons. The auger-spear was his invention.

One of the metal bits, ranging in size from 6 to 12 inches in length, was fitted to a wooden or metal pole using weathered leather straps; also found through our rummaging. These spears were fierce and ugly in their efficiency. Zeke demonstrated to us just how efficient they were, when he ended the life of an absentminded clansman—who had forgotten his guard duties on three separate nights. In everyone's presence, the Overseer had punched a hole in the back of the man's neck, then twisted the auger and pulled it away rapidly. Pieces of flesh, bone, and inner parts came with the spike, teaching me well that there was little to no hope of surviving such an attack.

Since bullets for rifles and guns were at a premium, each one of us was expected to carry and learn the use of these devices. They would become the signature of our defense should any unwelcomed visitors dare to encroach.

Aella:

After John had left and I awakened from my depression, life became even more of a struggle. Not only due to the physical realm's deterioration, but also because humanity itself was becoming unraveled.

Keeping Jessica in my protection turned out to be the best choice of many worst options. She did not understand the parting of her wreck-father and, being so close to him, she became combative with me. I was in no way prepared for her anger, I had my own to deal with and so I designed an even more diabolical solution, inspired by the actions of none other than the World Premier.

I was disillusioned by the failure of Darius Mede's technical crusade to change the world. His rocket failed, society failed and so I included him along with my former spouse, in my model for vengeance. If these two, who were the most righteous of men I had known, were so flawed, then it was time to refashion the paternal-favoring filter that I and my daughter had errantly embraced. In my domain, no longer would any men that had been considered "worthy", be so again.

I became obsessed with a regimen of physical training and mental reorientation. There was no longer an internet to access and so I took advantage of the university library. I determined that historical and modern-day feminists seemed more bent on criticizing the old hierarchy rather than designing anew. There was no template for what I was to invent.

So, the boldest, darkest thoughts of all surfaced within me. Women would become not only the dominant species but would now subject all men to the basest of servitude, utilized for three functions only: One, for manual labor; Two, for procreation and, Three; in the likelihood of a famine event, they would become a plausible food source. This model not only gave me purpose, but also in my new way of thinking, created a subjugated purpose for the newly subjugated *wrecks* as we would now label all males.

To enact such a plan, I would need a viable tribe of followers. They would need to be convinced of its value and of my worthiness to lead them. They would have to, as I had, abandon all past associations with mankind and its traditions.

The more I read and researched the social norms of ancient cultures, the more I realized that striking these traditions out of our new narrative would not be an easy task. It would require a complete cleansing of long-term ritualistic attitudes and beliefs. There could be only one way to accomplish this. We would have to extinguish the records of history.

I began to gather my followers, approaching each with the idea of shared survival and the opportunity for new freedom. I was amazed how receptive the women of the region were to this approach. We began to strike all masculine based language from our speech and titled our new movement *She Demands* which somehow was warped into a new identifier for its followers: *She-dames.*

Verse III

The promise of a healthy tree is in the proper planting and nurturing, not in the chopping down of someone else's tree.

—Portunus

Ilona:

Mede was long gone by the time of the Blanking, and there was no way of discovering news outside of each folk-town. Getting word to and from places is now chancy. Doves and other birds can be given messages to wing to places, but doves are food too. Folks think food is way more good-right than messages, so dove-notes don't oft get past a good arrow shot from a bow.

Our folk-town was in the desert of what was once named the United States. We lived so far away from the eyes of the big rulers, that when the Blanking came, and all the Pointers and little-folk left; those who were still around, decided it would be a great thing to rule. The problem now is that most everyone, it seems, wants to rule. My mom-dame started really changing and turned to more of a ruler in a different way. I'll scratch more 'bout that later.

I don't know what happened to Ruler Mede and his clone-making. Soon after the Blanking, rumors traveled on the lips of Bedouins—wanders from faraway places—who passed through our folk-town. They spoke out that Mede is still somehow a ruler. I'm not sure of that reality, but I grasp well my mom-dame hates any speaking out about him now.

What we hear of all things from outside of our folk-town seems downside-up. Trying to unpuzzle it now still muddles my brain and causes the darkness to creep deeper inside me. I try hard to ignore what I hear of the outside world, but that's an even darker sadness. Some days, I just want to not be...at all. That's my worst pondering of all.

Teagan:

We finally reached the Barrens, which I learned were the remnants of the once beautiful Black Hills of South Dakota. Now the rubble and canyons created by recent violent earthquakes made for a natural defense position. Multiple caves, what we came to call *the dens*, offered cover from the storms and a place from which to stage attacks should an enemy choose foolishly to approach the higher positions. Though there was still a risk of the inner dwellings collapsing during another quake, the danger outside was far greater. Timber from the once mighty trees that had dotted the area were hauled into the dens to shore up and minimize the potential for future cave-ins. I realized by the effort being made through the supervision of Matada, Portunus and Zeke, that they intended this to become our permanent home base.

We were fortunate to have arrived when we did because several weeks after establishing our ramparts, a fierce wind and ionic storm struck. Lightning and toxic gases in the area took twelve of our numbers in that terrible twenty-four-hour period. Another lesson learned: when clouds appear on the horizon, dig deep into the dens, and hold tight.

After the storm strike, we took assessment of our surroundings. Zeke was unyielding in his push for constructing a well-fortified perimeter wall. I personally wondered at the necessity. Surely every other creature on the planet had been blown away or consumed by the winds, constant lightning, and convulsions of the earth that we had barely managed to endure. But Portunus and Matada seemed in concert with the soldier on this front. I sensed they knew something the rest of us did not, and that was enough reason for me to comply.

In the evenings after the heavy hauling and lifting of stone and timber, we would collapse by fires built to boldly announce our presence in case any supposed attackers might reason we were not alert and ready in the night's edge. These resting times together became known as *fire-sharing*.

A clansman, anyone who felt compelled, or inspired would begin telling a memory of their past life. The sharing was only allowed around the fire. The reasoning was that thinking too much about the past could become an obsession or depress the man. Sharing in the company of others was thought to protect the storyteller by encouraging the positive details of his tale and discouraging the dark thoughts.

It was at the first of these fellowships that I discovered an astounding characteristic that I would be expected to adopt if I were to survive. Davis was, like me, a new recruit to the clan. He was a chatty guy and opened up eagerly when he discovered this was a free discussion moment. He started talking about his home in Illinois and his growing up in a middle-class neighborhood. He talked first about missing his father and then came the subject of his mother and sisters.

Before he could continue, a small stone hit him squarely in the forehead. We all traced back the trajectory of the stone and I saw shockingly that Matada had been the thrower. He had stood up and now had his hand, palm out, extended before him.

"No more of that talk," he commanded. "

Davis was confused but not injured by the small projectile or our leader's request. He looked around and saw that others were signaling him to continue. He obviously didn't know what "that talk" was that there was to be "no more of", and so shifted the story's focus to his first girlfriend.

The "thud" and crack" that followed jolted many of us as we watched Davis collapse as an unconscious rag to the ground, his head showing a nasty gash and the much larger rock laying inches away from his dazed eyes.

This time it had been Overseer Zeke's aim which had been true. "NO MORE OF <u>THAT TALK</u>!" he threatened as he rose and walked the circle just outside the flames, piercing each of us with his warning glare.

The fire-sharing ended with that warning. We each pushed up from the ground and headed for our individual dens. As I headed into the darkness, I turned once at a noise behind me. There, silhouetted in the diminishing blaze, were Matada and Portunus kneeling over Davis, tending to his wound. On the opposite side of the campfire squatted Zeke, poking a stick at the embers nearest him, watching the two administer their mercies. Then Zeke turned his head in notice of my lingering presence. He stared at me and stabbed his poker hard into the coals, causing sparks to fly. The message was clear. *This is nothing for you to become involved in.* I turned back quickly in my retreat, trying not to betray any further interest in the moment.

It had become immediately clear in the firelight that women, young or old, related or otherwise, had for some reason become a topic never to be brought up. I would learn later, the awful origins of this strange new taboo. But for now, I would hold tight to my own story for fear I might accidently let slip a maternal or courting memory.

I internalized the warning and determined that from that time forward, I would only share my deep memories and nostalgia in the form of notes played on my flute. To me, each melody encased a historical code only understood to me. The musings of my past, the people I had lost, the accomplishments and the pain of lost relationships were played out in the music. I dared not share in words, what I was truly thinking.

Aella:

As the assemblance of my tribe was all happening, there was pushback to my ideas from a surprising faction—women who resisted.

It was frustrating to say the least to hear the convoluted explanations these weak-minded ones tried to put forth to promote their position. Some were highly religious; like John, they served a male-concocted deity and could not erase the image from their minds. Others were simply subservient from years of indoctrination. Others were fearful of having to potentially fend for themselves or to sever ties with their mates.

There were other justifications, but regardless, it became quickly evident that to ensure the survival of the female species, we would have to steer a more dispassionate and efficient course. I, and my quickly growing tribe, were debating the options for this when the solution seemingly took care of itself.

Since the disappearance of so many Tucson residents a scant sixty days prior, most of those remaining tended to congregate in the central area. One thing that brought us all together was a need for survival information and resources: Who to see about what, and how to get what was needed.

We were not motivated by societal convention to congregate or to hear one another's stories; the ferocious bugs and unpredictable weather discouraged that. And separation trauma—loss of former loved ones and the threat of losing others—kept each person, kept everyone including me, from any intimate sharing of circumstances. There was a strange individual anguish that each seemed to clutch to, as their private space within.

All people in the area used the gatherings as a distraction from their internal pain. My tribe was no different. I capitalized on the depression of the times by recruiting despondent women to my tribe and trumpeting our cause. I and some of the newly converted she-dames were meeting in the Main Gate district of town near the university between the Santa Cruz and Rilito rivers. We met in the open without concern that it was somehow problematic. Jessica sat by my side, sullen and silent as she was prone to be, swatting away the occasional flyers that searched for flesh to torture. I factored that, for her own good, I must expose my daughter to the harsh realities of our new environment. Certainly, she could not refuse what she saw—the weakness of subservience corroding the womanly ties of our newfound tribe. Such beliefs had to be scrubbed out of our collective psyche if we were to evolve.

I meant to address this new thinking at our meeting. The event started innocently enough. While we were sitting outside in the early light of a hazed sky, several wrecks approached us.

"Ladies," One of them called out in a friendly tone. The term still grated on my sensibilities and their approach immediately set me on edge. The interloper continued in a slow and easy southwestern drawl. "I don't mean to barge in, but there's been some talk. Ya see, my wife says someone told her they was plannin' a demonstration of some kind to talk down our traditions around here."

We were seated at an outdoor dining table that we had pulled into the street. No vehicles were able to run now, by virtue of the Singularity, and so we thought the action was acceptable. Other groups had set up similar gathering places. I remember thinking about the dust that continued to accumulate in layers on top of all surfaces since the disappearances, and that someone should take a broom to the whole town. The smokey smell of it pervaded everything and gave grit to the taste of any food we took in.

My distracted thoughts were interrupted when, incredibly, the man sat down directly across from me at our table, uninvited. His ten other 'buddies' stood around almost as if in a parameter guard. He continued to drawl on with a friendly smile planted on his face. "No harm in that of course, but then we was told that you (he looked me square in the eye) want to take charge of things without any kind of vote. That seems extreme." He ended with this as if it demanded an answer and continued to try to stare me down.

A thousand, thousand replies danced around in my head. I felt the heat of my brain coursing down and throughout my entire body and I fought for control before responding. I somehow hoped that the ice in my return stare might incase him so we would no longer have to be exposed to such chauvinistic insolence. It was a futile fantasy, interrupted when an explosion shocked me from behind. I saw the man's head before me erupt into a mist of red spray before I could turn to identify the origin of the blast. His corpse crumpled, then seemed to melt from the bench to the ground.

The other men backed several steps away with shock written on their faces. I stood and turned in slow motion to behold Agnes, one of my first recruits, holding a shotgun now leveled at another of the men to my right who had mistakenly taken a step forward instead of in retreat. The smell of gunpowder now overpowered that of the dust, and weirdly mixed with another sweeter aroma, one I was all too familiar with in large quantities. It was then that I surveyed my gloved hands, following them to my leathered arms and then my body suit and finally to my booted feet; all of which were coated with a sticky red gel. I realized the shotgun victim's blood had intermingled with the airborne soot and painted me into a new horrific creature.

In surreality, I looked back up to Agnes who continued to aim her weapon and now spoke. "Don't worry, any of you. There'll be no demonstration. As for a vote, that's already been cast over the thousands of years of our oppression. The ballots are in, and we've already been elected!"

She then pulled the trigger once more and her target fell back into his own rapidly forming pool of ooze. "You may now leave our domain," Agnes said coldly as she pumped another cartridge into the chamber.

The men scattered as their merciless persecutor, Agnes, aimed and fired again and again, taking down one after the other, screaming her rage out with each blast. Chaos was not a complete enough word to describe the escalating scene. My multi-thoughts coalesced to one, *we are not ready for this.* I knew that we would quickly lose the advantage in a town reputed for its seasonal hunting with the equipment necessary to pursue their prey.

Pulling Jessica up from the bench by the arm, I started running, pulling her with me in what I hoped was the safest direction. "Quickly," I yelled as we dashed. "Everyone to Banner". My tribe knew immediately what I was signaling. I think most of them were as shocked as I. The male interlopers had been totally confused at Agnes' actions, so it took each a few precious moments to process the events. And that was far too much time. Many dropped without taking another step. The friends of the interloper reacted more quickly. They already had a defensive mindset and so had come prepared with their own concealed weaponry. While my tribe gathered their wits, the wrecks gathered their ranks and took aim.

In some strange way it was a strategic error, yet an opportunity for our ranks: The wrecks focused their retaliation on a single target; Agnes. Ammunition of all sorts cut and pierced her body in a furious fuselage of revenge. Even as she went down, the bullets continued to dissect her corpse and that was what saved us.

I ran and the others followed my example. We sprinted at best speed toward the complex in the middle of the university that I called my second home. My new regimen of exercise enabled me to run the distance faster than most. Many of my recruits had yet to condition themselves in this way and so they became the second deadly focus of the wrecks, after Agnes.

Ilona:

When I'm most dark, I think back on when I got my suit and who the Ripper bugs changed me into. My mom-dame and dad-wreck figured out fast that the buzzing critters would hurt me afore I could hurt them. So, we all dressed up in hot, sweaty leather skins made from dead animals. 'Cause water was scarce and needed to be saved for drinking, the skins could not be washed good-right. They smelled dead and so did we. I grasp now that to become safe, we were actually hiding inside, even when going outside.

We were walking bags, all clunky and slow and dark. Our suits made going to, or staying put, not easy things and stopped all of us from touching one another. Soon, we forgot touching altogether. We became prisoners in our suit-cells. And even if we were to figure a way to escape from our suits, it would only be into a bigger prison. There was nowhere to escape to, 'cept deeper inside, farther into the darkness that each of us kept hidden from any others.

Strange, now I have come to like my suit, 'cept for the heat and stink. Inside it, I can be more alone and that is what I like best. Afore, my folks seemed mostly good-right together, but after a while of not touching, I saw them change. By watching them grow apart from each other, they taught me how dark, dark could be. They, and the others in our folk-town taught me that the more I could stay away from all the sad ones walking through the world, the better for me. I was sad enough without them.

That didn't mean I was completely alone. I still had my crayons and pencils. I crayoned and scratch-spoke lots on parch, but I kept the pics and self-stories imprisoned too, I needed them to be only mine, no one else could be trusted with them. Everyone else seemed happy to stay inside their own dark cells, no point to my adding dark to dark. My pics and stories helped me fight the dark. I didn't even share with my dad-wreck who I spoke out lots to afore. He got sadder after the Blanking, and I didn't want to cry with him. I wanted to remember us best together, laughing.

So, all clunky and close and smelling dead, I scratched self-stories and crayoned pics of what things looked like to me. And I hid them in a special backpack that I let no one else touch or see into. The most strange thing was, I grasped someone else was still somehow listening and looking in. No matter how deep I hid my self-stories, there was a wreck—no, not really a wreck, someway different, someway knowing and who smiled sadly with me—who was more than good-right. He was more 'cause, the more sad I spoke out inside, the darker I crayoned; the brighter he was, the more he spoke light inside to me helping me fight the dark. He shined a very special light for me to scratch and crayon by—the best crayon color to pic him with is bronze. But the crayoning of his bronze light was not good-right enough. He was brighter than that inside of me. I never met him outside of myself, but I wanted to meet him lots, 'cause of his bronze lighting.

Then the man, and his light, went away with the Blanking: And there was more dark, more sadness.

Teagan:

Certainly, as we had been traveling, there had been a need for vigilance of what may be lurking beyond our vision. Now that we had a stationary base, it became critical that we prepare against any impending attack by other clans or gangs who may believe our stronghold to be a better place for them than us to possess. So began in earnest, an important component of our new existence. Defense.

One late afternoon prior to the onslaught of ominous storm clouds we saw approaching slowly toward us from beyond the Barrens, we were called to gather. Matada, Zeke and Portunus all stood together before us and our tall black leader announced in his crisp, matter of fact way, "Listen up so we will all live better."

It was Portunus' turn. As our scout for dangers on the road, he had been instrumental in alerting us to potential hazards. Now he became our signaler of impending assault. He stepped forward and retrieved from the leather rucksack he carried always, a ram's horn.

I knew the instrument not to have come from a contemporary source; it was an ancient trumpet fashioned from the rack of a male sheep. He cradled the curved animal piece respectfully in his cupped hands. Then he put the tapered end to his mouth and blew. A clear long-note sang into the air, richer and more resonant than any I might attempt with a modern-day instrument. Portunus sustained the clarion call for a good five seconds. Then he paused and said, "If you hear that sound, it means to stop whatever you're doing and focus yourself, for a new and wonderful thing is about to appear before you—victory."

I had been curious at the time as I watched both Zeke and Matada stand quietly to the side during the demonstration. In this instruction, they obviously gave way to their cohort's wisdom. Then Portunus made sure he had all our attention and spoke, "When you hear this, come together quickly. Bring only your alertness and your weapons with you for it will mean war is upon us." He blew the three repeating sharp short notes that I was now hearing echoing in the distance Each strident succession told that an opposing enemy was closing in.

It was apparently Zeke's turn to instruct. He pointed to the Barrens and commanded, "Just as the storm clouds approach us now, so will other attackers. Your senses will tell you, 'Run to protection, dive into the dens, weather-out the onslaught.' It is a fool's thought. Your adversaries will happily starve you to death in the trap of darkness. I will train you now, that as you are attacked, you will become chargers, bringing the fight unexpectedly first to them."

With that fine speech, he ordered us to run toward the approaching tempest to find appropriate killing niches in the canyons from which to surprise those who would surprise us.

In that storm, we lost five of our numbers. They had reacted too slowly in seeking a strategic place from which to conceal and strike. The lesson was learned well by the rest of us and put into unforgettable words of warning by Portunus as we retrieved and prepared the dead.

"Be sober minded, be alert, your enemy, the devil prowls about like a roaring lion, seeking someone to devour."

I learned more things to be sober minded and alert about. One concerns another danger in fire-sharing. The other things I'll get to those soon enough.

In fire-sharing; if anyone repeats a story twice, they are immediately punished, worse than Davis was. The reason: Zeke allows only one telling for what he calls a *release*, to let go of the pain. By my observations, he uses the sharing as a weapon to manipulate, through learning knowledge of the one who shares. As I began to realize his manipulation, I started writing down the stories of the fire, keeping them as confidential, historical chronicles in hopes of one day teaching others how to avoid our plight.

And on the topic of my wording, I must now confess another stressing discovery. It is a deadly personal sin which I am now guilty of, punishable by death. I became aware of my transgression brutally. No writing, nor page or parchment of script of any type is allowed in our camps. Scripting these words is a danger. Were others to see them, I would be branded as a *Parcher*, a certain death sentence.

By others, I mean specifically, Matada. By his reckoning, wording risks others learning of our habits and our vulnerabilities. Such things, if discovered, would be used to end us and in his words, "We hunger not to be ended."

Anyone found *wording*—in possession of a written page, by their own hand or another's—is immediately put to the auger. In an extreme example, I witnessed one who, while we were huddled for fire-sharing, absentmindedly drew a few letters in the dirt before him. His ending was mercifully swift, an auger through the back of the *worder's* neck by Zeke himself.

So, if no wording is allowed, how are these pages I am penning allowed? They are not! I am literally taking my life into my own hands by grasping the pen I keep hidden with my journal. They have been longtime companions, from just before the Blanking and I believe the rendering of our history to be vital enough to risk it. But because of the fire-sharing example, I have become even more careful with my wording than ever before.

How did I come to cherish this craft? Why do I stubbornly continue? It is a habit, a throwback to that other time: or maybe before that other time? As a child, I found writing to be my addiction. I could not...not write. The craft propelled me through school and resulted in my seeking a profession the halls of congress. I hoped my supposed wisdom, broadcast on paper, would win the hearts of those I served. Now, those who say they value me would slay me if I were caught sharing my ideas in this way. So, obviously I have to be hyper vigilant in my accounting.

Now at fire-sharings when others ask me to reveal my stories, I step into a tune. I reason with them that each note and song is symbolic within me of my past, that my flute is my voice. In this way, I'm not at risk of violating forbidden memories, absently or accidentally referring to my journals, or simply divulging too much of myself to Zeke. Not to say I don't believe he will always be suspicious of me. It's obvious when he asks for us to speak and instead, I jump into a tune as a supposed backdrop for other's tales to be unraveled. I fear that someday I may test his suspicions too much.

Aella:

It was only a mile between Main Gate Square and Banner Medical Center—a measly mile. I knew all the streets and shortcuts to make the quickest work of the route. But still my legs ached because of the pace it required to outdistance our pursuers. It took all my discipline to keep my head and stride forward. I heard the shots ring and the screams of my tribe behind me but refused to look back. They continued to echo in my tortured ears as I rounded the corner of the complex.

I reached the corner to turn in order to enter the side door, I typically used to enter my office. There, I hesitated, not wanting to lead my pursuers into my lair. I hid with Jessica in a side ally behind a dumpster and waited. It was all I could do to hold my breathing and keep my daughter's panic in check while listening for footsteps. The first to approach sounded bumbling and clumsy. I peeked from behind the container and saw one of my recruits assisting another past my position. I rapped my knuckles on the metal of the dumpster just enough to catch their attention. They flinched at the sound, turned their heads, and saw me.

Quickly they also made the corner and soon after followed groups of threes, fives and even a band of ten. All told, twenty-seven besides Jessica and I, found our refuge. I hoped our numbers were not too great to hide in the alcove.

Lastly came two more of our friends, but when they heard the signal and spied us, they shook their heads and ran on. Almost immediately after, five armed wrecks flashed by and then we heard the shots. Five minutes after, the killers returned the way they had come, talking out loud to themselves about the pursuit of their next trophies.

"I saw more of those butch-girls head out toward Sentinel. We can get a tracking party organized and find them tomorrow. They won't make it far on foot."

They trouped right on by the alleyway without even showing a thought to the possibility it was providing sanctuary to their prey. We continued to hide for hours, just in case. It was dark when we finally made our move toward the side door. I scouted the area first and then we gathered our wounded and entered, going blindly up the stairwell to the third floor where my research area greeted us. I was thankful we could stay there without outsider's eyes peering into the windows which had a reflective film on them for protection from the harsh Arizona sunlight. The only problem was the slow progress of our groping around in the night's blackness. Still, we managed to settle in, even finding and administering antiseptic and gauze to those with the most significant wounds. Soon enough, all of us collapsed in anxious exhaustion and fell victims to the disturbing dreams of deep sleep.

Ilona:

I've already told of my most vivid head-pic—my mom-dame's slaughtering ways. No need to re-pic that. But I grasp it good-right to remember as best I can, other head-pics; of how folks acted afore and after the Blanking.

Afore the Blanking, wrecks and she-dames like my dad-wreck and mom-dame got along a whole lot better; they actually lived together. And when they touched in special ways they made little-folks. My mom-dame says wrecks had work-power, they could lift and haul and run and punch; all good purposes when they were used in good-right fashion. Then wrecks started thinking their skills made them rulers of she-dames, more power-filled. She says that this kept she-dames from being equal and it had to stop. She says that being equal should mean that, whether dame or wreck, each should be able to do exactly the same thing in their life-work.

I am still trying to grasp how such a thing can be—she-dames and wrecks being different in their bodies, yet able to be equally the same in everything. My mom-dame seems to want to hurry me into some new folk-pondering; wants me to grasp that all wrecks, Mede too, are darkness. She spoke out her story of it—that I was born from sideways purpose. That my dad-wreck and her being a thing, should not have been a thing. I hear those words of hers to me as saying, in a downside-up way, that I am somehow a mistake.

My mom-dame says that just afore the Blanking, something good-right had started happening. Wrecks had started becoming nicer. By nicer, she spoke out that they started bowing down to she-dames, pondering that she-dames were smarter and better at running things.

But the Blanking caused wrecks to stop being nice. Everyone, wreck, and dame alike, wanted their own ruling way. My mom-dame decided to smack away some competition for the job of chief ruler. It was her special way of tricking. She now seems to hate all wrecks far too much and so wants nothing to do with any of them. To her they are in no way purposeful, I think my mom-dame's scheming with Ruler Mede's chemical skills was the birthing of her secret trick meant fix the wrecks for good so there would be no more mistakes like me. And the Blanking made her trick the dark purposing deepest inside of herself. She shared with me, "If we don't need the wrecks for making little-folk, do we really need them at all?

What do I speak out? Not a thing. Speaking out my ponderings would be death 'cause of what I grasp differently from my mom-dame. To me, he and she folks look and act differently and there is good-right purposing in the differences. I am from that purposing. I am not a mistake.

Teagan:

Matata, the big man, has organized a government of sorts, determining who will live and who will contribute in the "other way. I can't fault him for our survival, I still exist, as gruesome as that may seem.

But I am not like him and that is the strangeness of it. I seem to be one of the only ones, a sparrow within a flock of crows, who acts in ways that would be considered dangerous were someone to pay acute attention to my behavior. The clansmen in our lot are not prone to congregate unless ordered. We unify only in the midst of danger. Each cares only for his own existence, and only for the rest of the clan if their peril is also his.

No, I am not like Matada, or as best I can tell, like any of the others. I come from a time and a place that encouraged communal interaction and progressive wellbeing with a strange hope in the goodness of others that, to me, is visceral.

Why me and not Matada or the others? Possibly it is the whispers of their thoughts that betray the answer. Some murmur that the Blanking worked some magic to remove all right and good ones from the world. Not that I am better, but I do want a better way, a more civilized life for all. And if that is some measure of goodness, my existence proves the theory wrong.

My personal ideas on the Blanking? Everyone I knew who has disappeared was the best of the best, that is certain. But more than that, each seemed to possess a devotion, practiced, and spoken almost ad nauseum to the god-figurehead they called Jesus. I was not of that persuasion then, for the same reason I am not now. Though the legend known as Jesus was a fine societal model to follow; doing so did not end sickness, poverty, slavery, pestilence, violence. nor any of the dark things of the world.

If this god-man was what they claimed, I can't then understand why the ills of the world persist. And if they, the very, <u>very</u> good ones were somehow taken away by him, why leave us; and not just do-away with all who did not claim him as their leader? The posit of Jesus was flawed by the very people who created him.

So, what did happen? Granted I was very young and naïve during my time serving as an intern in Washington, D.C., but just being around people that wielded that kind of power allowed me to hear about "potentials" as they were called. Potentials were scenarios that military and bureaucratic strategists would pose to the upper levels of power. Weapons like dirty bombs and electromagnetic pulse emitters just scratch the surface of threats that would make the general public cringe were they to know the truth about our vulnerabilities and capabilities. One subject that kept resurfacing, made my skin crawl every time I heard of the "progress" being made in the arena. Progress is a strange, but necessary word to describe both the creation of and defense against certain dangers and there was great progress regarding chemical and biochemical warfare.

I heard, granted indirectly, of toxins and concoctions being developed that could not only kill, but kill specific genome groups—people with traits unique to their DNA makeup. I was actually in a meeting wherein was a discussion of terrorists who had "melted" their prey. Drones had appeared in a foreign town and fired needles coated with some sort of contaminant that liquified everyone struck.

Conspiracy theories were casually tossed around at water cooler breaks and coffee houses every day. Who knew if any of them were true or just macabre fairy tales? All I know is, there were millions upon millions of people on this planet who were its finest, and suddenly they existed no longer. Along with them civilization itself melted away. And there are other strange ramifications that I believe no one speculated about prior to the Blanking.

Up to that point, there had been a significant trending, in the public opinion and culture of the US. It had to do with gender and identity politics. There had been growing resentment, especially by those who were conflicted in what they saw when looking in the mirror. More and more began to believe that sexual identity was flexible; men and women could become women and men, or both.

No longer did we have to assume certain roles that society had ascribed to us. Although great progress had be made in the area of equality in the workplace and the home, there were those who could not be satisfied. An odd polarization began to morph, women who wanted nothing to do with men and visa-versa. It had grown from years of sexual harassment claims, shaming of those clinging to formerly traditional beliefs and mob anger against those who, as a whole, refused to accept a de-sexualized society.

Congress and the courts, states, cities, and neighborhoods became increasingly divided. Ultimately there were no sides, only fractured individual opinions with no hope of achieving unity.

Into that heated pot was thrown the cauldron of the V4641 disaster. Just when we as a nation, needed one another most, we had abandoned ourselves to our intractable causes.

Yes, there were those pleading for reason and grace that we might survive the storm together…but did I mention those people suddenly vanished?

Aella:

The first hints of clouded light announcing the dawn awoke me. My first cogent thoughts replayed yesterday's hunter's words. "We can get a tracking party organized and find them tomorrow. They won't make it far on foot."

He had mentioned Sentinel. He had to have meant Sentinel Peak located in the city park of the same name. At nearly 300 acres, the area held many hiding places, but if the wrecks established a watch point on the 3000-foot peak, they would have a definite advantage in scouting for the movement of those they wanted subdued.

I worried that we would not be able to reach the place before the wrecks and so would become as much targets as any other escapees. Then nature provided hope. I heard a distant roll of thunder and then more.

Moving to the window, I saw an approaching storm like many since the Blanking. The weather had become much more violent and the smartest thing to do when such tempests approached was to seek immediate shelter, dig in and wait out the deluge. The outside temperature was tolerable, I guessed around 80 degrees Fahrenheit. Anyone hiding in the park area, if they could find one of the many caves that had appeared in the area since the Earth's upheaval, should be protected from the worst of the weather. That would give us some preparation time, depending on the length and severity of the coming inundation.

Forcing myself up, I first checked to see if the wounds of the five most severely injured of my charges were healing well. I encouraged them to continue resting and then I went around to wake any of the others who were not already stirring. There were twenty-three including myself who were at least marginally capable of making the six-mile journey to the peak. But what would we find there, what was our plan to seek others of our tribe and defend ourselves?

Latisha, one of the most fit besides myself, was eager to help with a suggestion. "If there is food and bottled water in the building, we need to gather that first. Without energy, we won't be much good to anyone."

She was right of course. It hadn't been long since the Blanking occurred, and I had spent much of the time afterwards consumed in self-pity over the loss of my son. It had only been the last several weeks when I resolved to endure, and I had yet to do a thorough search of the premises for critical supplies. It was unlike me, having been self-coached by our family camping activities in survival tactics. Fortunately, I had not yet detected other marauders who might have the same instincts. They probably had chosen a more evident target—the actual hospital—where food and medical supplies would be an obvious objective.

My research lab and office were in a separate complex, less familiar to the public and it too should have resources we would need to carry on. Latisha and one other dame volunteered to scavenge the premises. We urged them to be cautious. Just because we thought we were secluded did not guarantee that another roving party would discover the place.

That thought inspired me to choose others for watch-shifts to supply some warning should the building be breached. As rain and wind started pelting the premises, the remaining group of us planned our egress to

Sentinel Park and we devised a strategy to overcome our adversaries. Considering our numbers and our lack of weaponry, it was a feeble strategy. We would have to depend on our wits and improvisation as much as on any tactics we might employ along the way.

Lightning strobe-lit our efforts to map out the route we would take. There was a university campus, downtown area, a freeway, and the Santa Cruz River bridge to cross, and much more open ground to cover to reach our destination. The idea of the trek for such a motley crew was daunting. We concentrated on our traveling because it kept us from the worry of what might await us on our arrival.

While we were debating our options, Latisha and Babs, the other supply scout, returned with two large rolling carts of non-perishable food packs, changes of clothing and backpacks from an abandoned outfitters shop within the complex, water, and additional medical supplies. They unloaded and simply stated, "there's more," then exited to continue their search.

As we chewed on trail-mix and swallowed down cold beans out of pop-top cans, we also searched the lab for valuables. Besides glass and plastic beakers for storing, we also recovered some unusual, but very valuable tools I knew would be of importance along the way: two magnifying glasses; a number of surgical instruments including scissors and scalpels; syringes, needles, vials of antibiotics along with anesthetic compounds and other medicinals.

We changed watch-shifts and the scouts returned multiple times with new valuables. Each of their trips, along with our own lab equipment discoveries shaped our scheme for regathering our missing comrades.

Ilona:

A downside-up dream in my head showed that a dark and wicked one was chasing me. I ran and fought to stay ahead of the bad one. Just as he reached out to grab me, I woke, not good-right.

Teagan:

First light: I have always appreciated mornings, just before and at the herald of the sun's rise. I still try to appreciate it now even in the barren wasteland. There is hope in the dawn, in the coming of life's daily rebirth. I struggle to reawaken with each sunrise, holding that flicker of hope close in protection as from a hostile wind that would snuff it without a thought.

That dim hope is all I have now. It is mine alone; no one else seems willing to share in its kindling. Ours has become a clan of sad indistinctiveness. No one dare stand out unless they desire the challenge of leadership. I do not hunger for that power. I've mentioned that my subtle behaviors betray me. Were someone to observe me deeply, I would be judged not well acclimated to the purposes of the clan.

I had feared that my hope will also someday be my doom. But then came a new awareness—another who distinguishes himself as a misfit. Portunus, our wilderness Monk, has become a friend. His skill is in making use of every resource, seeing the best skills of each member, encouraging order and by all means, loyalty to Matada.

That is why I was so confused when I first watched him walking toward the wild, the hardest, most infertile of places. Why would he risk such a journey when all he teaches us is to avoid risk? I can't explain my curiosity, I have always been so. I followed him. I became uncertain when he did not turn back away from the obvious course of his hike, but instead pursued the worst of the rocks and craigs.

My curiosity became panic when he turned a corner into a wide crevasse ahead of me. I waited a bit, taking in the dry heat, the smell of dust and hidden, unknown, waiting things. When I could stand it no more, I too turned the corner and...nothing. There were no tracks to follow for this seemed to be an old, dried riverbed of unbroken flagstone. Portunus was nowhere to be seen and only the wind echoed in the winding place.

I had been a fool to follow him. Now I was lost, not having kept a good account of our trek in order to safely navigate a return. I circled in the spot I stood and drops of sweat signaled I would soon lose all reason if I did not get a grip on my thoughts of danger.

"So, what brings you out this way?" a voice from behind me called.

I jumped and actually hit my head on an outcrop of rock just above me. It was hard enough to cause a drip of blood. I was so shaken, I didn't even think to seek out some sand to stem the cut, but instead, whirled to find Zeke watching me with a heinous smile as the red trickle dripped down my face.

Because of our union in travel, and my flute playing during fire-sharings, which he had seemed to enjoy, my guard was completely down. His fist was out before I could even define it as a weapon. I had a new adversary who I had thought to be a colleague. I was mistaken and was not doing well in my reaction to the attack. From my fallen position on the ground, for whatever reason, maybe shock, I actually tried to apologize for doing whatever it was I had done to offend him. "Sir, I think…"

This time it was a booted foot that caught me square in the stomach. "That's your problem teso. I do not like your thinking." His voice was almost the cadence of a song, a poem without any rhyme and for certain no reason I could conjure. "You guard your thoughts too closely; you pretend innocence and tweet your tube as if your entertainment is a justification for holding back your words."

"But you said…" This time it was his auger that dug into my thigh. Now my scream-song echoed throughout the canyon.

"You will speak when I say, you will bow when I command, you will breathe only at my bidding and share any thought I demand you to reveal. Are we in agreement?" Zeke hovered over my head and then crouched closer. His urine spilled into my eyes and onto my cheeks and he bid again, louder, "Are we in agreement?"

I nodded my head rapidly for I could not choke out an answer through the yellow flood. With that, he stood back up, looked down on me and said, "I'm glad we have become so close, Fluter."

After a rich laugh, he bent down and began to pull at the legs of my pants, removing them from my body with one strong tug. "Let's get better acquainted, shall we?" And with that he grabbed my feet and twisted them painfully so that I was flipped face down in the dirt. His boot on my back ensured I stayed in that position, and I heard him unfastening his own pants. I began struggling in panicked anticipation of the violation about to commence.

"He's mine, not yours to play with," Another voice spoke from beyond my view.

"So, you think, Matada's favor on you, somehow gives you authority over me?" Zeke responds to the new presence.

"Not authority, just an understanding. You know full well the boundaries to be honored out here."

Zeke rasps his contempt, "I do indeed, but it doesn't mean I have to like them."

I felt him lift his boot off my back and then I caught the sight of it swinging around in an arc toward my face.

And I was dead…

—Or so I thought I had died. With Zeke's final kick, I fell into a sleep bathed in blinding light.

I awoke immediately wishing I had arrived in some other world. there was no part of me, body, or mind, that was not screaming. I wanted to let the cries speak out my misery. There was not enough breath in my lungs to make it so.

"Say nothing." It was now another clansman kneeling over me; Portunus.

I wondered what punishment he would now inflict and if my killing was a slow process sport. First Zeke, now this man, soon after Matada and then maybe the rest of our kin? I wanted nothing but to wail, but my throat was completely clogged, and a gag was all that escaped.

Portunus seemed to read my fear. "I will keep you," his voice was warm like Zeke's stream, but its tenor offered something far more refreshing. Hope.

Another wetness touched my face and I rediscovered kindness. It was cool, fresh water, not a secretion. *This one cares,* I thought. *Or at least he pretends well. Maybe he'll do me the kindness of sticking a knife in my heart quickly.*

Instead, he took a small towel from a pocket inside his robe, folded it carefully, and placed it under my head. "Best we have a look at those bruises," he said.

Bruises? What about the rock gash on my head and the auger gouge in my leg? Am I not nearly bled out? I reached up toward my head and I flinched. The older man smiled, turning both palms of his hands up to show me he had no ill intent.

"Relax, son," It's a small cut, but you only have so much blood to devote. Better we save some for a more important time. "It's nothing," he said while continuing his examination, and with that he pulled a small vile from another pocket of his garment. He uncapped the container and reached to pour a drop of stinging liquid onto both cuts. "Iodine," explained the would-be doctor. "Hope you're not allergic". Then he rose, picking up a dried stick laying on the ground as he stood. He walked the stick over to an arm sized crack in the rocks of the canyon wall and poked it tentatively within.

"Can't be too careful—snakes and scorpions," was his explanation. After a good prodding, he seemed satisfied and stuck in his hand to then pull out a handful of soft dirt that he unceremoniously applied to my scalp and leg. There was just enough moisture in soil so that it stayed put and soon the trickle of blood eased.

This whole time I could not find my voice. I wanted to ask why he was out here. That would require me to explain why I was out here and *to spy on him* did not seem a good thing to have to explain. But of course, he already knew why. Portunus was observant to a fault, there was no need to ask.

His hands scooped more dirt, and he spit into the pile, working it with his other palm to make mud which he plastered into the wound of my leg. The would-be physician assured me, "Just a prick, much like he who delivered the strike."

I was so disoriented; I did not catch his meaning at first. And then realized his jab at Zeke. In trying to process the terror I had just endured, within his off-color diagnosis, I found an unexpected and great gift bestowed upon me by my healer—laughter finally erupted from my bloodied mouth.

Ilona:

I said, afore the Blanking we really had no complaints. But we complained anyway. I look back and see the silliness of it all. Not like my dad-wreck, who spoke out that we didn't treat life nearly silly enough. To him we needed all sorts of smiles—more unhurried folk pondering good for others. To him, laughing more and liking more would have fixed it all.

Another big memory to me: Afore, we needed each other, all of us. Now, no-one needs anyone. Sure, we purpose together—some, but not much. My mom-dame tells that we dames must purpose all together—all following her, no turning off the road. If one doesn't, they are severed and are no more—no purpose, no living, and there is no laughing or silliness about that.

Some of the ones my mom-dame has sacrificed spoke out afore their dying. They shouted that wrecks call us *clippers*—guess that's what we are to them: Some dames, when they used to find a wreck, would clip off the parts between their legs. But clipping didn't really un-wreck a wreck; not in their brains. There was still something inside that didn't work good-right with dame-living; that's why my mom-dame now speaks out that we are to clip off their breathing—no taking chances for dame purposing to go sideways.

Teagan:

Portunus began my tutelage, showing me the ways of the Barrens. Everyone else in our clan has called it a desolate wasteland. But the wilderness monk seems at home and alive here. He revealed to me the hiding places for creatures that still exist. He taught me how to scope a cave to make sure it was safe for dwelling. He instructed me on finding the rare plants that hide beneath rocks.

"Aiyn ad mizrach," my newfound mentor called our early day quests: *Eyes on the sunrise* in Hebrew, a language I was vaguely familiar with from my exposure to the many cultures passing through the halls of congress. How Portunus had become fluent in that tongue remains a mystery, but he would often defer to its nuances in order to better define the natural order of things as he saw them. "Things in the morning are new, and if you want to cling to life, you'd best arise with it."

The succulents he taught me to seek out in the blossoming light of each day, can be a nutritional source and have medicinal qualities as well. They somehow peek out from beneath rocks and crevices, extending to catch the meager morning moisture, then as the beating sun appeared they retreated to selfishly protect their secret treasure.

"These survivors might be your best teachers in how to protect your own gems," Portunus cryptically shared.

At that time, I had no grasp of what gems I might have to protect or who might want to take them from me.

Portunus was an extraordinary medicine man. As our relationship developed, I began to see why he was given so much latitude in the clan. He could heal, hunt, cultivate and scout far better than any of the others and he was willing to pass his knowledge on to any who wanted to expand their skills. Unfortunately, for whatever reason, few seemed inspired to absorb his experience.

I was the rare one who understood the value of his crafts and talents. Adding to his value, this was a man who did not seem to judge others, but rather, opened the door willingly to any who were hungry for deeper human interaction. Again, the nature of most of our clan did not encourage such relationships. My wilderness encounters with this man, however, are teaching me to trust him with my deepest secrets.

As we traversed one canyon trail, we encountered an incredible rarity. A small mountain lioness stood before us and bared her teeth in defiance of our intrusion. I pointed my auger in her direction as a defensive act and Portunus stood by me. I could feel both the cat's and the other man's eyes searching to understand what I would do next. I wanted to know as well. I had read adventures and watched many movies in the time before the Blanking: Tales of battle when confronted by one of nature's beasts. But I had never in my life, taken another. I stood, frozen in time, and lost in thought. Then I lowered my weapon slowly and met the gaze of the confident feline. She must have decided that I too was worth sparing, for soon, she turned and in the same motion leaped into a crevasse, leaving us to our exploration. In the rising sunlight directly behind where the cat had stood, I thought for just a moment that I saw another man standing. The shimmering morning light behind him caused an illusion that he, not the glowing orb behind him, was the source of the light. It was a mirage of course, and the *bronze man* hallucination vanished as quickly as it had appeared.

To my side, I caught Portunus glancing at me with what seemed an approving smile of respect, but beyond that, he nor I ever mentioned the incident again.

The Barrens became as much a home to me as it was to my new mentor. In times to come this place would reveal a great many of its natural secrets to us both.

Swimming was both our recreation and our leisure. The eddies that were fed by the *Rushmore*, our name for the frequently turbulent river that now sustains us with its liquid life-source, were clear and even provided an occasional fish for cooking over a campfire.

Portunus taught me the craft of spear fishing. He used a long, aged, wooden pole; not with an auger attached, but sharpened to a fine point. The first time he displayed his skills was an education in itself. He would disrobe, down to his loincloth. I observed that he was well muscled; but also, evidence of many scars suggested he had had to earn respect in the wilds. The frontside of his chest, below his right shoulder bore a tattoo, an odd symbol unlike any I have seen before or since. It was mostly green in tint and the prominent feature was three interlocking circles displayed with two beneath and one above. Single symbols within the interlocking spheres were unfamiliar to me until he kneeled to draw them in the sand and defined them:

א Aleph

> The symbol which was centered in the connecting rings of the circles looked somewhat like a stylized letter N. Portunus explained that it was the Hebrew letter Aleph and also symbolized the Oneness of God.

ב Bet

> "The letter *Bet*," he said while pointing to the glyph to the left of the Aleph, "represents the safety of a house and specifically a place for a family to dwell."

מ Mem

> The third symbol, situated to the right of Aleph looked somewhat like a lowercase n with a line off of one of the lower stems. "Messiah," the Monk spoke the word with deep reverence, as if it had no need to be further defined by other characterization."

I didn't understand his purpose in the moment, but I somehow felt within, that I was being transformed. Like Portunus, I was becoming a part of, not an intruder in, the land, and I looked forward to each time we would explore its wonders.

And in that particular metamorphic moment, my memory of the bronze man standing in the sunlight came back to me, along with a new, odd thought that entered my mind.

Will I know you?

Ilona:

I scratched afore, I am a Shorter. I spoke what it means, but I did not tell the how of it or the why of it. As I sit alone with my ponderings, I want to crayon the how and why, but it is too black to be a good-right pic. I try to scratch-speak 'bout it, but my tears color the parch and I'm left sadder, not good-right. Maybe soon I will find a way and the words. Maybe not.

Verse IV

"I can't explain why faith exists. I can only experience that it does."

—Portunus

Aella:

The storm lasted until well after sundown. We decided that crossing the terrain in the dark of night, though risky because we would not be able to anticipate dangers lurking in the blackness, was our best hope. The five wounded dames were improving, one even insisting she was well enough to hike with us. I examined her and suggested a more crucial role: She should remain with the recovering others; tending to, and protecting them in our absence. She reluctantly agreed and I was grateful, not only that we would not have to concern ourselves in monitoring her progress, but also that she would be there for the needs of the four others. Selfishly, I had decided that Jessica should also stay behind. She was too young and naïve to be of use in a potential battle situation and I wanted her protected.

As quietly as possible, the rest of us emerged into the street from the side door, each carrying a backpack. Without functioning lights, we chose not to fashion torches as they would only alert our enemies to our presence. The still clouded sky further masked our presence but made it difficult to navigate. Several times we ran into mud clogged roads and debris blocking our route. That made us have to backtrack and slowed our already painful progress. Two dames fell into an unseen ravine requiring several others to shed their gear, crawl carefully down the slippery gap and help the others back up to safety. Tending to one's sprained ankle further delayed us and a trip that should have taken two hours at most was made into a four-hour trudge.

Finally, after crossing the cascade over the only bridge that remained reasonably intact, we made for the pathways on the other side of the Santa Cruz. Creeping closer to our objective, the base of Sentinel Peak, we rounded the last curve before the ascending steps and stopped abruptly. Ahead were two medium sized camping tents, one on either side of the path. They appeared to be occupied for we heard snoring coming from one. The darkness hid many crevices shaped by the recent reshaping caused by V4641's approach. And because of the rugged terrain, the approach to Sentinel Mountain was a natural gauntlet. The tents, and their occupants had to be dealt with.

The risk of course was any noise whatsoever. We were in a natural echo chamber; the rock sides would broadcast cries of alarm or screams of pain. I had the most experience with stealth hunting. Another dame, Ellen was also skilled in outdoor survival. It would be our task to eradicate the threats. Using hand motions to select two others to watch and be ready to assist, if necessary, we both drew the scalpels we had acquired in my lab and crept up to the tents. Ellen to the left, toward the "snoring shelter", I to the right, the quieter of the two. I had to trust that my accomplice knew her craft, and so, focus on my duties.

As I neared my objective, I chose to go to the back, planning to quietly cut my way in through the nylon fabric. Trying to negotiate the zipper on the front screen would have more likely woken any sleepers and ruined the surprise. I paused at the tent-back and listened, the blackness did not allow any idea as to how many lay within. Holding my own breath, I tried to tune in for the faint inhaling-exhaling and any rustling on the inside of the tent. As best as I could tell there was only one occupant. A good hope.

I began my surgical strike with the premise that most people instinctively tend to sleep toward the rear of these structures, away from the entrance. The danger here was that if I cut too close to the occupant, my noise might wake a light sleeper. I began higher up and very slowly made an incision. My blade was faithfully sharp and so the tear opened as silently as a hot knife through butter.

With agonizing patience, my cutting route descended and when I had made approximately a 24-inch rip, I dared to pull at the fabric on both sides to allow me to peer within. I had been right—only one wreck deep-sleeping on his side cocooned in a sleeping bag. I cut down another twelve inches and was preparing to make my mark on him when I heard a rustling and the beginning of a struggle from across where Ellen was doing her work.

I had my head and arms inside the tent and looked down. My prey's left eye, the only one I could see in the dim shadows, opened. No time to think, I fell with full force on his head and shoulders. As he struggled to free himself, I muffled his mouth with my upper body and groped for my objective using my left hand. I sought the jugular in his neck. Even with the wrestling, I discovered its powerful pulse and brought my right hand, gripping the scalpel, in for the strike.

Warm liquid spewed in all directions including onto my face. I ignored the ooze and held tight to my victim. His jerking and tussling continued for terrible moments, I could feel him trying to free his hands from within his bag, but my weight upon him hindered his efforts. Finally, I detected a weakening of his fight and then after a few feeble twitches, it was over.

There was no time to waste in assessing my damage. I quickly withdrew and ran to the other tent to see what had happened. Apparently, there had been two occupants in that lodge, so that when Ellen had gained access, aiming at one, the other reacted by sitting upright.

Fortunately, others of our tribe had been alert enough to fall on the structure trapping the wrecks inside. Ellen had managed to pull herself free and all the tribe began pummeling the wrecks within with rocks, scalpels and whatever else was available. Ultimately, the tent dwellers were completely overcome and killed, The sentries' shelter itself served to stifle the occupants' yelling and it became their shared sarcophagus.

We all lay in quiet, anxiously waiting for any attempted rescue from other wrecks who might have heard the melee, but no response came. There could be no lingering pause for the dawn was approaching and would expose us prematurely if we didn't gain the summit.

Climbing the mount took another hour of exhausting labor; trying not to loosen any rocks to tumble that would alert anyone to our intent. When we did achieve the crest, we found exactly what we were looking for. No wrecks had bothered to attempt the assent and so we had the heights to our advantage. Resting, for only a few precious few moments, I encouraged everyone to pair up in twos, finding individual hidden vantage points. There were many nooks and crannies to conceal us, but still we needed to be careful not to reveal ourselves too quickly. I supervised their choices so that we created a 360-degree chain of observation while still keeping close proximity for communicating.

We had brought along a number of pairs of binoculars secured from the outfitters shop and in the early dawn's light we began a careful sweep of the landscape below. I had to coach those with the instruments to make sure they held them in such a way as to not let the sunlight reflect off of the front lenses. If our enemies detected the glint, we would become quick targets.

Our surveillance efforts paid off as we counted seventy wreck encampments. Our best guess suggested about 150 wrecks were present in the area but were just waking to begin their tracking of any dames in the vicinity. The ground was rapidly drying out from yesterday's storm. I reasoned that our perch had not been acquired by anyone earlier because of the perilous weather, but that would soon change. Someone in charge down below would certainly be figuring on the value of the roost.

We also detected dames hiding in the rocks and crevices below. Their numbers and condition were harder to figure because they stayed deep in cover.

Quickly a plan developed in my mind, and I passed the word to prepare everyone for the inevitable battle.

It wasn't forty-five minutes later that a wreck-patrol came upon the damage we had done at the steps to the mountain. It took another half-hour for someone to organize an assault on our location—no rocket science was involved in determining what we had accomplished. The only unknowns to our adversaries were our numbers, and how well armed we were. We wanted those secrets to remain. I watched as parities equipped with rifles, guns and knives were sent upwards from all sides.

We were outnumbered, but our advantage was in our rested concealment, and the exertion our attackers would have to endure to scale the mount. I had six pairs of two, including Ellen and myself carefully repel to lower points and wait in hiding. As the climbers ascended, our teams, armed only with kitchen knives and hammers from our supplies, remained in the shadows. Only when someone was upon them did they strike and again, surprise won out. Systematically the encroachers tumbled at our strikes; some already dead of their wounds, others breaking bones and necks as they fell to their doom. To our fortune, some even flailed into other climbers, causing an avalanche of wounded and dead.

The trick was, even as we smacked them, to remain as reclusive as possible. To add to our advantage, I had instructed the dames remaining at the summit to spy down and, as they saw wrecks nearing our positions, to throw rocks at them. This provided two benefits: Because on their climb the assailants could not accurately see our alcoves, they would miscalculate our locations, thinking us all to be nearer to the peak. Also, many of the rock-throws landed on heads and these too caused significant casualties.

Remarkably, whoever led from below stubbornly kept sending tired troops our way. Out of frustration I'm sure, they also sent rifle and handgun fire our way. Even at the chance of a lucky ricochet catching one of us, it was a wasted effort which did nothing but spend their valuable bullets. Only one of ours ended up receiving a wound and hers was a superficial graze.

After an hour of this approach, I estimated roughly fifty of their numbers succumbed to their injuries. Then apparently the wrecks realized the ineffectiveness of their strategy and the upward aggression ceased. Still about a hundred remained, too many for hand-to-hand combat on the field below. I was calculating what might be our next move when an amazing sight unfolded.

Here and there, I caught distant sight of wrecks falling to the ground, at first glance for seemingly no reason. Through my binoculars however, I discovered stealthy efforts by dames hiding in ambush, using whatever was available, discarded firearms, their own knives and in most cases more rocks to bring the foe down. There were more of our numbers than I had supposed, and they were coming up from behind to catch the remaining wrecks unawares.

Ellen tapped me on the shoulder and pointed toward the paths from the river, where now, other dames and some wrecks were approaching from the direction of town. They must have heard the gunfire. We watched as the opponents met to war with one another using any means possible to harm their adversaries. There was a distinct new coloring of the ground below, from stark brown to pools and rivers of red. Screams and the sound of blunt objects meeting soft bodies rose to our ears. There was no need for further planning, it was simply time to act.

I remembered a scene from a movie depicting an ancient rivalry. They were an outnumbered group of warriors, out of ammunition and pinned down by enemy fire on a wooded hill in a place called Gettysburg. I was struck then at the power of one word shouted out by their commander to rally those troops, so I used the word now.

"Charge!"

I was self-shocked that, as I made the cry, I had also emerged from behind my protecting boulder and was obeying my own command. Every one of our group responded without hesitation and our small wave grew in momentum as we slid/bumped and bounced from all sides downward. Some of us found and picked up abandoned guns on our descent, not even sure if the weapons were loaded.

Reaching the base, we found the remaining wrecks so distracted by the blindside attack that they had actually forgotten about our mountain occupation. Suddenly they were confronted from all sides. The ones trying to respond from town were also consumed. It became clear that dames from town outnumbered the wrecks who had not originally hiked to Sentinel Park and the males paid a fatal price.

As our assault gained momentum, I began to feel a sense of slow-motion alacrity. A club swung my way, was dodged, because my actions seemed so precise and efficient in the moment. The adrenaline coursing throughout my body became a rush of delight. I could taste and smell its power as I took down one aggressor after another. One more sound came forth in the riot. It was a blood curdling screech that pierced the arena. Both frightening and exhilarating in its shrill ring, it was not until after all wrecks were decimated or had fled that I was told by the other dames; the inspiring howl had been my own.

Ilona:

Warring. Why is it now the first way folk go to? "I don't like you" - war. "You don't like me" - war. There is so much blood-sacrificing, so much ending. I hear she-dames brags of winning. I hear their cries of losing. The dark of it all grabs me deep.

My mom-dame thinks we are all together with her, but there is no togethering, only selfing. If a dame helps me; good for her. If another helps me not; she is a wreck in disguise. Maybe no-one will speak those words out loud now, but that's the way of it. Seems like our tribe is only a tribe 'cause we share the same enemy. We all tell one another that we need each other's help for enemy-warring. But if there were no enemy, what would we be?

Teagan:

It was a world ago, my congressional internship and the subsequent debates before the blacking out of electricity. My life then seems so trivial in memory as compared to the struggle which dictates my current existence. We are barbarians now, groveling out individual survival as if civilization never was. Herds of us wander, but any lagging, are left to lag. When others dare to join, they had best be as strong or skilled as our leaders. Killing is no longer for spite or sport, it is a weeding out of the weak.

Aella:

The carnage complete, we surviving dames congregated beneath our mountain lair. We had faired only a bit better than the wrecks. There were now forty-two of us when assembled from the ranks of our Banner tribe, the field group and those from town. Dame after dame came to me with thanks for my leadership, but I did not relish any duty of that sort. Yet, no others emerged in the moment to plot our next actions, so I took the responsibility, hoping it was only for the moment.

There was much to be done. Bodies upon bodies blotted the ground and we had no idea if bloody survivors commingled with the dead. We would have to make a thorough search of the crimson plain to help any hero who was suffering; either to raise them to help heal their lacerations or to bring a swift merciful blow to end their struggle with honor.

I suggested we pair up once more and make sure there was at least one weapon between the two, for the inflicting of a kind killing, and also in case a wreck might be feigning their casualty in order to take one last opportunity to further injure us.

I chose Latisha to be my search partner and we made our way toward the river in our reconnoitering. She decided to check out a path leading over a small ridge, and I encouraged that we at least stay within calling range of one another. I continued toward the river slope and coming around a tall rocky mound, I froze.

Ahead by the path, close to the water was a small cave and from within I could hear a single voice, the distinctive lower tones of a wreck. What caused the hair on my neck to rise however was the familiarity of the speaker and my recognition of his faint utterings. I inched closer, careful not to reveal my presence by staying close to the rock-face into which the cave was carved. The incantations of the occupant continued, and I clearly re-called the words from my past:

> "The Lord is my shepherd; I shall not want.
> He leads me beside still waters,
> He makes me to lay down in green pastures.
> He restores my soul,
> He leads me in paths of righteousness for His namesake.
> Even though I walk through the valley of the shadow of death,
> I will fear no evil; Your rod and Your staff, they comfort me."

The complexity of the words struck me as they always had, the speaker pleading with an unseen superior, first as if they were separated, then as if joined in common company. I hated myself, for halfway into his cant, I realized I was mouthing the words along with him.

> "You prepare a table before me in the presence of my enemies.
> You anoint my head with oil, my cup runs over.
> Surely goodness and mercy will follow me all the days of my life,
> And I will dwell in the house of the Lord forever."

I was both outraged and anguished by the revelation. My former husband was alive. More incredibly, He had not searched out me and his daughter or made himself known after the Blanking.

Now he was aiding the enemy by offering his skills as a medical practitioner and spiritual comforter. Along with his own mutterings, I could hear the groaning voices of some wounded wrecks he must be administering to.

I struggled within whether to barge in and remove his head instantly or to wait and see if his ramblings might reveal valuable intel. I checked my rage and continued to listen.

"Lord, forgive me for my failings and arrogant assumptions. I thought I too would be counted among your called ones when the time came. Instead, you convicted me of my religiosity, of my inability to recognize you as a close companion whom I am bonded to rather than an idol created by a corrupted organization that had bastardized your name, your love, and your purpose.

"And Lord God, forgive me most of all for allowing my family to be torn apart. There was no doubt that my wife and I had chosen separate paths, that she even resented my presence, after the loss of, the loss of…I can't even bear to speak his name now—the memory of him is salt to my wounds."

Salt to your wounds? My mind screamed. *You cur, you left me after my heart had been ripped open. You left me to fend for myself!* Even as I thought the words through, I knew them to be a lie. He had not left me. I had insulted and blamed and hated him away. I pushed him out of that dark domain we had built together.

But the bitter, surviving, clawing to life part of me still defended my actions: *He deserved it. He didn't measure up. He didn't see it coming, he…he and his stupid god didn't stop or save us from the Blanking.* As the anguished sweat and tears of my pathetic memories bathed me, I remained hidden and tortured by his words on the other side of the wall.

"Savior, I thought it harmful to subject our daughter to the constant arguments and bickering. I thought I had to leave, for the sake of all of us. Was I wrong?"

Dammit, listen to the futility of his questions to a non-existent being—asking for an answer that he already knows. You idiot, you should have fought harder for us, not left, not…listened to me. Now you love your wretched invisible god—love him more now than before. Is there no love left in you for me? For us? For our Caiden who was, was…before that unmerciful idol took our baby away? You love that god and pray to him even after that! You love that idea more than you ever loved me!

I could stand it no more. I picked up a significant rock with which to enter his sanctuary and crush his head and permanently cease his ridiculous prostrations. My intent was all for it, but my body reacted in a bizarre way, instead hurtling the weapon out into the river. The noise of it stopped my former partner's babbling and I knew he would peek out to discover the source. I slithered back along the path and into another crevasse I hoped would hide me.

I could just make out his form as he leaned out and surveyed the riverfront. After a time, he apparently satisfied himself that he was safe with his casualties, withdrew and began again, his rituals. Quietly, I turned to head back toward my rendezvous with Latisha and the world went black.

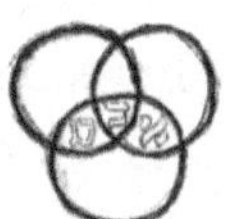

A face, blurred…saliva, hot breathing, smells—bacon, beer, blood, musky cotton? There is a great fleshy weight over me that I can't escape from. My vision and my brain clear painfully. I'm on the ground, pinned by a heavyset, well-built wreck. At first my focus is on his camo coveralls which are torn on the side where a field dressed bandage conceals what must be a significant wound. But then his face comes close to my ear, his tangled beard brushes my face and I feel vomit coming to my mouth.

"Sweet Thing, I'd keep quiet and still if you want to make it through this in one piece."

The horror of the moment has its own life, and like the miserable man who has me pinned; I am trapped in the memory. His heft continues to press on my body, his excitement and sweat rains on my skin.

I know the voice. It's one of the gang that confronted us in town just…was that yesterday? His wretched grin hovers over me as he steals pleasure from my agony and shame. And we share the final moment with an orgasmic cry—his of release, mine of physical pain mixed with dreadful resignation.

Yet it is still not done, for now he sits up on top of me, his wet hands around my neck, tightening his grip, robbing me again, this time of breath and life. As the merciful fog gathers in my weakening, I think, *this is best.* Existing with this memory would be unbearable. Ceasing to exist is the right thing to do and the darkness of the thought lures me deeper down.

As I comply with death, something else…a more primal desire—revenge— rises up. Should I die and let this pathetic creature have such a moment to boast about? No! But how to stop him? I am sinking. I struggle to keep my focus on any opportunity for survival and I am rewarded. The beast sitting above me closes his eyes, lost in his killing ecstasy. Now my hand detects a frail hope—a leather handle. What is it? My rapist's knife, in its hilt on the belt of his unfastened pants, has shifted and tilted toward my hand. My grasp is its captor and I pull quickly.

The angle is awkward, but I twist just enough to thrust the dagger upwards using the waning strength of my right arm. It is just enough. The blade of the bowie knife is well sharpened and enters him in the bowels. The edge slices up toward his midsection. In his shock, he releases his hands and tries to escape by pushing away. But we are locked together by the weapon wrapped tightly in my determined fingers. As my slicing meets the bones of his ribs, I plunge harder in and up, just as he had done with me. Liquid and soft organs warm me. The stench of his innards I greedily suck in as a strangely appropriate aroma for the climax of this moment.

I stare at the fading focus of his eyes and now it is my pleasure which we share. But there is no cry. We both gasp in the effort of it as I stir his insides with my attack. All too quickly, we are done, and he falls one more time upon me.

For only a moment we rest in the reality of our act. He is the one who has escaped. His lifeless body will not remember what mine will never again forget.

Making sure to be silent, I snuck back to find Latisha. Sobbing, and heaving, I could not work the words to tell her what I had just gone through. It was obvious to my friend that I needed help even beyond the physical evidence. She half carried, half pulled me with agonizingly slow steps back to my lab at Banner.

On the way, my hatred transferred itself from my attacker to John. How could he not have heard? How could he not have interrupted and how could he and his god not have rescued me? I told myself that if I ever encountered that particular wreck again, he would never again see light of or take the breath of another day. As for any other wrecks? Well, god help them as god had helped me.

Teagan:

I have tried to be careful and private about my putting words to paper, not even sharing it with Portunus. Although I think he would encourage me, this is a new realm I inhabit and the rules here are simply not predictable.

Once I asked him if he shouldn't encourage Matada and Zeke to let him instruct others in the healing arts and pass on his highly developed survival skills, not just to me, but to the whole clan? He laughed out loud at my suggestion and replied cryptically, "Why shout at a wall? The only thing you will receive is the echoes of your own beliefs."

That was his way. Seldom did he answer a question directly, but instead Portunus would respond with a question, or a statement designed to challenge his pupil's own way of thinking. Since coming under his tutoring, I think I've burned up more brain cells than I have enhanced, trying to deduce his deeper approach to existence.

Based on what I have learned from him so far, as his pupil and because of my wording, I am more of a target to be ended than I am a useful contributor to clan-life. So, I guard my own thoughts and disguise my actions, seeming to be one of the clan-kind, a willing contributor to their volatile ways, when in fact, I am becoming something altogether contrary.

But how I can continue to survive in chameleon fashion is still an unanswered question. When I asked Portunus how he is able to walk in both worlds, he shared one more of his mysterious missives

"—*Is it plausible that from a spiritual perspective, the physical world is mystical, whereas the spiritual world is reality?*"

More of my brain cells continue to burn up trying to figure him and his reality out. I have also discovered the reason behind the taboo of women-talk, why they are not spoken of and why none have traveled with us. Apparently Portunus, Zeke, and a number of others in our clan hail from a region a great number of months journey from here where a full-scale battle ensued between men and women. I have only caught bits and pieces of the tale, but the word is that a large group of females, *clippers* as they are often called now, have chosen to hunt and emasculate clansmen for sport. They are led by a hardened woman known as Aella. They too have been spotted migrating in this direction because of the dangerously unpredictable climate shifting in what had once been called the Southwestern United States.

I sense an approaching conflict between us and them and I'm not sure how to prepare, or if preparation is something any of us should be thinking about. It certainly hadn't helped us up to this point.

Ilona:

I have scratched what I see 'bout our tribe. Maybe it's also good-right to scratch what I hear around me. I grasp that I'm an even better listener than I am a watcher. Dames, they all play-talk to each other real nice, but I ponder it's only make-believe wording. I hear the whispers after the play-talk, and the chuckles bout "how odd that one is," or "how pretty that one isn't," or "how creepy Ilona is."

I see through the playing, and it grabs me that no-one else is watching or listening; least not as well as I do. No one even seems to care to watch or listen in that way; least not as much as I do.

Aella:

Our forty-two have become one hundred and twenty as other dames who had come out of hiding to join us in battle, now were invited into the Banner complex. Barricades and watches were set up, scouts were deployed to search for additional food and water, and a natural hierarchy was established. I was recognized as the leader. My lieutenants, Ellen, and Latisha became my right and left hands.

My daughter accepted food and took care of her physical hygiene in minimalistic fashion, but that was the extent of her existence. With no electricity, running water or other "conveniences" we used to take for granted. I found it difficult to focus on the manifestation of her psychological trauma. There were just too many needs of so many others to address and I was overwhelmed. So, I decided Jessica would simply have to work through her issues to discover her own reality in the moment.

I began calculating and coordinating a plan to hunt for any wreck-lair that might exist. If they had regrouped, they certainly would be doing the same, searching for their revenge on us. Six of us gathered in my office a few days after the battle to talk through strategies. It was early morning and there seemed to be more light coming inside from the dismal landscape than was typical.

A rumble, then a jarring shake took us by surprise, then a stronger pulse threw us all to the floor. The acrid smell of sulfur pierced my nostrils, and my ears caught the sound of rising confusion and panic from other dames in places throughout the building.

The pleasant light rapidly faded with the rushing sound of a gale wind that began to shake the walls. I heard pounding and screams from outside and realized there were some of our numbers who had been on reconnaissance who were exposed outside to whatever danger was approaching. I wiped my stinging eyes and tried to gain my footing. I felt like a marionette without the strings of the puppeteer to support me, but somehow, I crawled and bounced to the nearest outer entrance. There, a horror displayed itself as I saw vague human forms trying to walk toward the door. For terrible moments they seemed fixed in place and then simply blew away. Some were lifted, others rolled, and then the sulfur smell increased. I watched helplessly as shadowy bodies, that had been blown against light poles and outer brick walls, strangely evaporated.

Through my shock, I was jolted by my own inner voice of alarm. *We will be next if something isn't done.* I then lurched along in my puppet body back to the others in my office and shouted, "Towels, rags, anything you can find, now!"

There were supply closets nearby which we all staggered and careened to as the ground continued to heave and pitch beneath us. Grabbing as many linens and towels as we could each manage, we fought our way to the entrance door in the continually diminishing light and I commanded through my chokes, that the rags be stuffed tightly into any door crack where dust was sifting in. Everyone was gagging and vomiting but all complied.

When that door was secured, we felt our way through the halls to the back entrance and there found others who had the same plan, jamming fabric, best they could, into the crevices. As the excruciating work continued, I heard wheezing and ugly coughing, then gasps as some fell, not being able to manage a breath in the rancid atmosphere. I struggled to keep consciousness, but soon I couldn't decipher what as waking and what was dream. Crawling away from the door, I found a soft spot on the floor, laid my head on my pillow, and drifted to sleep.

Verse V

Just because you can't hear another's heart doesn't mean your own heart can't be heard.

Just because you can't change another's heart doesn't mean your own heart can't be changed.

—Portunus

Teagan:

One day, Matada approached me and told me to follow him. This was an unusual request and immediately my stomach churned. What had I done? What was he going to do? As much as I had observed both Zeke and Portunus, this man had stayed out of the main events of the clan other than sitting and his onetime stone-throwing during the fire-sharings. He seemed aloof and removed, only speaking through either his military adviser or his philosophical confidant.

So, I could not have anticipated his approaching me, nor his plan. He did not explain why, nor was he in need to. No-one disobeyed the Head Clansman, and I knew that obedience to his request was my only choice. Still, I don't like surprises and this moment counted as one, bigtime.

We took a familiar path into the Barrens. Sentries now stood on the heights dotting the passageway, guarding for what we knew not, but feared most, some new enemy coming to invade. Without any words of conversation between us, the imposing man led me beyond the protection of the sentries and into an unfamiliar alcove by the roaring river. It was difficult to hear other noises in the din of the rapids and I wondered if our dark robed leader intended to end me without witness, or to share some secret only between us. I feared the former as I could not imagine any secret he would want to divulge to me.

We stood in the center of the area and from out of another cranny appeared Portunus. He approached us and then received a strong embrace from the tall leader. Now I was curious.

"What is yer plan?" Matada began the conversation with his confidant, sparing any pleasantries, and both men seemed to ignore my presence. I was apparently a tool to be used in some greater endeavor, but only that. The interesting thing was that there was a plan, my mentor had come up with it and wanted it kept between these two. Why? And for that matter, why was I even included in this rendezvous?

"There is more scouting to be done, more searching. I have sensed a new danger coming and I want to explore the resources available to us. I want this one along to be properly taught and more than that, to protect him at least temporarily from Zeke. I believe our strongman has designs for this boy."

This tidbit about Zeke frightened me as nothing else. *What designs? Why me?* I was not comfortable with any of this but seemed to be the only one interested in my state of mind.

"How long?" Matada was not one to expound on things. I knew from conversations overheard with others that there was another plan in place to, as quickly as possible, build our numbers. The sense that we inhabited a territory that might be desired by others, meant we needed bodies for defense. Anybody that left, for whatever period of time would not be able to help in that effort.

Away from the eyes and ears of the clan's camp, it now became clear as to why Matada and Portunus came to this place to be private. These plans and designs might seem counterproductive to another plan...Zeke's plan and designs.

Again, no one was asking me about my plans and designs. It was disconcerting, but I was learning to trust Portunus and so chose in my mind to obey whatever he was concocting, wherever it was he would take me to implement it.

My new teacher however, seemed to recognize and appreciate Matada as his superior in these matters. And, between these two, I detected some much deeper unspoken relationship. What that was, I couldn't decipher—a subtly to unravel in time.

"Do it," was Matada's simple response/command. With that, the men hugged once more and the Head Clansman then left to return the way we had come, but without me. It would be up to him to stave off any complaints or attempted pursuit when it was discovered Portunus and I had departed.

And from that very place, Portunus marched me in a new direction. He had quietly secured backpacks, canteens, provisions, and supplies for both of us, hiding them in a small cave near the crevice from which he had appeared. His coursing led us on a grueling two-week journey. We camped along the way in caves and derelict buildings that seemed familiar to him from some earlier trek in this region. It was a great exploration, Portunus sharing insights and history of the region along the way. I was raised in the plains not far from here but had never really delved beneath the surface into how the area had been the site of one of the great gold rushes of American History. And how the United States military before that time had tried to exterminate an entire culture of people native to the area. It was the region from where President Gregory Blueroad claimed his heritage and so, with Portunus' additional teaching, the pieces came together as to why the area had been torn apart by what the Monk defined as the "battles between good and evil".

We ultimately arrived at what he called The Ruins, a crumbled testimony of a once great nation which ultimately perished on account of its loss of its greater vision.

Here a nose, there a broken portion of a once meticulously chiseled face. Once known as a national monument, this place has been leveled by powers I now respect beyond any scientific definition. The world has been completely reshaped and these pieces are memories that can only be reconstructed in the surviving remnants of a dying breed.

We sat atop another broken shrine; the head of an ancient, bearded elder. That one had seen the once great States of America through an earlier vicious and dividing conflict. Atop this perch, Portunus shared his adventures of exploring another intriguing geological wonder:

> "Not too far from here is a cave that is perhaps one of the most dangerous places remaining on the planet," he began. "I didn't know it at the time, and was foolish and overly curious in my interest of the place."

Portunus continued in what I came to recognize as his trance-tone, staring far off as he was prone to do, not seeming to see what was physically in front of him, but envisioning some other location—physical or ethereal:

> "My blue allowed me to peer deep within the cave, and there I discovered a steel stairway leading much farther down. Remarkably the gantry appeared to still be in good repair. A bent and tilted metal sign anchored to the cave wall next to the stair entry read, *DUSEL: No Unauthorized Personnel Beyond This Point. Proceed With Caution.* I might

have heeded the warning but the Spirit within urged me to proceed down."

At this point a bucket-full of questions flooded my mind and I was having difficulty following the tale. *How had Portunus acquired his blue aura? What was DUSEL? What spirit was the man referring to that would instruct him and why did he trust it?*

Though he appeared to be deeply projecting himself into the memory, Portunus somehow still had the presence of mind to sense my confusion. Without turning his far-off gaze to me, he reached over with his left hand to where I was sitting cross-legged next to him. He placed his palm on my knee and calmly assured me, "Patience, you will come to know the truth and it will set you free," then continued his story of descent:

"—The stairs submerged more deeply than I had ever imagined into the pit of the earth. I constantly had to swallow to help clear my ears due to the pressure change as I went down. A cool breeze blew up from the depths, but I soon found myself sweating, both from nerves and from the exertion required to navigate over boulders that had fallen onto the gantry, I supposed from the continued rattling of the Earth's core. Various signs along my climb down alerted me to the progress I was making:

"*YOU ARE NOW AT 500 FEET BELOW SEA LEVEL*

"*YOU ARE NOW AT 1500 FEET BELOW SEA LEVEL*

"An ironic thought crossed my mind as I passed the 3000-foot mark: The mine diggers had used a sea level measurement to define their achievement in a region where no sea was near to be found. What's more, after the violent shiftings and changes of the planet, who actually knew what sea level was anymore? Further I sank into the darkness; far below the surface, I'm sure, of whatever seas remained.

"Finally, I came to a dirt landing, and I was informed by one more sign:

"YOU HAVE ARRIVED AT 8000 FEET BELOW SEA LEVEL

"At over one and a half miles below the Earth's surface, there was a rhythm within and beyond the rock walls entombing me. I could sense and faintly hear the vibrations. Occasionally a louder, more insistent oscillation would warn that, whatever had happened to this site, and probably the world as a whole, was not yet finished happening.

"Equipment, computer consoles, office chambers tilted at strange angles greeted my sight as I walked the perimeter, about the size of a school gymnasium. But no evidence of people. This place had been left and left in a hurry. Dusty papers, coffee cups, pens and even computer tablets depicted a rushed trail to the stairwell from which I had just come.

"There was a dry, hot feel to the place, oddly mixed with the fresh breeze cascading from the stairwell. I was not sure how that could be. Then, as I rounded the corner of a larger console, I felt the source of the hotter air I had detected. I almost walked into the hole before I saw it. There was no telling its depth. The ascending smell suggested sulfur and other more toxic elements hiding within its bowels. I reminded myself that I was over 8000 feet below the surface of the Earth, and I could not fathom how much further down the void plummeted.

"I picked up a stray rock from the floor and tossed it into the abyss. My hearing is still acute, and there were a few bounces of the stone as it fell, but to the best of my ability, I never heard an arrival at the bottom.

"Then a new sound awoke, a ratcheting, grinding of metal on metal from below. As with locusts' wings the grating ebbed and flowed, each time its crescendos echoed to me that the origin was progressing upward! My mind had just enough time to register the source of the approaching assault and I dove out of the way as thousands of Rippers, launched out of the hole, streaming into a dark airborne cloud. They circled the room as one shattering cyclonic storm, and then flew upwards through the mined entry toward the surface. I thanked my Maker one more time for my 'blue'; the tormentors completely ignored my presence as they hurried away to seek more suitable prey.

"And that is when I realized, this was the birthing place of those torturing creatures. I was entrenched in, for a lack of better terms, the depths of Gehenna."

I drew my sting-suit closer around me when he had finished telling me the tale. Were the bugs about? What if they decided Portunus' strange blue glow was suddenly attracting rather than repelling? I had trouble sleeping that night, waking up frequently thinking I had heard the distinct nerve-wracking buzz of their approach.

Aella:

Of course, it wasn't a bed, nor pillow on which I slept, but the corpse of Simone, one of ours who had valiantly run outside the back door into the ally and helped several dames into the building when the initial howling and quaking began. According to others, having pulled five in, she had turned to head back out when the blowing fumes invaded and consumed her lungs. Her dying act was to pull the doors shut and fall away to let others seal the portal.

The *Fracas* had hit with no warning. We didn't know what else to call it, no name could adequately describe the electric feel, the friction in the air from the flying dust (if only we could have harnessed that power!).

It was all over within minutes, but there was no consolation from that in the mourning of our dead.

The storm was like none other. Those who had by circumstance been outside when it struck, were suffocated by the fumes, and if not carried away, had been skinned alive before our very eyes.

Yet fortune found a way to smile on us. Unexplainably, I survived, as did 112 of the others. As well, in Simone's last brave act, she had unknowingly pulled in two strangers, a dame and a wreck who were not of our tribe. Not knowing their origins or intent, we administered to their unconscious bodies, then bound them and waited.

When they awoke, they shared the story of their own struggles. Their names were Maria and Ramon. Amazingly they were the only survivors of a caravan of fifty or so that had made its way from Mexico up to Tucson in search of food and resources. They had just entered the main square area when they heard the storm approaching and quickly sought shelter. The tempest picked off one after another as they tried desperately to gain entrance to boarded up buildings, and it was only by chance that Simone grabbed them. The others? There was no evidence, in peering out the dusty windows, that they had ever existed.

We had no way of verifying their rendition, and so I took in their information with a skeptic's caution. What they described as the conditions toward the old regions of Texas and New Mexico were stunning. The storm we had experienced was not the first, nor the worst. Apparently, they had witnessed a greater dark cloud passing even closer toward the equatorial latitudes and then shifting eastward. It somehow passed them by, also sparing others that eventually comprised their caravan and who had now been decimated.

Something else they said was disconcerting. The storms were increasingly shifting toward our region. One of their former companions had been a television meteorologist. By his calculations, based on the readings of instruments he had been able to salvage and utilize, the magnetic axis of the planet had shifted dramatically. The poles had completely shifted, north and south, almost 170 degrees! He had warned his group that more storms and weather shifts were certainly in his forecast and that moving in the direction that used to produce frigid winter conditions was now the preferred migration destination. The area once called South America, once full of lush tropical forests, was now a polar desert surely to be avoided.

The climatic flip-flop and dire circumstances had galvanized their group's sojourning and served to warn us that, if they were to be believed, we too must move to avoid worsening conditions.

We were not yet organized enough and had many wounded. It seemed practical to relocate to a place where our she-dame tribe could temporarily avoid a large-scale retaliation, heal our injured and establish a stronger civil infrastructure by which to rule. But to where? Was any place safe? Were any of us safe?

Ilona:

Looking through my sad eyes, I watch back in time in my mind and see one of the saddest things. The wreck-battle was begun and ended in just one sunrise and setting. My mom-dame took off to meet that fierce day head-on and never came back. I'm not saying that the body of her ended, but when that body returned all blood-sacrificed and dirt-mangled, her inside person had disappeared, and a different mom-dame made a new home inside of her. I have tried to crayon a pic of it, but all the colors are black and blue. It is not a good-right pic and hard to look at; harder to figure. I don't grasp this new mom-dame in my heart.

The big battle of dames and wrecks was hard-fought, but a harder fight came just after the red-sacrificing had dried. Afore we had finished cleaning up to begin a new life beyond, the Blow hit. It stirred the dust so dark that lots died just from breathing; A small herd of wandering wrecks and dames close to where we hid inside our home-base, crawled to our doors seeking help. Only two made it through our doors still breathing.

Maria and Ramon, they were called, and they had trekked all the way from a far place that used to be named Mexico.

"Sanctuary please?" The wreck shook all over and spoke with eyes cast down. Muddy misery-tears dripped down his cheeks. My mom-dame appeared angered by the plea but decided to keep the two with us.

Lots more dames and wrecks, more of all folk, were ended by the Blow. Bugs and night critters started making meals of them and the no-more dames and wrecks oozed and melted into a black mess over the streets outside. I did not try to color it with my crayons. The rotten smell of it, like vomit mixed with old dung, filled the inside our home-base, too.

More cleaning had to happen, and my mom-dame pondered she was the one to do the cleaning. That's when I saw the biggest cleaning—she threw out her garbage-past as if her past was never a thing, and though I still breathed, I disappeared from once being her little-folk. To her, I was now a dame like all the dames. There was no 'I', only 'we'.

She spoke out that we needed to scrub away the old and find a better place to be—that we had won the war and so our reward was to choose what to do with what was left. In my watching of her, looking at the hard eyes of her now, hearing the hard thinking of her spoken out in cold word, I pondered that neither dames nor wrecks had won anything. We were all lost.

But we pretended different. My new-not-mom-dame used her brain-crayons to color a new world-pic for us to live in. We sorted out only necessary stuff to take along and readied ourselves for a trip. The new folk who had showed up just afore the Blow, spoke out that they had a map and that they would share it. They claimed the map had brought them our way, that it was colored in a dream to Ramon, the wreck who said he was wed-bonded to Maria. They spoke out that the only purpose in their life now was to help others move away fast from an even bigger Blow that was going to come.

New-mom-dame made it clear that she did not like Ramon. And she liked Maria even less. I grasped that Maria was the best-right match up for Ramon the wreck. Together they looked like I remember what Mom-dame and Dad-wreck looked like afore. I did not dare speak this out.

My mom dame said, "OK" to the sharing of the map, but I didn't figure she planned on spending a long time together with Ramon and Maria. She spoke quietly to some of us, without the two new ones in the room, that she didn't believe in dream-pics and couldn't grasp how the two had found the map. But we had to move from our now-home for sure and the map showed something new to try.

Teagan:

In the early morning light, we had planned to journey back toward the dens, we once more ascended to the pinnacle of the monumental ruins. Portunus picked a spot for us to sit on one of the once mighty heads, and there before us was a dove that had died and fallen to the rocks. I suspected he had already been here in the pre-dawn and thought it a good place and example to share as some sort of sage lesson. He did not disappoint.

"What would you do if you found the bird still alive, but unable to fly?" He asked.

"Kill, roast, and eat it?" I dared not sound too certain because I was learning the obvious answer was not always the best answer to offer this clansman.

"Fair enough. Now, what if there were no more doves, fish, or other meat left to eat. Then, what if you found a dead human body?"

"We had to resort to that ugliness before," I murmured, uncomfortable with my memories. "It would be my last choice, but if I had to, I'd roast it, same as the dove."

"And if the human body was still alive," Portunus added quickly, "but like the dove, it's essence was fading away?"

"What are you asking?" I nearly shouted at him, surprising myself as well with my frustration and anger. "Are you asking would I kill to live?"

"You'd kill the dove. What's the difference?"

I was shaking all over. Obviously, Portunus the Monk was testing me. "Would you kill another human for food?" I dared him back.

"I have eaten someone else's human-kill," he too sounded somber in his confession. "As have you."

I was now sobbing uncontrollably, and we both knew why. Just because I had not committed the act; but let someone else do it for me, conveniently out of sight, I was not excused from the…murdering. Nor did it shift the blame. I was fully culpable in the homicide.

Earlier, I had naively confessed to this man that I was incapable of the taking of another human's life. I had even sounded humbly, innocently noble and believed my own lie. Portunus had called out my hypocrisy and we both wept over it. We had devolved to the point of secretly condoning the act for our own indulgence. A long and painful period passed before either of us could speak again. It was my mentor who first spoke first.

"In the days before the Blanking, it was common in certain religious groups to blame a devil or evil spirits for our temptations and our poorly chosen actions. Satan the tempter became everyone's scapegoat in explaining why we acted sinfully. I'm not saying such an evil spirit does not exist, but maybe we give that devil too much credit, assigned him too much cleverness so that we can blame him for our personal conflicts and failings?

"But what if a more frightening scenario is equally or perhaps even more plausible? What if we are capable of being evil all on our own? What if demons are not always the cause of our bad behavior and instead, we willingly choose evil by our own volition?"

His words were not consoling in any way. But we both needed to explore the reality of his reflections, just as we had explored the ruins beneath our feet, to understand what consequences had caused them, and what we might do to avoid more of the same in our future.

Ilona:

Our stores were nearly dried up, Mom-dame spoke out a simple message to us all. "Time to move." The trick is that compass directions, and the weather with them, are sideways. We packed up all our good-right food, water, tents, wears and readied ourselves to go. All of us gathered outside at our town center, and mom-dame said there was one last cleaning that must happen. She told all of us to gather up broken wood pieces and anything lying about that would flame if it was lit. Then she scratched up a fire and had each of us light up one stick of the wood we held. Then she said to run quick through our home-place and the places near around, and light them all up with our sticks.

When the fire was everywhere, we turned away to leave and Mom-dame gave a harder order.

"Do not look back."

Aella:

Our numbers increased along the way as other wayward dames were found and invited. It seemed almost futile to teach the concepts of common womanhood and to instruct in our survivalist approach. We grew to as many as five hundred, but the elements and threats along the way cruelly cut our numbers again and again until, on arrival at our new home, we were no more than three hundred and thirty.

As futile as it seemed, I insisted each dame learn and adhere to the principles of dame separation. We could not trust wrecks, not even the ones that claimed affinity to our ways. It was time to rid the world of the archaic written record and nostalgic ideology that had memorialized patriarchal virtues.

As well, sexual latency and transgender acceptance were just too complex of issues for us to take on in the hostility of the times. I found no simple way to distinguish the intent of gender-neutral practitioners and that of the sly pretenders hoping to take advantage somewhere along our path. We could not afford the confusion and so I devised a plan to eliminate the issue all together. I planned as we camped along the way, designing a justice system that would become strictly enforced once we made it safely to…still the question…safely to where?

Our destination was inspired by the odd map that our two refugee companions had provided. Mine was a difficult truce with them—their traditionalized relationship represented everything I had come to resent. No, that was an unfair understatement...I abhorred their blindly contrived interactions. I had experienced everything they displayed between one another and I knew it to be a house of cards built on the worst of lies. So, I waited for the opportunity to expose them by some hypocritical act in order to use them as an example for all of my dames.

Meanwhile, their geographical chart proved to be amazingly accurate and valuable as a guide for our journey. But pulling a realistic account of its origins out of these two was impossible. Their shared story of its acquisition appeared to me, a strange mystical tale. They claimed the map was offered through some religious vision. I have always been suspicious of such superstitious drivel.

Of course, the map was only a basic guide. It meticulously described vast areas of topography but did not point to a specific destination; that we would have to choose on our own. We knew that we had to aim in the direction of the "new south", toward the old Canadian territories, but how far? What was the safest route, and what was to be our journey's end? My suggestion to all was to listen keenly to wayward travelers we encountered along the way.

A place must exist where we can settle to establish our realm. The answer came from those we ran into who had encountered some frustrating blockade, reversed course, or had simply given up. To a person, they had displayed what I now define as wanderlust. What they discovered in their journeying was never satisfactory.

Those shattered vagabonds spoke of toxic volcanoes, death pits of tar, scorpions the size of rodents and of course, the enormous Rippers with their razor-sharp metallic wings. As I listened to them, I resolved that we would not become such Bedouins—always searching for the proverbial greener grass.

Over and over, we listened to each we met along the way, and one location kept surfacing in their descriptions. It was a hostile place but apparently contained a source of ample water. There were caves and abandoned buildings for shelter and a somewhat predictable climate. It was not perfect—as no place was or ever will be on the hellish planet. That is why these wanderers abandoned it as they abandoned every place, futilely hoping to rediscover their suburban palaces and pleasures which I knew to no longer exist anywhere.

We had no such fantasies. The place they described had once been called the Black Hills of South Dakota. Now known as the Barrens, it would allow us the things necessary to establish a survivable if spartan existence. A particular area we kept hearing about loomed large on my list as a best choice. It was called now as it had been referred to before; Hot Springs, and we aimed in its direction, envisioning it with hope as our future home.

Teagan:

Zeke kicked at the body. "Good," he spoke out-loud. He did not further justify his comment and I wisely did not ask for an explanation.

Since Portunus' warning to him, the military Overseer has not made any more attempts to injure or seduce me, but now seems interested in somehow correcting my character. Unlike the Monk's encouraging invitations, Zeke's method has been to order me to follow him on several sorties into the Barrens. With each trip, I become more fearful that his restraint will not hold. What options do I have but to behave well and hope for his continued resolve? None.

The slowly increasing bird and fish population had allowed us to forego our pursuit of human flesh, but this day we came upon a most unusual subject, a man walking by himself, not of our clan. He looked to be an indigenous plainsman by heritage, and this one began to approach us with a look of relief on his face. I could only assume he was a weakened straggler who could not keep up with the large group of what were now dubbed by our clan, *digies.* We had observed them days ago heading toward what I had always known to be south.

With the total flipping of the Earth's magnetic poles, it was now north. I had heard, when the V4641 Singularity first started re-altering the landscape of the planet, far away in that direction, a once great country had been violently reshaped and was broken up into a menagerie of islands known as the Mexicos.

When we had watched the digies marching, we noted they had not split, male and female. Their abandoning of their long held tribal land might have been thanks to the strife they saw around them and their wanting to seek more peaceful conditions better suited to their temperament.

I thought it would be a helpful opportunity to learn the nature of their quest. Were there other dangers out here they had encountered of which our clan was yet unaware? I was going to suggest the question to Zeke, but he had other plans. As the elderly man neared us, my commander did not even hesitate. He launched his spear before the other had a chance to make an introduction. One more life was pointedly ended, and I was particularly saddened at the loss. The plains people had been one with this land for countless generations. What stories this old father might have shared by our fires. With his tribe now vacated, there was scant chance of better understanding their historical journey.

Zeke was about to turn from his completed deed when he remembered his auger was still implanted in the victim's torso. "Well, we can't have that, can we?" He chuckled as he bowed to extract the staff from the corpse. As he did so, he mocked the body with a benediction, "May the place you be, do better than the place you was."

The flesh-peddler retrieved his tool, wiping the blood away using the rags that barely covered his prey. It seemed the best use for the cloth, and for his own self. I remember now, and the puzzle still eludes me, that I wondered at the time, *why do the digies not wear protection from the bugs?* The thought passed quickly for Zeke turned my way and whistled. It was a command I understood immediately and of what it was ordering me to: It had been drilled into me through my early training just as the auger had drilled into its target. The body was to be "prepared". It was a hot day and there wouldn't be much time before the smell would ruin Zeke's work—that could not happen lest I would be the next to be "prepared".

Trusting that I would obey well, the broad-shouldered commander turned to leave the site and head back for the dens without a care of this man or my well-being. As an afterthought, he paused and turned back to face me.

"You will tell no one of this." Zeke's stare spoke the command and his intent in the moment—the carcass was to be his and his alone. He wanted me to understand in no uncertain terms that my reporting this act to Matada, Portunus, anyone, would be the ending of me, by him. His training and expectations of me were simple and clear.

There was an added, ongoing menace in his voice. Zeke, nor I, had forgotten Portunus' command to this warrior that I was not to be "handled". All that sounded good, but what was to stop him here in the Barrens from fulfilling his earlier intentions? The threat lingered in my mind and it was enough to overcome my revulsion of performing the human-butchering act I had sworn never to undertake again. As I sliced, I recalled another incident which still bothered me within:

> While doing my chores at our dens, I had observed Zeke, Portunus, and Matada standing together in discussion. Though they had separated themselves from others, it was obvious the conversation was animated and heated. Zeke used his hands a lot to communicate and seemed to be arguing, especially with our Head Clansman about something or someone not present. His arm would extend with a pointed finger in the general direction of the dens that included my dwelling and both Matada and Portunus shook their heads in disagreement. Then the military clansman looked toward my direction.
>
> I had quickly busied myself with picking up a boulder, hoping the three had not caught my glances. And apparently, they had not, for the next time I peeked their direction, they were focused again on their private conversation. Still, I could not help but suspect that I was the subject of their argument and apparently the clan

leader and our scout were in disagreement with Zeke the Overseer about my role and value.

Here in the wilds, the influence of the other two men carried great weight with Zeke. He kept his personal hungers in frustrated check, but we both knew that any misstep on my part at any time might trigger the unleashing of his desire. I was determined not to give him any reason to misbehave, but I was not naïve. Zeke's eyes and mannerisms told that he had longer range plans for me.

Was I the only one? Maybe he had designs on others as well, possibly to ultimately put the entire clan including Matada and Portunus in our proper place. He was an astute reader of men's intents and I'm sure he has considered me, cover to cover. Maybe he has been assessing me for much longer than I have realized. And I worry more for my longevity because of it. My relations with Portunus are not well concealed and Zeke is certainly intuitive enough to consider such an alliance as dangerous to his growing authority. He has not become military Overseer of our clan by friending up to others.

Maybe the time is coming soon when multiple alliances will no longer be a choice. Maybe I have spent too much time with Portunus, discussing our community and its condition. Our conversations are contrary to the *One Minding* of the clan and so a danger to Zeke's stronghold over the troops. Maybe he has already been eavesdropping, overseeing our dialogue, and this duty he had me undertake was his signal to me, "Choose and choose quickly!"

Maybe; maybe. And then in response (or is it a harbinger?), one of Portunus' witticisms spoken to me recently, floated to my conscious mind, "*Maybe* is just a path to *yes* or *no*."

So, to whom, or what do I pledge my "yes"? What will be the consequences of my "no"?

Ilona:

As we trekked the hard road, awful things tried to end us. Cold and hot, Ripper attacks, earth-shakes and storms, other critters and even dark minded wrecks who tried to make us their food. Best as she could, Mom-dame kept us strong together, but still some were lost. On the good-right side, we found some more dames who were cave-hiding. They were nature-savvy proven by the fact they were still breathing when they should have been ended. They joined us and our tribe grew as we searched for "new home".

"A plan is needed". That's what Mom-dame said during a night-camp, to her circle—the dames she trusted most. I was in that circle, but I grasp I wouldn't be if Mom-dame knew my ponderings and pen-scratching 'bout her.

Ramon had helped much on our way, even offering some blood-sacrifice when fighting alongside us against the wild-wreck attacks. But still Mom-dame hated him and Maria too. I ponder that allowing no wrecks, however good-right, to exist in the world; and not tolerating wreck-likers; would be Mom-dame's pleasure.

"When we establish our new home, there will be new rules. Any wrecks we find near us must agree to be clipped of their manning. Only then will we allow them to survive. It is for our safety...and theirs of course."

On our trek, I stepped backward in the line, preferring to be at a distance from New-mom-dame. Stead, I walked alongside Maria and Ramon. I learned the closeness of them. I felt the deep-care of them. At first I was puzzled in my head 'cause I'd been told by Mom-dame that a wreck's brain was 'tween his legs. But I heard Ramon speak good things out and I grasped his thinking to be just like anyone's.

Mom-dame got louder in her telling them to stay separate and they obeyed in fear. So, I listened when walking with each of them apart. Then I shared messages, one to the other, back and forth. I became ears and mouth for them and to them. It felt good-right seeing, and hearing one speak out well to the other—Maria part of him, Ramon part of her—without a touch. The more I heard and shared their messages, the more I wanted those messages to be for me, coming from some...good-wreck.

I kept close to Maria and Ramon. Simple fact of it—I liked them. They spoke out 'bout their Mexico days and how they met, and they used the word "amor" to explain their closeness. I had not grasped afore that two folk, most so, a dame and a wreck, could ponder and tell as if they were one-and-the-same person. Ramon would start to tell something, fumble for a word and Maria would fill in the blank. Each was fast to do things for the other, even if the other didn't ask for the doing. They wanted to help one another lots and seemed to want to help all of us dames. They did something else strange, together as one; they laughed and got others to laugh with them—me most of all. When the laughing came, Mom-dame would turn her head quickly toward us and frown, putting her finger to her mouth to shush us as if laughing was noisy death.

One night on the path, Ramon and Maria shared a quiet secret with me. They whispered that the map they dreamed and pict, was put in their heads by a bright man. I asked what color bright he would be if I crayoned him, and they said at the same time together, "Dorado."

They also whispered that their *Amigo Dorado*—what they named the bright-man—gave them another map. They had drawn it up but had not shared it with Mom-dame. Maria then looked all around in the low light to make sure no other ears and eyes were peeking in on us. Then she reached into her pack and pulled out a rolled parch. She handed it to me and put her hands tenderly over mine. She took a slow quiet breath, in and out, and then spoke out quietly to me, "Por tu, Ilona dulce: El camino de vuelta a casa." Somehow, I can't grasp how, I understood her in my head, *For you, sweet Ilona: The way back home.*

I knew a wow-gift was in my hands. I didn't grasp why, but I felt the giving of the gift powerfully inside me. It was only for me—at least for the moment. I hid the parch in my pack with good-right care and whispered back to them some amor words they had taught me, "Gracias, Mama y Papa."

Aella:

We have arrived! What should have taken us no more than three months of determined marching turned into a crushing eighteen-month trudge.

Along the way, marauding bandits, wild weather swings, storms that would wipe a life away in a heartbeat, and unspeakable creatures, attacked without warning.

But we are here and so our organizing begins. Soon, very soon, we will be a tribe to be reckoned with in this land.

An odd side note. As we approached our new domain, there was a sensation that something had changed...much like when someone changes their hairstyle or appearance in some way, and it takes a bit to figure out exactly what they have done. Progressively, many in our tribe mentioned to me the same query: "What is it? What's different?"

We discovered the old pig slaughtering plant in a very secluded and watered spot. It appeared to provide the best options for shelter, defense and building a community. I had encouraged everyone to focus on settling in, but honestly, the doctor-scientist in me became preoccupied with identifying the "what is it?"

The "something else, something different" that everyone had been sensing came to my awareness a half a day into occupying and arranging our new home. Actually, it was someone else in our midst who also could not dismiss her curiosity. Jessica came toward me in her silent way with an unfamiliar smile on her typically sullen face. She was holding something rare in these times tucked under her right arm; a greyish brown animal, looking to be the size of a raccoon. Always being a bit of an animal whisperer; it did not surprise me that the creature seemed perfectly comfortable being carried in such a manner by the girl.

As Jessica came closer, I recognized the species: Short narrow head tapering to a small snout, abundant body covered in a tough armor-like shell, dangerously long claws on stubby feet, and an almost reptilian tail. It was an armadillo! The girl-turned-woman during our journey-petted the prehistoric relic on its head and then held it out to me for observation. She made a two-word comment, her simple style, which revealed a world of revelation.

"No bugs!"

Teagan:

We have been told never to wander far and to make sure any movement away from the dens is done in pairs or preferably more. On several occasions, wounded men, not from our clan, were discovered or limped to our location. Some didn't survive, but those who did spoke of their traveling parties being ambushed, being hacked, and tortured mercilessly at the hands of the she-dames, as they are called. The fear in the survivors' eyes when they spoke of their narrow escapes, suggested truth in their wild tales. Portunus himself has warned us around the fire that any encounter with the dame-tribes means death. He is the only one of our clan allowed to speak the title and he does so only as a messenger of hazard.

—Women attacking men? How had this come to be? Again, the monk shared his insight by the light of one of our evening fires. Portunus reminded us that, in the old days, countries, regions, and tribes more carefully deliberated on the purpose of their warfare. In the country of the United States, we had tried (but had not always succeeded in) declaring war only if there was some vested interest—territorial disputes, natural resource access, conflicting ideologies. or some other lofty issue.

"Waring has changed," he explained. "Now we war simply to survive, the cause of an assault, one toward the other, has become unclear in the moment. The unknown intent of our advisories makes our vigilance all the more important."

With the emerging enemy as a shared threat, Matada, our de facto leader has successfully united most of the fractured clans. We are becoming one efficient unit, both for protection against the she-dames and other yet to be discovered dangers.

Ilona:

We have found a place near the rubble that was once black mountains. Our new home-place is a good-right dwelling though there is much to clean up from the numerous quakes that have rearranged the land.

We heard tell that afore, the place had been called Hot Springs. Hot it still is, but none of the dames have spotted any springs. If they are here, they hide under a raging river that can only be crossed with great carefulness.

On our journey here, Bedouins told us that during one of the big, big quakes, another river called afore, the Missouri, decided to take a sharp right turn, 'stead of where it had been flowing. Now it is a noisy rush, but it feeds us good-right liquid and washes us too. Mom-dame has spoken out that we need to be careful with the water, not just in its crossing, but in its using.

"We can't know when another quake might send the river another direction, or away completely" she warned. I ponder she learned this lesson from the Blanking as much as from all the quaking.

The new name we have given this place is *River Canyon*. It is a good-right pic-place, and when I make my dwelling up, I plan to crayon it as green and blue.

Papa Ramon still breathed, and I was glad-right for it. But I fretted over his chances of living 'cause of the look in Mom-dame's eyes whenever I saw her look his way. He had made himself purposeful. Mom-dame, spoke out to her inside group that he was only pretending to embrace dame beliefs and would soon try to rule. Mom-dame would not explain how she foreknew it to be, but most all the tribe, 'cept for me and Mama Maria, also thought it would be that way.

Mom-dame used Papa Ramon as her red-flag to put fear into all the tribe and warned us that we needed a big way to end the danger. That's when she started calling the pig plant, *Law House* and made rules for living there.

In our first group gathering in the Law House, Mom-dame gave us commandments on how to live and not die. The smell of the place was still pig, not pleasure, and so she made a joke of it…

"We need to clean the pork from this place. Let's make some bacon!"

The dames liked the cooking joke and listened real quiet for the next.

"These commands I give to you so that you may live, and live strong."

Cheering went up big in the smelly Law House, at Mom-dame's telling:

"First, be proud of all dames together doing right for all other dames. We are dames only, and only dames. There will be no other ways but dame-ways.

"You will not take being a dame for granted. We are important, one to the other.

"We will be dames together all day and all night. There will be no rest from being together-dames.

"Honor your sisters. They are all you have.

"Beware, death awaits you outside of your tribe. End those first who would end you.

"Your tribe and your sisters love you. Love no one else.

"Dames share all and tell all to all dames, with all dames. Stealing from one is the death of all dames.

"Lying to the tribe is death. If you lie to one, you lie to all.

"What I have is yours, what you have is mine. We dames will share and there will be no owners.

"Don't desire your sister's stuff, it's not hers or yours to want. Desire is death.

"…And the eleventh is as strong as the first:

"Life to dames, death to wrecks!"

All the dames picked up the theme in a chorus chant, "Life to dames, death to wrecks! Life to dames, death to wrecks!" The shared voicing in the Law House was enough to shake my bones. Mom-dame let it go on for a good-right time, then raised her arms and brought them down, slow, and easy, to signal she needed quiet to share more. The Law House obeyed to hear her next speaking-out.

"If a wreck comes near, we will come nearer and cut or end them. If they survive, they will be "trialed" in our Law House by me as Judge for the dames. And judgement will be swift, I promise."

A roar of "whoots" and hollers followed her words. But Mom-dame was not done, and she spoke out one more surprise.

"Any wrecks found in the wilderness are fair game for any dames hunting food. It will be your choice when you gain the high-ground over a wreck. You can clip them and leave them or cure their meat for a meal later…"

With a smirky dark smile I had never afore seen cross her face, she added to her telling…

"Or both."

And that is how the Big Warring started.

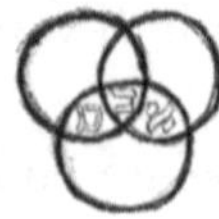

Teagan:

"—You will tell no one of this," said Zeke. The haunting repetition of his command caused another quiver to run the course of my spine. I remembered the order he had given me after his taking of the wandering digie in the Barrens. My stomach and my soul burned with acidic dread. As was his way, Zeke's stare spoke the command and his intent in the moment. Nothing more need be said.

He has just fleshed a dame he had snared in the crags of a nearby canyon across the waters of the Rushmore. We were hunting when the dame came out from behind us. A well-hidden crevice had disguised her presence and she meant to take advantage, stealthily jumping, and landing onto Zeke's back, pulling her arms tight in a stranglehold around his neck and shoulders.

But he is also a practiced warrior, and with no small struggle manages to bring down and pin the dame to the ground. Her knife had cut deep but could not manage to find his ending spot. Zeke's auger has found her fatal regions. Red oozes from her body and mingles in a pool beneath the two as he pummels her into unconsciousness. His blade has cut deep into her chest, and she is quickly becoming a "past thing".

We had been warned by Matada, Portunus, and Zeke, of the she-dame danger, but besides the heightened hostility of one gender toward the other, something else has changed. Beyond domination over one's adversary, and the lust of sexual brutality, there is still an added temptation that remains very clear.

Until recently, grubs and insects had only gone so far in nourishing our bodies in these hostile environs. We had tried to plant crops but the results were dismal. Then, as I have already recounted, we had lowered ourselves in desperation to consuming human flesh. The sudden and prolific appearance of the armadillo herds and dove populations (as they developed a taste for the Ripper bugs) have just begun to occur. Portunus, by his methods, has determined that the local shelled creatures are not carriers of leprosy as they once had been. Bird flu had also been a well-known killer, but the flocks here seem impervious. So now, "possum on the half-shell" and cooing birds have become a welcome addition to the menu. Thus, to the victor not only goes control of the area, but also the food source.

Now, we can at least sustain ourselves with animal meat, but Zeke is not satisfied. With the emerging threat from the she-dames, his undisputed hatred of the opposite sex has evolved into an avenging butchering quest. It is his belief that we should continue to "utilize our prey" as he diabolically justifies the savagery. In his words and way of thinking, it is the pragmatic thing to do. He has lectured me about his beliefs on numerous excursions.

"It is the ending of the weak, the infirm, and unproductive that will sustain us," Zeke insists. "What better way to obliterate your enemy than to consume them?"

But Matada's edicts have become less…consuming. "Even in such a primitive existence, there are 'understoods'," he preached at one fire-sharing. "Whoever is the leader of a successful hunting encounter, is expected to honor your opponent's final struggle." They should no longer be considered meat acquired for the group."

Zeke still thinks himself above such restrictions. His intent was made clear by one of his own fire-sharings:

> "An occasional capture and rape of a she-dame? Why not? That's a reward according to our customs. Violation of them is justified considering how they strike us in the night. Their robbing and clipping of our ranks is far more vicious than anything we can do in retaliation. We war upon them as they war upon us and that's the way of it."

Although Zeke no longer publicly mentions the continuation of cannibalism, his statement certainly leaves that door open to interpretation. My interpretation remains constant. Excusing the pun, I did, and still do find the slaughtering of any other human to be…distasteful. Up to this moment, I have even succeeded in avoiding joining any ongoing hunting or sporting parties, other than when he had taken me and ordered me to butcher the digie.

So, being present at Zeke's current conquest of the dame, I once again find myself having to choose between my life and loyalty verses another's behavioral un-sensibilities. I would like to claim nobility in this, but how can I?

I should have known, by his other unorthodox ways, that Zeke's desire is always to make a personal statement by his slaughtering, to satisfy his own importance. In this terrible present moment, I watch helplessly as he sticks his forefinger in one of the dame's arm wounds and she is instantly again awake and screaming to the emptiness in the place. Her pain is her own with no one courageous enough to interrupt and bring a quick end to her suffering. Then to her screaming, he adds violation, taking her with a hungry blood-soaked smile. The rhythm of it sickens me, but I hold that in. I cannot show him weakness; he would end me in the aftermath as well.

The dame stops breathing. Along with the stillness, her anguish vanishes. It does nothing to stop the Overseer. Ended or alive mattered not to Zeke's release of lust. He contributes himself to her brief history, and when he is finally done, he does not bother to clean himself. He simply takes his large blade and starts portioning the carcass for later consumption.

What we have become is the cruelest shame of all. But this moment is Zeke's trophy and in a twist of the words his dead dame had proclaimed, he boasts to the world, in his loudest voice, "I am Zeke the Overseer, conqueror of the Barrens. Death to dames and life to Clansmen!"

Zeke's most recent success in conquest is not the norm amongst our clan. Since their recent arrival, the dames more oft are the winners. One against one, they are powerful, clever, and strong in defending themselves. We cannot know how our captured kind are treated. The only evidence of our defeated ones is an ending site, usually a secluded area with plenty of bones and signs of futile struggle scattered about.

I have suddenly realized that Zeke's commands to me might be based more in insecurity. Strong actions can camouflage weak belief and wavering conviction. I would have to keep a watch on him, such inconsistency in

thought could lead to inconsistency in decisions critical to our existence…
my existence.

Aella:

I can't…I can't…there is nothing I can do, she is gone, brutalized, and butchered by the savages beyond the Canyons. I have lost the sweet love of my friend and willing soldier, Latisha.

All I had asked her to do was scout. Nothing more. "Careful," I said. "We aren't familiar with this area yet. Take someone with you and…scout.

But she was so eager, so beautiful in her willingness to serve. She spied two wrecks, a commander of sorts and his boy companion. She saw an opportunity and wanted to please me. Thank the stars that Babs held back, ordered by precious Latisha to stay in the rocks. "This will be a simple ending," claimed my confident one.

And it was simple. The warrior-wreck took her quickly, and in the ugliest of ways. I shiver at the callous way he stole her purity, then filleted her for a later meal. If I had been there…if only I had been…

—It was all Babs could do to not vomit in her hiding spot. She silently wept as she watched Zeke, as he called himself, pronounce his manhood as if it was some noble title instead of a genomic defect. My sweet Babs is forever traumatized. I saw it in her eyes as she worked her way through her report to me. I see it in her walk and now in the robotic way she performs her duties. The old girl is gone, the woman survives. I can only hope she will resolve what she had to endure in the watching and use it as fuel for revenge. I will help her use it. We will all need to be fed by her story, and then…

I can…we will do one thing. We will kill the killers. All of them; not only the ones who have killed, but the ones who will. The repulsive, ever sex-crazed Y chromosome pollutes all their DNA and so they must be irradicated, every last one. Latisha deserves no less than total retribution.

We will start with our own pet wreck. I have held back on his ending for too long. And then, the boy. He is as guilty as his general, he did nothing to protest the slaughtering, so he will become the beginning of a new slaughter that will only end when we dames are free of them, all of them.

Ilona:

There is sobbing, then wailing in the place; it does not come from the wreck kneeling and roped to a metal bar in front of Mom-dame, but from Mama Maria. Mom-dame glares at the weeper. I grasp that our rule-warrior is annoyed at the weak-sad song of Mama Maria who mourns for Papa Ramon. Turning her head back to stare spikes of fury into the kneeling one before her, she spits out words meant for both the wreck and his mate.

"You know that cohabitation between dames and wrecks is forbidden. Your sharing of mood and thoughts, comparing, and polluting one another with your...man and woman ideas, is as deadly as a child born between the two of you. We spared you as a gift and commanded you to total separation. But you rebelled. We observe you now to be beyond trust and therefore, beyond the privilege of life."

I look with wet eyes and open ears. I hear the words of Mom-dame, but my brain is busy with remembering my listening and sharing back and forth with Papa Ramon y Mama Maria as we were trekking.

What I did not ponder back then was that, while I listened and shared with them, Mom-dame listened too. She did not say a word to me but followed my eyes and ears with hers and grasped too well what we were doing. She did not ask, she did not speak out her seeing of our doing, it was a secret in her 'til we came to River Canyon.

Then, this night, the dame-drums sounded, and we all came to the Law House. We had been trained to know that drums meant *meet* and maybe *war*.

And there was Ramon on the ground with gashes on his back and bruises on his face. He was roped and already looking very close to not living.

Teagan:

"—You will tell no one of this," Zeke the Overseer's orders keep haunting my dreams, waking me in a sweat and I find myself terrified to speak, even to myself. But another voice, not my own and not Zeke's, calms me in the moment.

"Come to me, you who are heavily burdened."

I have heard those words before. Where? The source and the sayer escape me, but the words are a warm blanket, tangible and able to guard me from the cold of my dank dwelling place.

It's one thing to be comforted, but what do I do? I can't be silent about the horrors I've witnessed. Do I risk my life by reporting the events to Matada or Portunus? Would they be empathetic or simply brush me aside; being more concerned about what they believe to be more pressing issues? And what would their reaction tell of them, of their conscious morality? Does a greater good exist any longer?

So many questions. But only one answer vibrates within me.

"Let not your heart be troubled."

Ilona:

"You have chosen your own fate, and by your choosing, you will live or die!" Mom-dame's words from the center arena of our Law House sound important as she stands tall over the bruised and battered Papa Ramon.

"Let this be the way of us!" That's how she readied us for her slaughtering. And quick it was. After all her shouting, Mom-dame untied Papa Ramon and made war on him. I had never afore seen her make one wreck be what she thought of all wrecks. I grasped that by ending him, she was ending every one of them.

When she was done and I helped Mom-dame cleanse herself and dawn new wraps, she said not a word to me; nor me to her. We both knew it was because of me that this had happened and so, for me a new choice had to be made and a new wrapping had to be dawned.

Aella:

She is disturbed. Deeply. I'm not sure what to do about my daughter, but she is becoming less and less connected with reality. I thought that involving her with me in our judgements and survival duties. would help center her; would help us bond.

What I'm seeing instead is a deepening schism within her psyche.

Teagan:

There is another peculiar attribute humans share in common with armadillos. The meat of the ancient, armored creatures does not taste as I remember beef or chicken. It seems though that they and we do taste very much alike.

As I play my flute in the confines of my den, words form in my brain. I'm not ready to write them yet because they are so confusing in these times and conditions in which I live. The words though refuse not to be heard and so I play them over and over again in my head and they share my music's melody. Or maybe they are the melody and my fluting is simply the accompaniment to a more powerful message.

One odd thing about my music. Whenever and wherever I play, Armadillos assemble as an audience. I've not shared this phenomena with anyone because it seems a cruel way to lure a next meal. I'm finding myself willing to forgo cutting into them for their tasty meat as they are becoming more companions than cattle for consumption.

Since birds and fish also are making a resurgence in the area, I guess I'll have to have Portunus teach me more about his skills in nabbing those tricky prey.

Ilona:

Rocks fly, I have seen them do it! Not just down and sideways, but up, like they were woken-up! Most days the Earth shakes regularly, but this day even boulders took aim. The ground cracked to kill us if it could.

A few dames were crushed, some were swallowed whole by the avalanching. Many were red-sacrificed and bent in ways that aren't normal. But after the rocks fell asleep and landed, most of us still lived. I remember all of this, but I didn't on that day 'cause one fist-sized stone met my head in the air and took my brain on a trip. On that dizzy ride, I remembered things that I had put far away. Foods I missed tasting, smells, and one other pretty thing, a girl doll that Mom-dame had tossed away without my knowing.

Since the rock flying, I am not just doing lots more remembering; I am trying to un-remember too, some memories I no longer want to keep. Yet some of the unwelcomed recalls, I do want to hold tight to; like the ones about who I'm loneliest for most—my dad-wreck. Mom-dame, spoke out 'bout his ending and 'bout his afore-ending. He was a Pointer, but I remember how he pointed differently from most others…he was always pointing up, not at others, not telling them hard things. His pointing was always asking, always what he called praying, and helping me ponder that there was a bigger Pointer no one could see, who would someday answer the praying and pondering. I never heard Dad-wreck speak out that he got an answer, but that didn't stop his praying and pondering.

I remember afore, a few others like him. My grasping of such things is that they were blanked 'cause, like my dad-wreck, they pointed and prayed. But to Mom-dame their Blanking was the good-right ending for what was, and what never should be again. She oft times acted as a Pointer too, though she never pointed up, just at others, and at me.

I only remember my dad-wreck through my little-folk eyes. We did a strange thing together called…*play.* I would pretend to be something I was not—an animal—and we would act out a story, with me and him being in other places, even being on different planets. And we would do another strange thing; we would laugh and giggle together. I remember liking the pretending. I wish I could do it often now, but there are too many dangers near at hand to risk pretending much for much more than for a blink of an eye.

My memories of my dad-wreck are foggy, but mostly good-right. In my mind-pic of him, he is tall, but not big-built. He has eyes that seem happy even when his mouth was frowning. My dad-wreck knew the earth—how to use plants and things to heal and grow. Mom-dame is one that knows folks and how to use them, to bend their pondering ways so that they ponder like her. Dad-wreck and Mom-dame were good together back then, until they 'grew dark'— grew apart from each other's wanting of the other.

When Mom-dame spoke out to me that my dad-wreck was ended, she made it sound all matter-of-fact: No sadness, no gladness; just that there had been an accident, that he was 'not' and would 'not' be with us anymore, and for me 'not' to be watching out for him to come back. After her telling me this, I was quiet in my remembering him. I grasped somehow that Mom-dame had become angry at my dad-wreck—it showed in her face when she spoke out about him. I did not want my mom-dame's anger at him to become her anger at me. She spoke out 'bout my dad-wreck in a way that made him small and I grasped she wanted me to agree that he was small. I did not want her to know that I still saw him as big. I did not want to be made small like him at the hands of Mom-dame.

River Canyon and the pig plant might be a good-right home-place for dames, but I grasp deeply now that it is not any longer a home for me. I don't feel as numb here, but my darkness in this place is still like a gun pointed at my head; when the trigger will be pulled for the final time. When it does fire, will I finally be killed? Death would be better than the pain, but something inside me battles, something fights ending the pain, stops me from pulling the gun trigger.

Then comes the crying again. I want to sink into my tears, but too soon, they dry up. So, I fetal myself in a corner of my room and try not to forget: I visit the old ways; I remember the happy Mom-Dad times; I ponder about when the world was a favorite song with green and blue things all around 'stead of the brown and rusty black of things now.

My hunger is now fast and fierce. My hope that seemed to always be just behind and around a corner, promising, but never showing its face, now pokes at me, tells me, "Join the race!"

Others keep trying to slow up my race. All the dames, including Mom-dame whisper to me, "You just wait and keep hoping," they say, but their idea of it all is a lie. I tell them they can't make my hope come true 'cause it's already here! How can they pretend to know what hope is and how can they hope to make it come for me? I can see their pain too—vacant eyes and hung heads—those tell the truth of their no-hope, to me.

Most folk's hoping stopped with the Blanking; I don't know why. That was the biggest change of all that I felt inside me and saw in other folks back then—men and women, all of us, seemed to at one time have needed each the other. Now, no more. I have pondered it since, harder than I figured I was able. I have washed my pondering with tears from the deepest part of me to try to make my old grasping go away.

I am scratching a new name for myself and learning to be a new chooser; someone who had a past way of living that is ending. Mine is

not like the living others do now. My wording, my pondering, my...me...
is not learned anymore from the words and acts of dames or from wrecks.
It is a new way for a new me, and so the new me will not live with the old
way or the old me.

Now I will call myself, Ilona. I figure, if I am going away to live in my
new way, I need to be ALL new. It is the only and best way. But to what
new place is Ilona going...?

—The *Way Back Home* map given to me by Mama Maria y Papa Ramon!
The rock to my head helped me remember that I had hidden its special
importance away deep in my mind. And I start pondering secretly inside,
Is it ready to be followed? To what home will it take me?

Aella:

My daughter has changed, and it is not a welcomed one. I have already
noted that I have been including her more and more in the administration
of tribal life survival, hoping that she might break out of her cocoon to
become the wonderful warrior I know hides within. Instead, the new
women I see before me has rebelled in a very different way.

"I am leaving," she said to me.

I had heard from others that she was behaving oddly. Especially after
the most recent severe quake where she (where many of our sisters!) had
been concussed by the flying debris. I had even noticed some of her acting
out myself, but she had seemed to be improving over the weeks, so I had
stopped being overly concerned. That is, until I entered her cabin to find
her packing her scant belongings. She said offhandedly, as she reached

for her trinkets and pushed them purposefully into her pack, that she was preparing to abandon the tribe.

I was shocked. Her carriage, her demeanor, her everything is dramatically altered. "You can't go," I instructed. "You are in no way prepared for what lurks out there. No dame is safe on her own."

"It is this place that is not safe for me," she responded without looking up from her search for personal items.

An unfamiliar sensation came over me. I wanted to hug her, hold her tightly and soothe her anxious fears. I fought the temptation and responded in my role as dame protector. "You are forbidden from leaving."

As if her actions were not already unpredictable enough, her next was beyond the pale. She turned in surprise to look at me as if I were an adversary challenging her intent. Then her face broke into a twisted emotional eruption, hysterically laughing and crying in combination with the spewing acid of her next words.

"And what will you do to stop me? Will I be your next show in the Law House?"

How can this be happening? I desperately searched for the words to settle her, to ease her back to reality. "I am not your enemy, but your enemies, our enemies, are out there, waiting for you." I point to the door as I whisper the words, hoping my warning will still her insanity.

Her frenzy settles at my beckoning, but her eyes betray the fire consuming her from within. I can see her grappling to bring her thoughts under control and hope she is reasoning through a way to make peace with me and our circumstances. Her next gasped words rip through my soul.

"Do you believe that because one is my enemy that another who also calls them enemy is my friend? I share not enemy nor friendship with you. I no longer call any an enemy or friend, as another—as you—would have me do."

With that, she slung her pack over her shoulder, sidestepped me and left into the night.

Teagan:

We sat in the early morning light and observed an armadillo.

"They should not survive here as they are voracious drinkers," Portunus informs. "But where we have been cursed in this new age, these armored ones, strange relatives to the anteater, have been truly blessed."

Without my prompting, he continues to share, as if he too has a need to grasp how he has arrived at this part of his journey. I feel somehow honored at Portunus' confiding in me, understanding that what he is revealing would be poorly received during a fire-sharing.

"My family was ripped apart by the actions of God," he says while continuing to stare at the foraging mammal nearby. "I always considered myself devout and well-studied in religion, but never tried to force my beliefs or practices on my loved ones or friends."

At this, he chuckles and corrects the comment, "They, I'm sure would argue that point, but I could not help live out my practices. Those had become...rote and internalized." Portunus' face became somber as stone and the weight of the memories appeared to pull his head down to stare at the barren ground below him.

"My wife did not hold my convictions. we had agreed to disagree. And when those we knew to be strong, and or innocent in their belief were taken away, we were both shocked into a new reality. Neither of us had a true relationship, neither with the Creator of the universe, nor with our closest partners. We had been living a practiced lie.

"At first the realization angered me," Portunus continued, again looking out to the armadillo. "How could God abandon someone who was so loyal to him? Why had he not warned me of the coming catastrophe? But...he did warn me...over and over. I now realize how little consideration I gave to the idea that God is actually capable of interpersonal fellowship with any...all individuals. Even me. And by dismissing that idea, I had dismissed the most important, the critical part of what he intended in the first place."

Wait, did he just suggest that Portunus the Monk and God had personal conversations? That sounded so crazy when spoken out loud. Why would any of us deserve the attention of a divine creature, and even if I did try to speak to that spirit, why would that spirit bother to actually respond?

"Ever wonder what that little voice you talk to in the back of your head is and why you have a conversation with it?" Portunus seemed to have an uncanny ability to read the thoughts of others and to respond to those thoughts without provocation. It unnerved me every time...maybe as much as his conversations with God have appeared to unnerve him.

"...And if I can't even properly relate to God, listen, and respond to his urgings, how can I possibly relate properly to the people of this planet?"

Portunus' spoken thought seemed not to relate at all to his comment before. Yet, it resonated in my mind as a tuning fork catches a note and insists on adjustment to match its vibrato. The song it planted in my head was now titled, "Is God speaking to me?"

Can I talk with God? the little voice in the back of my head asked.

"I regret not working that thought through earlier, before...before...," my mentor continued, seeming then only to be talking to himself.

But I sang along in my head, *Before...before.*

"I have lost everyone whom I wanted to share my love with, because I did not understand what true love was."

What is love, what is love?

"Now I love by listening, being changed by the hearing, doing as the voice of my Sovereign loves me to do."

Listen, listen to the voice of the Sovereign.

"Have you noticed how every creature, every insect, even what plants still strain to survive, at some point, wake up?" Portunus is doing what he does best, teasing with questions that seem to have obvious answers. But the obvious is not what he's after. "It's the common thread of life, each and every one of them, and us, begin in unawareness. We are inert and uncaring in our sleeping, somehow functioning on the most primitive of levels, but not truly...woken. And then we are touched by light...energy... fuel of a sort that causes our inaction to become reaction."

I couldn't fathom where he was going with this. There was purpose in all of his comparisons, so I remained inert, waiting for him to completely fuel my reaction.

"Our shelled friend over there, used to be a sleeper during the day, and awakened only at night—a creature of the dark. But the rules went and changed on her. Now because of whatever alterations to natural circumstances and physics, she has become a day-player. Her state of awareness is altered and so she must either awaken to the situation or perish as the world alters differently from her norm.

I wanted to ask why the armadillo's adaptation was important in the moment. For some reason I also wanted to know how Portunus was aware of the crawler's gender. Probably the latter was unimportant to the lesson, but I was learning that my mentor was often inspiring with the subtle as well as the sublime.

"She, like us," he continued, "has a choice. Maybe it is one that has been thrust upon her, or maybe it is one she had a part in influencing. But the choice is the same, the choice always has one of two answers: Yes or No. Yes, I will or No, I will not. The circumstances, the conditions may differ. The question of life or death may be asked from within or may be posed from another, or One other.

What Question? Who is 'she'? My mind raced with its own questions.

Aella:

I suppose I should be grateful. My daughter has abandoned me, my life from before, finally is completely written off. A new existence and identity are mine to design. I can be anyone I want. Do anything I desire. To most, I'm sure this primitive landscape is a curse, but for me, it is rugged clay to be carved and molded, marble to be chiseled and sculpted into Athena's new temple. *Aella's legacy*, like Athena's, will serve as both sanctuary and university in which all dames may safely dwell, all dames may thrive and conquer.

But now I hear of a drip of acid that may mar my soon-to-be masterpiece. One of my lieutenants reports that a so-called holy man wanders the nearby wilderness. He travels with the nearby wrecks and is repute to be especially talented in the healing and spiritual arts.

If it is whom I think him to be, I hunger to put an end to his self-righteousness once and for all. His clipping and slow suffering will be an example for all wrecks to fear. If it is not him…perhaps I will display an act of dame mercy, allowing him to take his own life in order to avoid my final judgement.

Teagan:

Our hunters are out to catch whatever nocturnal dwellers have not found their way back to their burrows. I am not on the trail with the trackers because others were selected, far better than I in the use of their auger spears for such work. There will be no fire-sharing tonight for Zeke and Matada are personally leading the quest.

Nor am I on sentry duty. Portunus has scheduled others for that important duty this evening. My mentor has granted me a rare gift—solitude. I cherish these "alone" times as they give me the chance to quietly play my flute. It requires no firelight, no audience, simply a personal pleasure while listening to the sounds of nature beyond the confines of my den.

I am at peace and hope in some way to share my music with the world, that it too may rest; there is so little resting to be had.

The first arrow comes straight on, from behind a mound somewhere out front of our scavenging party. It is true and deadly as I see simultaneously the head of Charlie, the man in front of me, jerk as the tip of the flint exits and explodes the back of his skull. I am splattered with his brains and blood.

There is no time to wonder at it, there is only reaction as we fire volleys of our own shafts high and toward the unseen attacking source, hoping to distract and injure the hostiles. In that same motion we all scramble for any boulders and protection we can find.

Not a moment too soon as a return volley arches overhead, then descends seeking their prey. I hear screams from the ambushing mound area and several from our numbers. The wounded unseen enemy have higher-pitched voices. Now we know, it is dames who are out for us.

Each side, ours and theirs, fire upward and toward their adversaries. More shrieking and the smell of human innards is the only thing that escapes. I hear the screams of those being clipped and killed in the night, I quickly reach for my flute, fighting death's dirge with songs of peace in its search of a place to inhabit. The echoes of my soft melodies I had so recently been playing no longer soothe my soul, but instead act as song-spears shot from my instrument into the hearts of my companions. They cry for me to play out their individual finales, helping transport them on into merciful, blissful death.

I start, awake again, and realize I had been lulled by my own playing, into a macabre dream. My hands shake as I pick up my flute again which had fallen into my lap.

I guess peace and rest must also be fought for in these times. Does my music have any purpose to be shared whatsoever? Might it be a lamenting voice representing our clan's…all of humanity's search for some kind of escape from our suffering existence?

And from outside I hear it once more, the groanings of my clan. Now I realize what had triggered the dream: Each one, in the secrecy of their private place, the recessed cage of their individual hell, relives the torments of their past.

Unable to hide from the flashbacks, played over and over in the slow tortured riffs of their anguished nightmares, they weep and whimper as they flee in futile escape. *Do I also whine in my slumber, as they?*

A phrase invades my consciousness from somewhere in my past life.

Do you hear what I hear?

Laughing at the utterance, it inspires me to start playing an old Christmas tune; a tale of a shepherd boy passing on a message that he hears whispered on the night wind about a gift offered to the world of a newborn baby.

The old song suggests that through the child, hope has been born, and my playing changes picks up tempo. In the war drums of the dames. I now hear a rhythm of life, not a warning of death, and in my thoughts I ask, seek, beg...cry to some unnamed source, greater than myself, for that tiny spark of life, not death, to be born into this place and time. I hope for a new dream to come with the light of day for both clansmen and dames.

Ilona:

I have never been alone 'cept in my mind when the dark fog takes me. Now a new kind of aloneness is my partner. Once I had hiked away from the dame camp and Mom-dame, I lost all sense of time. The days and nights disappeared for me, and I thought I had come to be a fictitious character, as when I used to imagine with my dad-wreck. Food was of little interest and the water in my pack was sipped only slightly. My walking gate was more like floating and direction was based only on following any level ground or path in front of me. There was no me. There was only the path ahead walked by feet that happened to be connected to the empty shell that had been my body. The rushing river guided me until a large fallen tree trunk which bridged its two banks suggested, "Come on over." So, I did.

How many days was it until I found my cave? No telling. But it was the most welcoming, plenty-of-space place I had ever discovered. It was nowhere and everywhere to me. Hidden in a rock cleft that even the craftiest wild beasts would be challenged to find, it was plenty safe. Because it was close to a small creek off the river, I would not go thirsty. There was even a healthy bush that guarded its opening. Anyone looking for it would have to really be looking, and in this part of the world, most would die trying even to get here. Who knows; maybe I was somehow ended while making the trek: And so, this place might be as imagined as I am.

The day is barely a day at all. Dust, clouds, and some strange floating grime cloak the sun. Breathing stings my lungs; the wind swirls and blows the foul brew into the deep bones of me. There is no escape from it, no rocking up the cave entrance from the air's stink.

How can I survive this? How have any survived this? Am I not in a desert of someone else's making? Yet the only footprints I see on the landscape are my own. Who is to blame for my pathetic existence?

My ponderings are not good-right. I want no part of living with them. My blade dares me from the table, "cut to forget." I used to think that was the way—slice and stick, drawing blood to slowly kill my misery. Now I think more toward a quick and deep gashing to end the miserable me.

Why did I leave the tribe? Was I that brain-blanked that I grasped being alone in the soup of my sorrow was the best way of it? I must stop trusting my stupid mind. I have made an angry grab of the knife twice today and almost did it, almost slit deep into my arm to drain the dismal flow of life once and for all.

But I couldn't. The *stupid* inside of me fights with the *smart* inside of me. The voice within says, "You live for a purpose, you have a path." Are they smart or stupid words? They sound stupid in my mind, but more stupid is what I do with the words. I listen to them. I start to hope they might be true.

Then I remember my mom-dame speaking out afore to me 'bout *the crushing*—that's what she called her inside sadness. She had spoken out to me that, like her, I need to turn my crushing downside-up; to crush what I ponder to sound smart during the time I fall into my stupid dark place.

Right now, I'm having trouble grasping that my crushing the dark will make me less sad: When I try, it seems to make me more so. Yet, when I battle the dark it does make me fight all the more to find light. It's a bitter feeling, like the anger I have seen in the eyes of Mom-dame. I don't grasp why the anger helps, but it does.

I keep speaking out to myself that I do not want to be like Mom-dame in any way. But that too is a fight inside me—there were good-right things she taught, as well as the bad. When her words and teaching circle around in my mind, I want to knock them out by banging my head against a wall in my new home. 'Stead, I get busy cleaning the cave. Somehow it busies me away from the desperate feelings. I go searching, crouching carefully with a fire-kindled stick into the corners of my new rock home, searching for stinging or biting critters, to scurry them out.

But there are no pests—two new dillo friends who found the cave afore me have seen to that. They come to meet me in friendly fashion. I reach out to pick one of them up and he actually lets me do it. There is no fear in him! I pet him and then pick up the other and pet her too. I do not grasp how I know the he and she of them, but I do, and as I pet each, I name them out loud, for my hearing and for theirs, to announce good-right that I am a true friend. "You are now Mama y Papa Dillo."

"Can you turn off the lights, please?" I speak out.

My dream is too bright. I'm guessing I'm still blacked-out from the rock-hit during the earth-shake. But that was days ago, this is new. And the rock-hit made things dark and dizzy. This dream is clear and bright and everything is easy to see.

And who is the…wait…it's the Bronze-Man. "I have missed you!"

"I have never left you," says the bright voice back to me.

"Oh now, I know that's a fib, you went away with the Blanking." I say the words sadly.

"Someone hid me from you by putting a hood over your brain. I'm still here. See?" the bright voice asks.

"Sure, I do! Why would someone want to hide you?" I think I know the answer, afore I even ask the question. "Oh: Mom-dame."

"Oh yeah; and you, too," warns the bright voice.

"Why would I hide you from myself? It makes no sense," I ask.

The bright voice smiles, "That's the best grasping you've done today."

I smile back, "But best on top of that, you're here! Will you help light my pics again?"

"…Your pics, and more. That's why it's so bright in here. We have lots to light up," promises the bright voice.

"I'm ready!" I promise back.

"Sure, you are," laughs the bright voice.

Verse VI

"We confuse the Creation Story when we conveniently omit the Creator. God is not, nor ever was, nor will be 'convenient."

—Portunus

Teagan:

"Life is brutal—it destroys anything that gets in its way."

—Yet another odd proverb shared at an odd time by Portunus. He had just explained that unless they were able to find a way to make peace with the she-dames, the clan would die. I was shocked by his outspoken assessment here in the Barrens. If he had spoken the words at the dens, it would have been cause for his immediate ending.

"There are no new clansmen or she-dames to be had," he had laid out the dismal facts, truthfully. Zeke and Matada would have had none of his outlining it to illuminate the dark reality. And so, for some reason, Portunus had chosen me to guard his secret thoughts.

What was my purpose in this? That was a high question, then, and now. What, of all my stew, had purpose? All civilization, all of nature seemed to be ending just as the blanked ones had predicted.

Ilona:

A new sense is perking up in me. I remember it from afore, but it makes me want to do more things; like going out to explore; and dressing up my cave more. I can get up from my straw pallet when I want, I can sleep when I want. I can do nothing, or all things. My dad-wreck used to call it a life-way, a choice I have. I had forgotten that, but now it is awake again in my mind and wants me to scratch its name. Dad-wreck called it *Freedom.* One of the last times I grasped that I had freedom was when I had my computer and smart phone. After the Blanking, most freedom also seemed to be blanked.

But there is one other freedom that I miss and that has to do with keeping what I call "pretty things"; girl-wears called dresses, shiny things called jewelry, and smelly stuff called perfume. I remember some of Mom-dame's tribe whispering outside of her hearing, that they missed pretty things too. I heard the whispers, and I grasped well, the missing of the pretty things.

Pretty things are again alive in my mind. To call them back in a good-right way, I use a pink crayon to pic them.

Most all the pretty things from afore were ended with the Blanking, but my freedom tells me I can make new pretty things. At first it seemed like it would be hard work 'cause there's not much around to make pretty things from. That's when a loud inside-pondering came to me. *Why not crayon pics of your new way of living on the cave walls?* The pondering was not my idea—I can't scratch how I know this, but I do. Did it come from Bronze-Man?

From wherever the idea came from, I grasped it to be a good-right thing; and so I'm doing it. I started by finding new colors in the rocks, sand, stones, and the stubborn green, white, and yellow stuff that grew hidden in cracks, in the shadows of it all. I ground them up good-right and mixed them with water. It took practice, but I have found ways to make the colors bright and to be long-lasting.

I am pondering memories, one at a time, that make a smile come to me. Then I paint them out. The first was simple; water in the river, running fast. It spoke out within me to remember that, without the water, I would have been ended fast. Then, I crayoned my new friends, Mama y Papa Dillo, who both keep me safe from Rippers.

More pics are coming to my mind and my painting hand works as fast as it can to color the walls of my new home. I step back now to ponder my pics and I see they are a very good-right thing. Now this place where I live is all a pretty thing. And me too—I am pretty 'cause I'm a part of the pics.

Teagan:

There is a nuance of this new reality: Prior to the Blanking, if someone mentioned experiencing an event at night or when there was no light, they would typically include some description such as "in the darkness".

Now, to a person, by some unspoken agreement, I hear people describe nocturnal or unlit circumstances by the phrase "in my darkness", or "my dark". I don't know how the wording became universal, but I easily grasp the resonance—the expression makes complete sense in the times we live. I suspect that each survivor in the world would say that their dark is personal, their darkness is more than physical, maybe even more than a "mental" thing. And that is the best I can do in the moment to explain the vernacular. All this is to explain that something extraordinary just happened to me…it happened in my darkness, and my hand still trembles in the penning of it.

I had secluded myself in the depths of my den to journal some observations of the day—whatever those observations were are now lost in the shock of what happened next. As I was scribing, I saw light from behind me and immediately gathered my parchings to hide them from potential discovery by invited eyes. As I fumbled with the pages, I became aware of an oddness about the light. It was actually not from behind me; not from…anywhere, and yet from everywhere.

"You don't need to hide from me," a voice, also from nowhere and yet from everywhere, startled me. I actually flinched and my precious ink pen flew from my hand onto the dark floor, rolling into some niche in the wall as if it feared being discovered as well. I had no words with which to reply to the invisible inquirer.

"Why do you write?"

In some frightening way, I knew the question came to the inside of me, from the outside of me. This was not a typical "talking to myself" conversation. Most everyone I have ever known has described in one form or fashion, the idiosyncrasy of self-monologuing and this did not match up in any way to my or their past internal conversation episodes. No, this was a new voice from a… new place. I felt it, I knew it, but I had never encountered it before. The eerie amber illumination filling the cave continued as well, and that did not help my sense of well-being.

"Why do you write?" I did not sense impatience in the voice, instead… how can I explain this…the voice seemed to have a smile in it, as if it knew the answer, but wanted to hear my response anyway.

So, I swallowed and then tried desperately to gather enough moisture in my mouth to respond in anything but a rasp.

"I can't not write." That was the essence of it. I had answered the question for myself long ago.

The voice smiled again but did not reply. *How did I know that?* I wanted to justify my answer, but as quickly as the voice-light appeared, it vanished. I was left alone in my darkness, but something had been left… in me. Something wonderful and powerful in a way I had never known before. The something had a name and like the smiling, I cannot tell how I was aware of it, how I continue to be aware of, and cherish it as my prized possession.

The something, was hope.

Aella:

I can't be rid of him! My scouts confirmed the rumors; mystical tales spilt from the mouths of wandering wrecks whom they had captured and tortured for intel: There is a "sage", the curs say. A wise man, who travels with the wreck-clan, who teaches and helps them survive when they shouldn't. How did he find me? Or worse, does he even know I am still alive? Does he know I am nearby?

We will find out soon enough. I have planned a ruse with the unknowing help of a particularly ignorant, naive young wreck, who dreams that he has found favor with me. He is eager and willing to please me; even sharing the location and weaknesses of the wreck dens. He has no idea of what that pleasure will turn to.

Ilona:

A big "ahah" moment. It's time for me to fight-out my inside dark, finally and for all time. When I sleep, Bronze-Man is back, brightening my dreams and speaking out loud inside me, so that when I wake, I remember. He's been telling me that something big is coming and I should be full of a new thing —joy.

I'm grasping that being joy-filled is not like being happy-filled. Happy shows up and then all of a sudden tricks me and runs away, then sad fills in the blank. Joy is all 'bout the light and being ready for it to show up even when I am most dark and can't see a thing. Joy does not always fix pain, but it does not trick me either. It teaches. It is teaching me now that the place I'm in, the aloneness I feel, is not the place I'll soon be in. Joy doesn't tell me the when or how of the new place; just that I'm on my way to it.

Bronze-Man is speaking out lots of other things too. One big thing he has spoken, "It's time to make your Song."

Inside, I can actually see, not just hear what he is speaking about— when he speaks it, there is a big S, at the front of the word Song. I am vexed 'cause I haven't made songs like I used to in the days afore, when...

—No, that's still a sad thing I'm working on being able to share; I can't yet scratch it.

But Bronze-Man's speaking of it to me has somehow planted a seed into my mind that, like joy, won't go away. It's growing and soon will peek out from the ground inside me. What's the seed? It is a question that repeats over and over:

What Song am I to make and for what purpose?

Teagan:

Two days after my voice-light encounter, I noticed Justin at dawn, discreetly edging his way out of the dens. He casually walked to a spot in the defense walls which had needed repair and in the early silence, placed some small rocks in an unusual pattern at a specific spot. Then he followed the path leading to the Barrens.

Without alerting anyone, I slipped silently out as well—something I've become adept at thanks to Portunus' training—to follow. Justin was not a skilled navigator of the Barrens, and it was easy to track him. I gave him plenty of distance because his boot prints were simple to follow. As I moved past a small cave, two hands grabbed me from behind, one over the mouth, the other pinning my throat. "Say nothing," the familiar voice of my mentor whispered in my ear.

Portunus then relaxed his grip and signaled me to retreat back into the cave I had just walked by. How had I not seen him? How did he sneak up so easily from behind? Obviously, there were skills he had yet to teach me.

My mentor motioned for me to crouch and then we waited. He seemed to be listening with all his senses, testing even the silent rock with his hands, and sniffing the hot wind that was now rising with the day. Then he relaxed, apparently assured we had not been followed or that Justin had not circled back around to catch us spying on him.

"Your friend seems to be on a mission," Portunus said quietly.

"He's not my f..."

"—Figure of speech," he interrupted. "Why were you tracking him?"

"Why were you tracking him?" I thought my retort a clever escape from admitting I had no purpose other than curiosity...and boredom.

"I wasn't tracking him; I was tracking you," Portunus clarified.

"But how did you get ahead of…" Why did I even bother to begin the question? This man had proved his skills of anticipation many times to me.

"You're improving," was his reply through a grin. "You suspected he had a personal motive to leave the dens and you are right to think so."

It was no answer, yet it said everything. Portunus was well aware of my strengths and weaknesses. I could not help but seek the answer to Justin's mysterious behavior.

"The world would have us believe that all spiritual powers are equal. The spiritual powers know it not to be true," my teacher said.

What? I didn't speak the words, but Portunus could see the perplexed look on my face and shared more explanation to his maxim.

"You and I are different than most. The one you are tracking is of this world. Your mind is being transformed, you are testing the things you see and hear, not just because there are questions, but because you are beginning to understand there is an answer.

An answer? One answer? I ask within. *How can multiple questions have a single answer?*

"The fact that you are trying to reason out what I just said, is proof of the work that is going on within you." Apparently, my mentor also has mind reading skills or has figured me out so well that he knows how, if not what I'm thinking.

"Right now, if you trust the lessons I've been teaching you to observe in the physical world," he continued, "trust also these things I'm about to share with you about the *unseen places*. That path, the most important path, will become clear for you soon enough."

Unseen places? Most important path? What in the world…or elsewhere, was his gibberish about? Before I could begin to work my head around his proverbing, he rose and starting again along the trail that Justin had pursued. I followed, trying to keep my focus on our surroundings as he had taught me, and it caused me to wonder why Portunus would stir in an obviously distracting thought while we were at risk in the wilderness? In my earlier wilderness training, he had warned never to let my mind wander when everything about this place was sworn to consume me. *He must have a powerful purpose to plant another seed in me at this place and time.*

As I finished the thought, we heard the drums of the she-dames, the sign of their hunting. The eastern wind carried with it the sounds of a clansman's screams. I could only assume Justin had been discovered and his fate would be far worse than had Zeke tracked him down.

Aella:

This will do it. If I can get him to scream loud enough, the rest will come. That was my thought; hostile and hungry to be fulfilled. The feeding of my plan, the bloodying of this pathetic wreck, brought a new tingling to my nerves. I had never before realized how much pleasure this slaughtering was starting to bring to me until I spit the words at his screaming face.

"I must have more!"

Teagan:

Portunus signaled me to follow and began silently sprinting the canyon to get nearer to the activity. How he knew which ally and turn to take was beyond my skills, so I followed closely. Soon we could hear talking and hollering mixed with the screams of the victim. It was most definitely Justin's distressed voice we had heard and we managed to circle behind a rock outcropping to view what was happening.

From our vantage point, we saw our fellow clansman tied to a tree at the edge of a cliff overhanging the Rushmore River gorge far below. Was life still somehow coursing through the roots and branches of the wood? I fought off a strange temptation to walk toward and inspect the curiosity.

In front of the prisoner stood a tall, muscular she-dame. The boy begged to her now. "I drew maps for you, that's what you wanted, wasn't it—to know where we hide from you? I'll…I can tell you everything, where we keep our food; names of people…"

The amazon she-dame circled the tree where Justin was roped. She held a baseball bat, passing it between her palms as she paced. I had not seen such an item since the Blanking, and I have never seen it used as it was to be now.

In a semicircle around the tree stood thirty or more she-dames. The bat holder began to take swings at the body of Justin and with each connection, cheers and whoops went out in encouragement from the audience.

The amazon stopped her beating for a moment and leaned her face up close to the sagging, sobbing head of her target. "I'll ask you again, cur," she calmly addressed him. "I had promised you protection if you would scout the dens and report to me on weak spots where we could enter. No maps, no old words, new words are what we want. Tell us, how do we attack?"

Justin whimpered in obvious pain. Blood dripped from one corner of his mouth and his left arm was wildly cocked in a direction that his elbow should not have allowed. His right ankle and foot were also bleeding, and his completely exposed body showed deep purple bruises surrounding his midsection. I could see him gasping, probably trying to grab a breath to answer.

"I…told…you. Built it…strong. Z…Zeke…smart."

Another strike crushed his left knee. I could easily hear the sound of snapping bone and cartilage even from our hiding place. Justin had no problem finding air to project his shriek of agony.

Portunus whispered in my ear, "He won't last long, wait here and make no sound."

With that he was gone and I shivered. *Please don't let them find me.* Who was I saying that to? I was alone and there was no help to be had should I be discovered. Justin's might not be the only siren call of the day.

I kept as low as possible and watched the horror continue through a crack in the rocks. The amazon continued her methodical interrogation, making blows to Justin's body every time he did not satisfy with his answer. It was obvious that the attacker did not care about his intel and that she knew he was not in any way a skilled spy. I got the impression she was more satisfied when he did not have a proper response, taking delight in her swinging vengeance.

Justin gave her our numbers, our leadership, our habits, but that was not enough. The she-dame wanted an edge, a secret angle of entry, which her batting target could not possibly give her: Justin had been honest, Zeke had planned well in the construction of our defenses.

Please hurry with whatever you're going to do, Portunus. I knew he couldn't hear my thoughts. I hoped somehow it would spur him to quicker action.

And as if in taunting reply to my silent pleas, the amazon went beyond the pale. She came very close to Justin and stroked his face in strange tenderness with her left hand. In the most outlandish of seductive moves, she sidled up to her barely conscious captor and danced provocatively and sensuously, body to body with him, male blood basted in female sweat to paint a hideously joined carnal canvas. The woman actually appeared to be losing control in her eroticism and brought her lips hungrily to coo in his ear. I could just make out her husky invitation. "Is there anything else you want to offer?"

Incredibly, the naked battered man gave evidence that he could still rise to the occasion, and in a single swift motion, the amazon brought a concealed knife down with her right hand. A gushing fountain of entrails announced that Justin had been clipped in the deepest of ways. After one last burbling blood-soaked wheeze, the shock on his face became Justin's immortal death mask.

How could it become worse? I will tell you now. The dead clansman's killer cocked her head and considered the results of her interrogation. She seemed to become suddenly bored with the game and so took her bat up again and knocked Justin's skull out of the park. With a mighty swing, pieces of bone, teeth and scalp flew. Her crew yelled their lungs out in celebration, and I decided I was out of time if I wanted to escape detection.

In the end, Portunus was too late, it was time to retreat and retreat fast. I turned to crawl out of the outcropping and encountered a figure standing over me. I tilted my head upwards to see who had found me and then there was my darkness.

A low volume throbbing noise pulsed around me. Like my vision, it was blurred and dim. Then the pain swarmed my consciousness. The noise I heard was from within, not from the outside. It was everywhere and nothing else mattered. Like a swarm of Rippers, it ebbed and flowed in volume, etching fingernail scratches into the blackboard of my sanity.

I tried to open my eyes, but outside light was a spear that stabbed needles into my forehead and increased the throbbing. I opened my mouth to cry out, but instead of a sound, all I sensed was liquid pouring out. The ooze tased like salt and metal and instead of dripping down my chin, seemed to climb up my nose and into my eyes. Blood choked my nostrils and completely clouded my sight.

Many other insistent things competed for my attention. The blurred world rocked back, forth, sideways, and around. I was simultaneously spinning and flying, but how? My feet stung as if the circulation was being cut off. Something struck me from behind, causing me to slam into a hard object—*a wall?* I bounced away from it, with pain now searing in the flesh of my face. *Why is the world spiraling?*

Through blurred twirling vision, I kept seeing a body circle by me laying on the sky-ground. Justin? Why was he all red? I sensed, rather than saw, an image of one who was speaking a dagger into my ear. "Are you having fun yet?"

Somehow, I realized it was her, the she-dame batter. And why was she upside-down? Why was she not swinging with me?

That was it—It was me who was hanging upside-down by a rope. Repeatedly my head banged painfully against something rough and scratchy. Bark! I was dangling from a limb of the tree by the cliff!

I was blind, drummed by noise and slowly suffocating, yet I managed a thought. *This was the end of me. Please let it be quick.*

Again, I questioned myself, who *are you asking?* My loudly exploding head pleaded with my thoughts, *shut up, you are making the pain worse!* The appeal was pointless, I could not stop the agony nor my pondering. Both demanded to battle with the other.

I perceived that the she-dame crew surrounded me, felt them pushing me back and forth between them like I had seen done to a piñata, a paper-mache animal figure that children would take swings at with a stick. The game was to break the creature open in hopes of breaching its belly to release birthday candy.

They were not taking bats or sticks to me yet, seeming to be enjoying the push and shove—foreplay in preparation for the real sport. I knew the swings would come soon. Each of them would choose specific points on my body to damage as the amazon had done to Justin. Through the cracking of ribs, maybe even by the stinging of well-placed knife cuts which the she-dames were known for, I would be slowly and brutally tortured to a miserable end, much like Justin's.

I was pushed again to the amazon who stopped my motion long enough to stab again with her voice. "Where are your friends? Are they coming to play too?" This time she punched her fist into my groin, driving all awareness away. Vomit mixed with more blood found its way out of my mouth and dripped down my face into my eyes so that nothing was clear. And I didn't care. Death would soon be my blessing.

"What shall we do with this one? Is he juicy enough to eat, or fit enough to do our work?" Her voice was too loud, too happy.

I became immediately alert and terrified because of cries from the other women who continued to whirl in my vision. The jeers suggested many of them thought I was better for the menu.

I opened my mouth, trying again to speak. I choked twice and then a few words spilled out with the crimson river. "I know this place. I was raised here."

The leader held up her hand for silence, and to a person, including me, there was no more noise. She approached my suspended, spinning body, balled her raised fist and landed an even more vicious strike to my genitalia. I gasped from the throe, wanting to curl up into a fetal ball, but gravity and rope were my enemies.

"Who gave you permission to speak?" Said the ruler of my anguish.

Through tears, I caught a glimpse of what looked to be curiosity from the leader. "I was raised here" she mimicked my words. You're a farm boy, then? What's the address on your mailbox?"

Laughter came from all directions. The She-dame leader shot a glance to the surrounding crowd and again, there was an immediate void of voices.

I knew my next words meant life or death and somehow, I managed a sentence. "The land has changed, but not all of it."

Now her face was bent to mine. "That _is_ interesting," she whispered. "Any other wonderful abilities you wish to share?"

Ignorant to many things but hoping the she-dames had a higher approach to existence, I spit out through bloody swollen lips, "I can write."

A crooked smile crossed her face. Then she swung a mighty slap to my jaw. The thunder in my brain was worse than any from the storms that now frequently attacked the planet. The most stabbing pain of all came with the blow she landed to my gut with the end of her bat.

"That's too bad, I was beginning to like you." The leader turned away from my writhing body and announced to her tribe, "I say we clip him… slowly. His friends will surely come to watch that!"

My ending was now very near. Blood continued to trickle down into my nose. Soon I would either die from lack of anything coursing my veins, or I would first suffocate from the gel filling my head and lungs.

An image of Portunus now clouded my brain. He was jabbering on about trust, as if there was time for such a thing to be important. There was a word that kept floating between his face and my sight. The word was red and blurred. I could not reason it out—read the letters—nor was I able to fathom why it existed in this reality. As the dames tore away what tattered clothes still clung to my body, the word became more defined. Smiling, my mentor nodded as the letters sharpened and their meaning sung sadly to me—Faith. The thing I had lost, I desired now most to find. *Belief in the unseen*, that was Webster's explanation. And now it was my face in my brain, blurred beyond the letters. I could just make out my lips speaking, "But if it can't be seen, does it really exist?"

Yes, I screamed at the fool behind the word. *Don't you see? It's right there in front of you. It has to exist, nothing else can exist without it!*

And to the song of my own shouting, the world again faded away.

A new sound woke me. One from the recent past that the throbbing would have me forget. But with the sound, the dull ache in my head vanished.

Three sharp staccato blasts in succession, from a ram's horn echoed through the canyons; then a pause, then three more blasts repeated. Each strident succession told that the opposing clansmen army was closing in. Our clan, my rescuers, were bringing the fight to their assailants. War it was.

I was still hanging upside down and by a quick assessment, I judged my body was bruised but not yet broke. The amazon had crouched immediately at the herald of the horn and now sniffed the air around her. "They've taken the bait. Get ready!" She spoke this to everyone around her and I realized why I was still alive. The she-dames had used me to draw our clan out.

The thirty warriors obeyed her command instantly by dispersing, in every direction. Each had picked up their individual bats and what looked to be bags of stones to carry off with them. Through my clearing vision I grasped that for each of the women, there were others waiting throughout the surrounding rocks, troupes of she-dames trained for engagement and ready to strike in surprise when the clansmen attacked.

But the amazon remained, crouched by me. Without looking at me she spoke. "So, wreck, are you ready to die?" Maybe first you want to watch your brood be bloodied? Let the fun begin."

I wasn't sure if she was talking to me or to one of her enemies approaching. Maybe both. I could not understand her hatred mixed with obvious pleasure at what was happening. What had shaped her so? My training at the hands of Zeke and Portunus kicked in and I knew my life was…literally…on a short string. There was only one weapon available to me in this moment and I had been taught to strike with whatever I had.

"It's a trap! It's a trap! It's a trap!" I shouted at the top of my lungs and my words echoed into all the canyons. The amazon rose from her crouch, swiveled, and caught my head with a vicious kick. I saw two teeth fly from my mouth and my voice was taken from me.

"Let's let them figure out the trap for themselves, shall we?" The she-dame leader had bent over and was smiling viciously at me. Then the warrior queen turned and ran toward the coming battle, trilling her voice to join in the attack-cry and charging with her she-dame troops.

Gun shots, and something else I couldn't quite make out—a "clacking" sound. Cries every direction, some commands, others begging for help. An object hit the tree I hung from and fell within sight. It was a small stone. I tried to look out at the landscape to figure its origin and saw a she-dame stand from behind a rock, twirl a sling of some type with her hand then a projectile, yes, a stone, flew from the sling out into a field I could not see. Simultaneously another gunshot rang out and the same she-dame slumped over a boulder she thought to be her protection.

From another direction, the flight of an auger-spear caught my attention. It missed its mark and the intended target turned, let fly her own rock which struck the spear's owner true in the center of his forehead. He crumpled and moved no more.

Action erupted all around now. Ricocheting rocks and bullets spat the ground, some perilously close to my dangling head. Soon all the ammunition was spent, and aggression became a hand-to-hand thing. Countless personal sagas ended with the spilled red of both sides.

Once, a clansman and a she-dame scuffled right into my body, both digging knives into the other. The she-dame fell first and then my clansman careened to me, cutting the bonds that held my hands behind me. Before he could free the rest of me, a baseball bat flew and smashed him square in the back. I heard the snap of his spine and watched his eyes glaze before he dropped. His knife fell under me, and I grabbed it up just before the amazon tried to kick it away.

"Oh, do you think you're living long enough to use that, cur?" She cocked her bat behind her and I closed my eyes, preparing for the final strike. Then a voice of heartbreak pealed out above the others. "Aella, no!"

It was the cry of Portunus. I opened my eyes again to see him, arms raised and waving, weaponless, charging in our direction from across the killing field. The attention of the dame leader was veered from me and now squarely rapt on him.

"You!" She spat. "Alright, time to take this cur's place." She had turned to charge at my mentor, a vicious animal snarl etching her mouth, and the earth groaned beneath us.

Aella, as Portunus called her, flew skyward. The ground under me strangely rose up to pound my head and then I too bounced into the air as from an old trampoline I had played on as a child. The world tilted every direction at once. Bodies, live and dead, jumped and popped like dried corn kernels roasted over a fire. The amazon landed hard on the dirt to my side, and I watched Portunus roll uncontrollably toward a boulder. His head made perfect contact and he went limp.

In my own panic, I tried to reach up with the knife and cut myself loose from my foot-noose, but instead painfully stabbed myself in the calf. Spinning and swinging wildly, I was pulling the blade away for another attempt when I saw the tree disappear with a crumbling roar.

In slow motion I thought, *who can make a tree do that?* My whole body then slammed the shaking ground and a yank of agony announced the reality of the disappeared tree. It, and the ground beneath had broken away from the cliff. It was tumbling down to the river and I, still tautly tied to its branch, was pulled into falling space.

Oddly, I glanced another body falling and flailing along with the tree and me. It was Aella. the amazon she-dame. I should have been completely hysterical, but instead, in the infinite moment of our shared plunge, watched her downward spiral with morbid curiosity.

"You will save her as you will be saved."

The voice-light again? From where was it coming now? Why would it say such a thing at such a ti…?

—and suddenly there was no time.

Verse VII

"What if the existence of God is not dependent on my belief?"

—Portunus

Ilona:

I thought the feeling of being low had been taken away, once and for all time, by Bronze-Man. But that is not so. today I feel maybe the lowest ever. Worse than that, there is no reason for it. I just woke…low.

And my mind plays word tricks on me. My darkness is trying to kill the light inside. It laughs at me, saying how silly it is to think a make-believe person wants me to live. *Who really believes there is purpose in the doing of anything? If that make-believe person really wants to help, why doesn't he stop my sadness?*

A dark pondering starts to make good-right sense in my mind; to tie some rocks around me and walk into the river. Another pondering follows right behind it; retry my knife, or maybe find a sharp flintstone to open some veins in my arms and legs. It would be a slower ending, but more sure. Who would care if either of those things became my purpose?

Bronze-Man's voice inside of me, battles my dark ponderings. *I care!* His voice echoes in the hollow darkness. I close my eyes and I see something reach out, growing brighter as it comes near. It is an open hand. The hand wants to be held. But my own hand seems too heavy to lift, to reach back.

Bronze-Man's voice echoes again. I listen to it and he helps me battle my dark by yelling together with me out loud, "There will be no freedom if I end my life."

And since freedom is what I now hunger for most, I listen to Bronze-Man, and to myself. I open my eyes again and look at the wall pics I have painted. I remember again my freedom, my choosing, my purpose:

I will live, no matter how dark or light, the day; I will live!

Aella:

My head, what are you doing to my head?

Concussion…must be…John, what are you doing at the battle? How are you here? And that other wreck, the boy hanging from the tree. You…love him. First, you love your god, then some waif…is there, was there ever, any room for me?

I must find you; wherever, whoever you are. Please tell me where, tell me why!

Teagan:

The moment is as alive and present in me now as it was then.

I find myself still on the beach we had been washed onto, conscious and not broken into a thousand pieces. Establishing the reality of that great fortune however, forced me to consider the most unreal sensation I have ever had. It seems I am standing over my body and over that of the still she-dame—standing but without touching the ground; floating, but not flying. I look at my still body on the ground and realize I am completely naked. I scan the floating-not-flying body I now inhabit and it is in the same condition. It is perfectly natural for me to be stripped of any garments—there will be no more hiding any of my thoughts or my physical attributes. I am vulnerable. I always have been, but now I don't care—even if I did care, it wouldn't matter.

Beside me, floats the man. He is as real as I, but then, I don't exactly know how tangible I truly am, just that...I am.

In appearance, he has a full head of golden-brown hair, his stature is not short nor tall, with beautiful glowing skin. He is not naked but dressed in a perfectly white robe that does not seem out of place in this wilderness.

The robe is tied with a sash in a knotted fashion. It has brilliant blue markings on it and interwoven white with blue decorated tassels on both endings. I stare at the embroidered markings on the Bronze Man's belt, thinking I should recognize them from somewhere, but in my confused state of mind, I can't reason it out.

My attention and full focus are brought to his eyes which are every color possible, shining, not in a frightening way, as I had seen animal eyes do when they reflected firelight in the night. His eyes...gave the light, and I could not get enough of it in the moment.

It comes to me: The order of the markings

א ב מ

—Aleph, Bet, Mem. They are Hebrew script. The letters should be read from right to left! And I understand them. They are the same as the etchings on Portunus' skin.

"What will you do now?" He asks in the same disarming tone. This banter reminds me of a casual conversation over a meal that I might have with someone I have known all my life; like a family member who I cannot not lie to, because they know me perhaps better than I know myself. In this case, I sense he knows me best of all.

"I suppose I should bring her back to life," I reply bizarrely, as if in this quasi-dreamscape, I have that ability.

"Good choice," he approves. But let's bring you back first. "Of course, I'll help."

I am confused; and say so.

"So, you think you're full of life?" The smiling man teases. "Now I'm confused. What about your writings that suggested the god-man was uncaring, that the ills of the world persist? And that if the very, <u>very</u> good ones, were taken away by...me, why leave you and not just do away with you who did not claim me as your...savior?"

I am now very, very frightened. I had shared my spiritual doubts with no one. How..."

"So, if the posit of Jesus is flawed by the very people who created him, what does that make of your present circumstance? If I do not exist, then who are you talking to? Could it be that you are dead, and this imaginary conversation is your last…fading away?"

I feel moisture from between my legs and in my eyes. It is not residue from the river, but an involuntary response to his troubling query. A strange question comes to my mind. *Can a dying man weep and wet himself?*

"Oh yes, I assure you he can," he answers sadly.

I did not speak those words aloud!

"Of what concern is that to me?" My companion queries.

Now I am flat on my face in the sand. "I'm not ready!" These words are most certainly sobbed out loud…

"—Not ready for what?" asks the Bronze Man, "To live or to die?"

Suddenly I see the answer in my mind, I feel it in my heart, but can I speak it? *I am not worth this…chance of choice. I have been the most selfish, arrogant creature on the planet, I am a coward, I am a…cannibal.*

"I love you, Cannibal," he sang to me! "Will you love me in return?"

"Lord, please forgive me, I didn't know…"

"—Yes, you did know. All of my children know. It is not what you do or do not know. It is what you do or do not do."

"Yes, I love you, Lord, Jesus." I plead, "What must I do now?"

"You have already done it. I will do the rest."

"Let's get to work then," Bronzeman says. He kneels to the ground by the head and shoulders of the woman. I kneel with him as He lays one hand tenderly on her forehead, stroking her matted hair away from her ashen face. He does not ask me, but I know that I am also to place my hand on her in the same way; care for her in the same way.

We both place our other hands on her right shoulder and then he raised his face to the sky.

> "Abba", he weeps. "Aella, your child, has seen and lived
> so much pain. She has been tormented by spirits darker
> than most. And she fights! Against all, You, me, even

her family. Yet she yearns for life with that same fight. She gives her fight to Your other daughters, to help them survive, because it is the only way she knows.

"She has taken life away as well, but I see her struggle within. She is whispered to by the enemy. I name out now: Legion, be gone from this one. She wants a new way and you have been blinding her heart to it. Darkness is now forbidden from her by my command and you, dark-one, will be punished for your evil act against her."

There is an aroma in the air, or in…me, or, everywhere in time and place, all is, and smells new, like wind carrying a waft of spring with freshly cut grass and fragrant new growth. I hear a song; or rather feel it. I have never heard it before but recognize it immediately. I want to sing with it as loudly as I can, but tears choke my voice, so I let the song sing for me, to me, in me.

The Bronzeman, Jesus, bends closer still to Aella's inert body and invites me to bend with him. Once more my Savior speaks, "I now breathe into Aella, a new name, that she may be redeemed as Yours, Abba. She will be our hands and feet in this final time."

Bronzeman uses my hand to open her mouth and then he—he through me—breathes out and kisses her in one motion. Water spews from her mouth, and from mine. We choke and gasp together, and then the fresh smell and song fully fill both Aella's lungs and mine.

Our skin takes on the radiance of our healer and the woman on the ground smiles, though she remains asleep. It is a smile more beautiful than can be described, other than to tell that it is the same smile I see on Bronzeman Jesus' face. I look into an eddy that has pooled beside us, off of the noisy river water and see the same smile reflected back on my face.

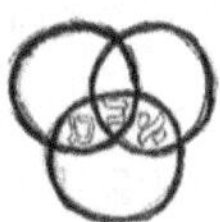

I awoke beside Aella and looked up to the sky. It was brilliant blue as it had been before the Blanking, and I began to hum the song-tune that filled me.

"You are not yet complete. It needs your story to be written into it," Bronzeman, the man whose name, whose song, I now love beyond all others said from deep within me.

"What do I need to complete it?" I cried.

"Not what. Who?" With that, the song faded, Aella and I were alone.

Ilona:

Today will be a good-right hunting day. The reason I grasp this? Mama and Papa Dillo are busy nabbing Rippers inside my cave. Why the ugly bugs fly right at my shelled friends is a crazy question. But they do, as if the dillos are saying something I can't hear but that the Rippers can't help but listen to and obey. The flyers hover right over my dillo-guards who zip their tongues out faster than my eyes can see, wrapping up the critters one at a time and chewing 'em down like candy. Maybe Bronze-Man is working somehow through the dillos. It's worth pondering.

I can hear lots of the nasty buzzing outside too. That's how I know to put on my heavier suit and go outside for a good meal—when the Rippers buzz more, there must be birds flying too—as they also love the taste of Rippers. My heavy suit comes from one of the giant four-legged fur animals called buffalo that used to own this land. I've heard it spoken out by folks, and in books, that there were so many buffalo at one time that they looked like a carpet moving over the flats. I can't grasp such a thing, but in a good-right moment, when I was on another hunt, I found one of their dried-up hides. It was so heavy; it took me a day to haul it to my cave and lots more days to trim it down and sew it together as a suit. I had to be extra careful as it was so tough, I feared breaking the precious needle I keep for crafting and mending clothes. The hard work paid off, for the new suit proved Ripper-proof.

Now when I hear lots of buzzing outside of the cave and see my dillos sucking in their treats, I grasp that there is a feast for me coming soon. Doves! Flocks and flocks of the cooing critters show up when the buzzing starts. I almost hate to nab them as they are pretty and good at Ripper nabbing. But I've got to eat too. Their meat is so tasty when cooked over a flame. From the sounds coming from outside, there will be lots of flaming to do! My heavy suit will keep the Rippers from nagging me and I'll soon be enjoying a full stomach.

As I scratch-spoke afore, the hunt was good-right! I arrowed a bunch of doves! Seems now the right thing to do is to add the birds to my crayon wall in respect for their blood-sacrifice. They are food, sure, but they also cause me to ponder my new freeness to fly. Like them, I am learning in my thoughts to soar above the heavy world that exists outside my cave.

My cave is becoming a proper home with my crayonings on the walls and my *keeps*—the things best for me in this place. Exploring the wilds next to the river, I am finding things which have been washed to shore, that will be of help to me. I have nabbed two old metal drinking mugs (not sure when I'll have visitors to share with—hah, a joke!), and a plate for eating from.

And I found another special keep that has just washed up. A metal box that has special rubber and tight locks to keep the water out of the inside. The rubber worked only so-so 'cause inside was a soggy book. I am trying to carefully dry the pages by setting them out in the sunlight, but it is taking time. I have not started reading the book yet, 'cept for the front, which is named, Good News Bible. There used to be lots of Bibles, but no more. This is the first I've seen; the first I'll read.

I cleaned out the metal box good-right; rust and all and dragged it into my home-cave. Now it hides my parch, pens, and extra crayons, moving all of these from my backpack which was getting crowded and heavy with stuff. Once I completely dry the pages of my Good News book, the box will be its home when not being read. It will stay there not to hide it, but just in case my dillos or other critters think the book and its pages, and maybe my crayons, are good-right for food.

Other keeps? Yup. There is some special ribbon once used for wrapping presents. Mom-dame had hidden it away in our old home, but not well. I found it and I'm not sure why I have kept it. It's so pretty and all different colors like my crayons. I don't want to use it. Hiding in containers at the dame pig plant, I found some very special cooking and healing spices and herbs that my dad-wreck had taught me 'bout on our camping trips. I snuck those with me when I hiked away from the dames. Now I grind the spices and herbs using a stone pestle into a rock bowl. I found both of those when traveling with the dames. I mix up the ground stuff with an old stirring spoon mom-dame had long afore tossed out (imagine tossing something away now!). Now that I have stashed my keeps properly in my cave, my backpack is made ready to go keep-hunting once more.

O, what a treat washed up on the river shore my way! It was an old plastic jar that looked to be half filled on the inside with some brown sticky paste. There was no markings on the outside to tell me what the stuff was, so I carefully screwed off the jar top. Afore touching the insides, I sniffed the leftovers—peanut butter! There was no other smell like it—sweet, but not too much, mixed with a kind of maple whiff.

But was it safe to taste? I could not help myself. I took my blade and stuck it into the goo. Just a dab. I pulled it out and saw that this was the crunchy kind with little nuts all stuck in it. I touched the dagger tip to my tongue and that was the end of my stopping. It tasted just as I remembered, all creamy and thick. I plugged my knife in deep and pulled out a slab of the stuff, then put the blade in my mouth, closed my lips and pulled the weapon out, carefully so I didn't cut myself.

The goo stuck on the backside of my teeth and it took a scrumptious minute to lick it all down. More digging in brought out more tasty stuff and terribly soon, I was shaving the insides of the jar to scrape off every gluey brown stripe I could catch.

It was sad but so good-right to taste that last licking and I lay back on the rocks, closing my eyes and mouth to hold the treat tight in my mind for as long as I could. And for a good-long time, I had a new old remembering that I wanted to keep forever. A word came to me that had once been used much to speak out the feeling. I was *full.*

The healing spices and my prized ribbon came in handy a number of days back when I was outside my cave a little ways. I was searching the rocks near the river for more keeps and reached around one too fast—not a good-right move. I heard, then felt the rattler. It was only a small one (vipers don't grow like they used to afore) and barely nicked the tip of my left pinky finger with one fang afore I could pull my hand back-quick. Small as he was, I grasped I would soon be in big trouble 'cause a small viper does not mean small poison. They are now bigger life-enders than they ever were afore.

I ran into my cave and took my knife from my belt. I stuck it into the coals of the fire and then reached for my herbs; *echinacea* and *goldenseal.* I poured out a dab of each on some burlap I took from the pig plant, mixed it together fast and added some drops of water. Now the worst part.

My finger was already swelling up and soon, my arm would be too. I had to end the poison from traveling further, afore it ended me, and there was only one way. I took three quick-deep breaths and a long one that I held; then I grabbed my knife from the coals and sliced my pinky from my hand like a carrot from a stalk.

I let out one good scream, plunged my bleeding nub into the herb mix, then wound it up tight with burlap and some of mom-dame's pretty colored ribbon. That was all afore I spewed my last meal out from my stomach and the cave started spinning round me. Then I blanked into nowhere for who knows how long.

When my eyes slitted open, I asked Bronze-Man, "Am I ended?" He didn't need to answer 'cause the throbbing of my left hand spoke loudly to me that I lived. Washing and soaking the nub in herbs helped seal it up and I got over the fever of it quickly. I ponder Bronze-Man had a thing or two to do with that too and I thanked him.

While I mended, I pondered my keeps. They are what help me remember the days afore the Blanking in a good-right way. Do I miss my pinky finger? Sure! But after surviving the viper bite, I ponder that I am here for some new reason. I grasp that Bronze-Man is readying me for some even better purpose.

I grasp deep inside that another hunt is soon coming my way. Bronze-Man is making me ready in my dreaming and there, I see and hear him telling me to put on another new suit that he'll give me—a Spirit-suit that will guard me from more than Rippers and Vipers. He says to keep listening and keep watching and soon, he'll be speaking out how to battle for something great-right that's on its way.

Teagan:

After tending as best I could to the injuries of the amazon, I thought it best for me to distance myself before she regained consciousness. I would try to make my way back to the dens while avoiding the other she-dames. They probably thought us both dead after the plunge over the cliff, but what if they were searching for our bodies? What if they found us?

I decided not to make that job easy for them. I had no accurate way of figuring but thought that we had been carried by the rapids at least two or three miles downstream from the cliffs. We had been swept away and deposited on the opposite shore of the river, which was a continuous frantic froth, not inviting of a safe crossing in either direction. I also had no idea of how many curves and turns the rushing waters made on its course.

I would have preferred retracing my way upstream using that guide in hopes of finding some kind of ford. But the river canyon offered no consistent banks to follow.

What direction should I head? I took in as much water as I could drink and headed up a canyon path that I thought looked easiest to maneuver through. It seemed to parallel the water, but there would be no way of knowing other than listening for the nearby rush. I was confident that, with Portunus' survival skills trained into me, that I would be able to find food and more water along the way.

Now I understand how someone who regains the use of a limb or their sight or hearing encounters challenges in using and managing the reclaimed gift. Their new abilities are as foreign to them as my new relationship with the One I had dismissed since my childhood.

I was sure he had my best interests at heart. That did not do much, to inspire me on though as I was becoming increasingly weak from lack of food. This place was far more a wasteland than the Barrens and as I trekked, even the river's proximity did not cooperate. The unfamiliar canyon forced a journey further and further away from where I perceived I needed to travel. I thought several times of abandoning its winding ways. I should have turned back to find another route, but what if that was equally wayward?

My thoughts also twisted in unforeseen directions. My tumbling dreams of slow-motion descent into the spumy waters; my confusion of feeling I had been ended after I had surged into one river boulder after another; the golden face of the man who comforted my mind, assuring me that I was not now dead, but somehow by him, was reborn.

I recalled the branch of the tree I had hung from as Aella had tormented me. It had broken off from the main trunk when we struck the river and that saved me and the dame. Why had I spent the energy in that moment to hold onto her, propping us both up with my waning strength? And before losing consciousness, what made me fight to hold on to her by her tunic belt so that she would not sink from the weight of her leather sting-suit. How we landed on the beach is…well it would have been a complete mystery had I not encountered Jesus.

But even that was in question. Why had he left me? Was it possibly all a fantasy, made up in my desperate mind to make sense of all the chaos I had just pummeled through?

No, it was true and real, I knew it beyond knowing. Like the tree branch, he was there in that moment for me to cling to for life, and he will be there again when the time is…right.

I thought then that, as much as he loves me, it is for some greater purpose that I survive, that I was trudging through that canyon to nowhere.

"What do I need to complete this test?" I had cried out loud to him.

"Not what. Who?" Bronzeman had replied.

Aella:

Where did he go? Oh, God! Where have You gone!

Teagan:

I am stumbling in my steps from lack of food and water. I had been overconfident that the canyon route at the river's edge would take me home. Instead, it meandered without alternative branches, never nearing the rapids again. I struggled to hear the sound of the torrent, but it had faded long ago, as had my sense of direction.

Words flood my mind. A seminar I once attended, put on by a motivational speaker…Cornelius someone:

"It doesn't matter whose problem it is, it's what <u>we</u> do about it."

But where is the "we"? There is no society here, only one individual scavenger, seeking his own survival. How can "we" do anything about this problem? How can "we" continue to exist?

I'm in trouble. I know it because I open my eyes and realize I have fainted and fallen into the canyon sand. *Can't let that happen again,* I scold myself.

Another memory, as I struggle to my feet:

On a strangely cooler day, when the breeze brought hope of meager rain—yes, every little often, it happens, and I desperately cling now to that precious recall. I was led by Portunus to an unfamiliar place in the Barrens. He took out one of the many pouches from a pocket within his robe, and commanded, "take off your coverings, all of them. Slather this on all of you, every place, every tuck, even your hair." In the pouch was a jelly, very slick with a faint licorice smell. I had come to trust his strange ways, so I did not question, but obeyed. It helped to see him also strip down and do the same to himself with another pouch.

"This is a natural mix, but difficult to find," he said and warned. "Never waste it on a doubt. I will teach you its location at another time."

Once covered, he took me carefully down a rocky path and into an area of dark grainy sand. We stood in the center of the area, not more than the size of an old city block and after a moment, he raised his right boot high and stomped.

In an instant a red wave appeared from beneath. I knew the cause and fear flooded me.

Fire ants. More than I had ever seen in my lifetime. Portunus placed his hand on my shoulder and assured, "I know your fear, show me your courage."

I stood frozen and tried to hold on to his words to keep from bolting. The creatures surrounded, then did not hesitate in coating us. I felt them climb and explore, causing a scream in my mind, but somehow, I held it within, daring not open my mouth or eyes for they were now searching every part of me. I could hear the scratching of their antennae and feel the tickle of their feet even in my ears. I badly wanted to brush and address the itching all over and in me, but I fought with all my thought to be in some other place for the moment. I waited for the inevitable sting and numbness to my body, having encountered these beasts before in much smaller quantity. Their venom would work quickly and painfully, causing a swelling and inability to use the inflicted area for days or weeks. There was little that could be done to treat the injury they caused and often, an angry red scar would remind to avoid them ever again.

But this time, they did not sting. Instead, they finished their body search and seemed uninterested in attack. An eternity passed, but finally they abated and retreated once again to the depths. With smooth steps we also retreated from the "ant cove", as Portunus then defined it to me.

"These we will plant." He said and revealed a container with a screw cap within which he had captured some of the crawlers while I was busy trying not to fill my pants with caca during the scare of the encounter.

Portunus explained that he had planted others in places known only to him and which he now taught me. The ant coves seemed to not grow much after covering a few square yards, as long as it was not disturbed terribly. He explained they were to be used as havens against harm and to have a pouch of repellent handy at all times.

I was not sure if I would have the nerve to do planting on my
own, but I held the lesson within for use in future times…

—Future times for me however are beginning to seem like a thing of the
past. My eyesight is blurred, I am having problems with time of any sort.
Am I in the wilderness, am I alive, or did I ever exist at all? It seems…
seemed, will seem a good idea to lay down. Maybe a nap will clear and cool
my burning head. Maybe I have already closed my eyes forever.

Aella:

—*You taught him. The boy brought me back. Why, John, did you teach the
boy I was about to kill; to save me? Tell me why?*

    *And who was the other man by the boy? Friend or Foe? He is a wreck; the
answer should be obvious. What was he trying to tell me? Something about
forgiveness, but I could not hear him clearly! I must find him, ask him. I must
find you too John, and the boy to tell you…something…something about
forgiveness. What is it I must tell you? Will I remember it when I wake up?*

Ilona:

There is still that one thing I have not spoken out on parch afore now,
but it is strongly crayoned in my memory. I grasp that the time is now to
scratch it back to life:

    After the voice had shook me back to life, I had jumped
    up, grabbed my water sac, and put on my gear. I was
    'bout to trek out on the search for "him", whoever "him"

was. Afore I left my home-cave, my eyes caught sight of my *best-thing*, the thing I prize most, even more than my crayons—and that must mean it is very good-right!

My best-thing was a surprise from my dad-wreck when I was a little-folk. Our fam had gone camping in the mountains, when mountains were fresh and big and more beautiful than crayons can pic. I was sleeping late after the sun peeked over the trees. I was all foggy eyed and crouched up in a tent when I heard a song-note! Not just any song-note, but a loud instrument sound like that from an orchestra horn. The note I heard was long and thick, like warm wind in my ears on a cold day.

When the note quit, I left the tent to find out how it was and there stood my smiling dad-wreck. He held out in front of him, a curvy horn from some kind of animal and he said, "I was hiking this morning and came up on a large sheep, a ram that had fallen from a rock ledge and had died."

This made me real sad faced and then dad-wreck reached back in his pack and pulled another curvy horn out. He sat down and placed both ram horns on the ground in front of him. He asked me to sit and said, "I have an idea. Since the ram can no longer share his voice with the world, what if we; you and I, share his voice for him? The ram had two horns to share, so I'll need help."

The horns were the most wonder-filled things I had ever seen, afore and now. I stared at them with eyes-wide and my dad-wreck said, "Choose yours."

I picked up the horn that had more blue and green in it—my favorite two crayon colors. My dad-wreck said, "In a country far away from here, the music-minded people and some who are called to be spiritual priests use these to get everyone's attention. They call the horns, *Shofars.*"

He picked up his shofar and before putting his lips to it, asked me, "Ready?"

I touched the tip of it to my lips as he did, and we blew! At first, all I managed was to blow lots of air, but no sound came out. Then my dad-wreck showed me how to get my lips just right, and soon we were making notes of all kinds!

Asides the stories and the coloring and all the things we did together, blowing was our most, and best thing.

And then he was ended.

I stopped blowing after that. I tried a few times, but I did more crying than noting and it hurt deep within me. Still, I kept my shofar, even when I made the big trek with mom-dame to the hot springs. It reminds me of things and folks I hope again to be close to. I ponder also that somehow it will help me find the "him" that Bronze-Man spoke out 'bout.

There, it's done. My saddest-pain is scratched to parch.

Teagan:

My mind swirled and spun, like my canyon walk. I remembered the teachings of Portunus who had carefully chosen only the wilderness for our conversations. As dangerous as that seemed to me, he knew every ridge and nook. It seemed a natural gift to him that he was able to smell before hearing the marauding she-dames. He kept us clear of them and taught me amazing ways to "work within"; that is to be a part of the place where you are.

"Do not disturb what is given to you in the moment but become it. Do not divulge yourself, instead know your place and embrace it. He showed me how to bathe in the good mud by the moving water, avoiding the snake shelves, then to blend with the world."

"Still, they may discover you." He said solemnly. "You must be ready for that, always."

I was not sure if by "them" he meant the she-dames or other enemies. He never spoke of a person or a thing that might attack. He warned that <u>all</u> was suspect, <u>all</u> might be of benefit. Why he chose me to share with, he did not share. Was I suspect as well if I did not fit the Monk's plan?

I was not thinking nor walking straight. In fact, I was not looking straight either and so crunched full force into the left portion of the canyon wall. My last memory before tumbling for my final faint?...

—Will the Bronzeman, Jesus, call me home?

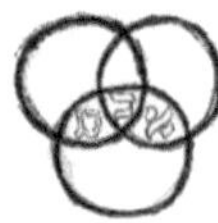

Ilona:

I was woken by a dream of danger. I first pondered that another earth-shaking was about to come, but the flag in my dream spoke out 'bout something more important than a quake. And as I tried to do my own shaking off the nightmare, Bronze-Man spoke out loud with his hurry-up voice.

"It's time. Find him."

"Find who? Find him where?" I was not grasping well what Bronze-Man was speaking out.

"Trust me, you will find each other. Go!"

Like I scratched afore, *hurry* is not a good-right word for me, but this was Bronze-Man speaking out. Straight away, I pushed myself up from my straw-bed, suited up and readied myself for what, I could not yet see. Just afore I left my cave, I somehow grasped that I must grab and take my ram-horn with me.

I will find the mystery-him with it. That is what Bronze-man was speaking out to me in my head.

And then I made my way out of the cave in the dim light afore dawn, out to find what and who Bronze-Man was hurrying me toward.

The voice of Bronze-Man is stuck in my head, telling me over and over now to "Go and blow." The dark is all gone, both inside of me and outside. The day is hot and ready for me.

"Go and blow!" Speaks Bronze-Man.

So, blowing, I Go!

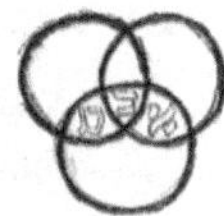

Teagan:

Portunus? I hear him. He is just around the bend. *Soon, I will be too.* I chuckle loudly to the canyon walls at my pun, and then howl hysterically, hearing my laughter bounced back to me in the echoes of my desert tomb.

There is no food here, no water. You tricked me, clever you! Am I taunting my mentor or my God?

His voice again. I'm getting closer.

"If you hear that sound, it means to stop whatever you're doing and focus yourself, for a new and wonderful thing is about to appear before you—victory."

What sound? I hear nothing but my own prattling. Then a clear and beautiful long-note sings into the air. The tone is so wonderfully familiar, richer and more resonant than any I might attempt with a modern-day instrument.

I rasp pathetically, "Victory!" Is my cry loud enough that the trumpeter will hear it?

In answer, a blurry image appears in the shimmering heat—*Portunus, is that you? Bronzeman, are you coming for me now?*

Ilona:

I will try, but there is no good-right way of scratching 'bout finding my gift. As I hunted for the mystery man, I spied a dillo. They mostly waddle in the dry places away from the river and that's where Bronze-Man was hurrying me. Why dillos like the dust so much, I still can't figure. But it was because of my hunting in the dusty places, that I found the dillo and the dillo helped me find my new-best keep.

Somehow, I new the critter's hunt was as important as mine. I slowed down and followed it around a rocky corner in the gulch and stopped quick. The dillo was now crawling over a small mound where it busied itself licking up ants. But that was not the end of the dillo's and my shared discovery.

I grasped that the mound under the critter was not a mound at all, it was a sand-body, a sand-wreck-body. I picked up and tossed a small stone onto the sand-wreck and it flinched, then it moved no more. I took a bigger stone and cautiously tossed it onto the head of sandy-wreck. There was a groan, but it did not move. I rose up and circled the body, kicking sand at it to see if I could get a stir. Nothing. Then I pressed down on the body carefully with the toes of my foot, ants moved from under it, but sandy-wreck only groaned again.

I pondered someone had tried ending him and wondered if he was someone else's trouble, thrown away. But then I saw the scars and bruising all over and he didn't seem to be the trouble, he seemed chased by other's trouble. Someone else had caught him, tried ending him, and somehow he got away, just far enough that he still breathed. I was pondering how near-ended he looked when I got a big shock. Bronze-Man spoke out!

"He is yours."

His voice came not from inside me, and not from sandy-wreck's body. It was from everywhere but those two places. It was Bronze-Man, sure thing,. But his voice was not connected to a body.

He spoke out again, "He is yours."

I spoke back to the Bronze-voice. "Why is he mine? What will I do with a wreck? What might he do to me?"

A wonderful cool wind washed over me where I stood, and in it, the Bronze-voice whispered, "Do not fear. He is yours."

And that was enough, all he needed to tell. I felt more good-right than ever afore. It was the good-right of a doing that had to be, needed to be, wanted to be done. So, I turned my attention back to sandy-wreck, crouched down and overturned him. Brushing the dirt and ants away from his lips with my hand, poured some water from my water-pouch onto his gritty face. Then I coaxed his mouth open and filled it with the liquid. That's when sandy-wreck choked some and swallowed. I gave him another short swallow and washed more of the grit from his face.

His shaky arm lifted and his hand went to his face to wipe. Then he opened his eyes. I had never seen that color green since afore the Blanking, and then, only in the color of springtime plants that were new and happy.

Even banged up, he was beautiful. That was my pondering of him. And I grabbed then that Bronze-Man's voice without a body was beautiful too. I nodded to my unseen friend and spoke out loud one more time, and my voice echoed off the canyon walls that held all three of us together, "Yup, he is mine."

His springtime eyes looked up and caught me, but then caused me sadness for the fear I saw in them. Was I a danger to him?

Well, my eyes are not afraid of you, I thought inside.

Our eyes stayed on each other and somehow, my stare of care fixed his fear. I saw the eyes change. I pondered that he was now seeing what I was seeing—a new thing, a good-right wondrous miracle of a thing. We were the thing.

I held out my hand and spoke with as much peace as possible to him. "I've been watching you." The words were strangers coming out of my mouth, not 'cause they were untrue, but 'cause they were fact. I hadn't figured it afore. This wreck had been in my mind-pics even afore I had walked away from the tribe. I fought the pics 'cause he was...a wreck. My mom dame had made them, even my dad-wreck, devils in my head,. But this one wasn't a devil. I know dark, real well, like regular food I eat. I can taste and smell it even when it's not near. This man on the ground does not smell, taste, or look dark. He's the other—he's light

No more pondering, no more just staring, Bronze-Man spoke out to me. I reached out my hand. First, Sandy-Wreck just looked at it, for a good while. Then he reached back and grabbed it. I pulled up and we came face to face. We stared more...and more. Then with no words, I brushed all the ants I could find off of him, turned so we were side-to-side, and worked his arm over my shoulder. We then began a slow-slow walk through the canyon maze to my home-cave.

Teagan:

Liquid, familiar only from a long-ago memory, pelts my face, drips onto my cracked lips. Some of it spills into my mouth. This is another of those moments that will always be a present tense thing, never in the past. Always this, and the memory of my first encounter with Bronzeman, will exist as if always happening in the immediate. All other moments will be subordinate; all other time must be filtered through the reality of these most important times.

Like a baby's first sip; I have to remember what to do when such a thing as water seeps into my consciousness...*swallow.* I choke the fluid down and try to lift the rock that had been my head, up off the ground. I fail at the attempt.

Cautiously, laggardly lifting my arm, it takes all my cognitive power to recall how to cock my elbow and bring my hand to my face. The tips of my fingers feel moisture on my skin. Ordering my index finger to obey, it wipes some of the wetness and brings that also to my eyes. A trembling touch to my lids and only then, do I dare try to open my eyes. Steel light pierces my vision. A miracle—I have sight!

The sun has come out of hiding and is directly overhead. I react by shielding my eyes with the hand I am now learning to use clumsily in my rebirth. More water washes the caked sand off my face and my eyes squint to identify my rescuer in whose lap my head now rests. *When did I arrive here? Is it the lap of my God who has come to fetch me? Hello Savior.*

I try moving the rest of, or any of my body, but it is useless. I am a one-armed rag. My eyes though are starting to cooperate. I look to my right to see the canyon wall I remembered before my collapse in my last life. I force my sight to the left and there, I stare up at certain death.

It is a she-dame crouched over me! Surely, she is hungry and will simply stab me into edible pieces of not so fresh meat. Or possibly she will drag me to her camp as a trophy from the cliffside battle. I will be impaled as a demonstration of her superiority over a pathetic clansman. Whatever her plan for my demise, I am helpless to prevent any of it.

But in this new life—new rules are born. To my shock, a hand extends from her side. The dame tenderly, yes tenderly (*Is that even a word that exists in this strange place to which I have been delivered?*) cradles my neck and head from behind and slowly lifts me with the help of her other hand, to a sitting position. Without a word, she brings a leather water-pouch to my lips. I take in a few hesitant sips. *Is she poisoning me somehow?*

The answer comes after a wonderful moment. Her refreshment awakens me enough that she is able to help pull me to my feet. I wobble, but stand there transfixed, inches from her. Our warm breath mingles in the small space separating our faces. Our eyes lock in what has to be mutual confusion. *How are neither of us attacking the other?*

"Beautiful." That's right. That is the strangest thought of all. I am not alarmed but captivated by her features. Her garb and weaponry suggested her to be battle hardened, but within that, is a softness. I suddenly imagine bees swarming a comb but all I can focus on is the honey.

I am shocked even more when she signals, a single index finger placed vertically in front of her lips, then brought in the same manner to my lips. I realize now that the observed thought I had about her had not been a silent one, as I intended. Now she warns me by her muted signal, that we are, by this encounter, both potentially in mortal danger. Only by our shared quiet might we survive the moment. And I am astounded in this reality:

She cares!

Her hand does one more extraordinary thing. It carefully descends away from my face and finds my hand while she continues to stare into my soul. Grasping mine, her hand pulls with encouragement, my arm over her shoulder and only then does she turn to carry/lead me to a higher embankment and from there to an obscure cave. Within, she leaves me weakly standing in my ongoing disorientation. As my eyes adjust to the dimmer light, she skillfully squats and tends to a small fire, constructed in the way I had also been taught to build, emitting a minimal amount of smoke by using dried birch twigs. She adds to the flames and then looks up at me. It is only then that I realize I am somehow still cold. The fire calls to me, and my body shivers in response. *Or is it her who causes my shuddering?* I come down to the spot beside her and again her hand grasps mine. Without a word we watch the flames, consumed in our private thoughts of what had just occurred.

And then I am asleep, sure that this is sadly nothing more than my most perfect dream.

Aella:

Boy, I am awake now. You are my target and when I find you, you will tell me why. Why would you restore me on the river beach? I am not your friend; I am not your family! I would have killed you, had I the strength. I would have tossed you back into the current as fish food. You must know all of this. What do you think you also know of my life that you would believe for a moment that your kind act would somehow forgive the sins of mankind toward me and my kind?

You naked fool. All you have done is set me free to continue my mission.

And who was that kneeling by you, teso cur? Another wreck who thinks himself above my wrath? Why did he touch me with tenderness? Surely, he knew I have no compassion to return. His efforts too, were in vain. Surely, he knew!

So why? Why! Why do those I hate, try to reclaim my respect, my love? I am not, nor do I long to be lovable. I do not believe in such antiquated ideals as an unconditional embrace. The proof of time's past miseries has taught me well the true intent of man and his kind!

So why? And who in the world is it that I am asking the question to?

Teagan:

I can't say how much time passed. Too much. Not at all enough. She added more branches to the fire, and I forgot again about my physical condition. She still seemed worried about making a noise, so I took my own form of risk and drew my name in the dirt by the fire. Oddly, she did not seem disturbed by the taboo and scribbled her own name below mine:

Ilona.

And then, these words:

I've been watching you.

Verse VIII

"It is difficult to perceive prophecy unfolding when you are living withing the prophecy's timeframe. It would be like standing within the middle pages of a giant book and trying to comprehend the book's beginning and ending.

"We need to hold hands with the writers, whom the Spirit has inspired, and let them walk us through the past and present vision, and to the ultimate completion."

—Portunus

Aella:

"Why do you persecute me?"

"Who are you that I would persecute you?

"You know my name. You have always known my name."

The light is blinding, searing, but it is the only warmth in this cold dark place. It speaks to me in waves that wash my bloody body.

"You don't exist. You are my imagination."

"Is that so? Why do you believe that?"

"What? What do you mean? You have always been imaginary!"

"I have always been?"

I can't breathe. There is no air in my dark. But the light breathes. It pulses, it wants, it...loves.

"Why have you never shown yourself to me?"

"Yes, why have you never shown yourself to me?

"What? I asked you first."

"Did you? Have you?"

The light is not glaring any more, it is fading, but it hopes.

"I…have just asked you."

"Yes, just. What is your answer?"

"What? What is my answer?"

"I asked you first."

I can't breathe, I am dying. The light is almost gone.

"The answer...I know the answer. I thought I was god."

"You are not God."

"No, I am not. You are...God."

"That is a different answer."

And the light changes, it breathes into me, for me. the breath, the light is...golden…bronze.

Teagan:

Best as I can calculate, it has been two weeks since she saved me. In that time, a lifetime and more. Ilona has nursed me back to health, shared her home, her food, and her story with me. She was patient and attentive when I finally opened up and told her about my journey, from the home of my youth; to Washington D.C.; to the dens; to here. I could not believe in this desolate and violent existence, that such grace, such beauty could exist. Surely others would have hunted down and destroyed one like her because...they would hate what it asked of them.

And what does she ask of me? To be like her? I have forgotten what caring for another means. It has become too much to care for others. Surviving for self is all I have been able to muster.

But she makes it, causes care to be so smooth, like floating on a calm sea. I can't resist the care, I long to learn how to return it again. And when she sat at her small table and invited me to sit alongside, I was ready to care, but I was not ready for the trust she was about to bestow on me.

Ilona opened her backpack that I observed she always kept close beside her. She turned her head and smiled at me, then reached within the satchel and withdrew two crayons: one green and one blue. I sensed these represented a cherished memory for her and when she handed them to me, I felt as if she was bestowing me with her treasure of gold.

I wanted to honor the gift but was not sure how. Somehow the right way came to me. I brought the gift to my nose and took in the reminiscent aroma of the coloring sticks. Nothing else smelled like this and I closed my eyes to replay in my memory; innocent days with a blank piece of paper and my own crayons...

> —Paper was a canvas of freedom, imagination and wonder
> that was to be filled with my hopes and future adventures.
> First, stick figures, but then more creative and embellished
> figures, images. Then for me, the most wonderful...

I was not an artist by any stretch, but the crayons offered a new expression for me: letters; then words—big bold colorful words, slowly excitingly evolving into phrases and sentences. I discovered I could shape my thoughts into roadways, avenues and then into a map and universe of expression. I could share and dream and sing and collude with others using my colors. At some time, I learned that a pencil, and then a pen, could color as well, faster. But in my mind's eye, the crayons were always in my hand, painting the picture of life.

Apparently, Ilona could see my thoughts and so retrieved and revealed her greatest secret and treasure from her backpack—A carefully wrapped package of parch, and a number of pens. My own trove was still (I hoped!) buried in my den.

Beautiful Ilona shared her writings with me, and I then asked if I could borrow a pen. I began to write these very words that I have been sharing now and shared with her. She read and wept. Then she wrote in response and shared her cursive thoughts with me.

We became...there were no other, no greater words for it...parch lovers.

Ilona:

An accident, no, it's a bright new present! But how do I unwrap it...how do I scratch it out for other folks to best grasp?

After hiking off from the other dames, I had only myself to keep me company. Now I grasp that was not the way it should have been. In so many of the conversations within myself, I miss-spoke and brain-twisted the *true* stuff. Who was to tell me different?

That was my darkness. Bronze-Man fixed...lit my darkness, spoke out to me, some teasing in my dreams that I have to figure through:

"The darkness inside you is gone," he spoke, "But what are you going to do with the light?"

Good question, that. I remember when my dad-wreck gave me an old flashlight on one of our camping trips. He showed me one night, that the light would take away dark wherever I pointed it. I could point it anywhere, but I soon grasped there were places and things that needed light more than others. There were dangerous things that needed to be pointed to; places and things to stay away from.

There were also good-right places and things that I could find and light up to make them even better by brightening them. One of them was me. The light brightened me! Also, I figured that I could turn the light off, and walk again in my darkness if I wanted. I have done that lots and now grasp it is the worst of things to do.

Bronze-Man is showing me now that his light is always on in me, even when I'm not pointing it. His light is different from my old flashlight, and he's asking me to always point it good-right—never turn it off. He even speaks out that he'll help with the pointing if I ask him to; lots of times even if I don't ask. He is the best-right Pointer of all. That's how he pointed me to my Teagan.

I had forgotten how bright light could be 'till Bronze-Man showed up and plopped my Teagan in the sand for me to find.

Teagan:

Don't get me wrong in what I'm about to write—it's not a complaint, just a confusion. I have found in this new life of mine that I'm having trouble figuring out who my enemies are.

I once thought the world and its made-up concept of God was my nemesis until you showed me a new world, Jesus. I thought the Barrens and the wilderness were against me before Portunus taught me differently. I thought my adversaries were the dames until I met Ilona.

Now I can't distinguish. Was it all of them? Is it none of them? What has changed to muddle my brain so? How can one day; something be evil, and the next; be righteous? It makes me wonder if something I perceive as good and righteous can become an agent of my doom? How can I discern what, who is actually for or against me?

I do know that Ilona is certainly not my enemy, nor will she ever be. The picture, the mystery, the purpose all come together in the face of the one who, in my canyon death, cradled my head in her lap and, by the power of Bronzeman, brought me back to life.

But those thoughts bring with them a more sinister consideration. Am I the enemy; to myself; to my companions; to my God? How can I tell if I am acting on their behalf or for my own selfish interests?

Bronzeman, protect them and me, from the old me; my worst *ene-me*.

We had been singing separate verses to a song that now crescendos into a chorus we both share.

And in a perfect moment we are now singing together through a simple stare. I hear words…

"I know you!"

My coming close to Ilona risks and deserves volumes of script. She has shared with me, her early history, and her struggles while existing within the dame tribe. I had no idea of their strife. We were told by our rulers that they were the cause of our quarreling, not the victims. I had suspected otherwise, but their attacks on our borders invaded my fears as they had animated the fears of all clansmen. Imagine then, my reaction when she shared her relation to Aella, the most feared of all she-dames.

Ilona assures me that she has abandoned that path, but how can I know for sure? What if hers is some well-planned ploy to draw us out, then to be overtaken by the clippers to who knows what outcome?

No! As I grow to know this lovely one, I detect in her sharing, no guile, no bitterness, only hope…as I have secretly hoped. So how am I to reconcile my want of her ways with the demands of my clan? Toward what purpose? Is it to discover a new path for all of us? I have no map; only the teachings of a lost friend, along with the dreams of a dame in whom I am eagerly learning to trust.

She, I will call a *peacer*—her wording, not mine—one who wants to reshape those who war into those who seek life, relationship, as one. My term would have once been *peace-keeper*, the moniker once used by the world to define someone charged with keeping change from happening, dialogue from challenging, growth from occurring. Now I understand, peacers…*peace-makers*…to be the antithesis of peace-keepers. Peacers heal. Ilona is exact in her branding. Her identity pairs perfectly…touches and makes peace…with my own. We are peacers for and with one another.

And Bronzeman's voice-light speaks from within to encourage me. He says, "There is more."

Aella:

My mind is busier than it has ever been. Voices from the past, voices from… who knows where invade any hope of a private reflection or introspection.

Stop! But then I realize it is someone or something, telling me to stop resisting, stop…rebelling. It is not me commanding. I don't understand how this is happening. What I once abhorred, I now am inexplicably drawn to. I can't bear the silence and long for the next perfect tone of the speaker's voice.

Go! Again, it is not me directing. I know now I must go. I must find them. I must confront. I must battle.

Ilona:

A noise. Is it critter; a wreck-cur? I snuff the fire to wait in darkness. The sound is the wind talking to the trees, nothing more. But now I must rekindle a light, the night is a cold one. I was so-at-home in the dark, but light is a craving to me now. I'm eager to work with it where I was not afore. The wreck—*my Teagan*—has become part of my light and I watch him now snoring deeply on his pallet. Guess I'll have to get used to that… or snore louder than him!

I want more of the warming light of him. How did he become good-right so quickly to me? Nothing can steal the pretty crayoning now inside my head. Sure, darkness still lurks on the outside, like the critter I thought might have been hunting me tonight. But my mind…my heart-pic of my Teagan, stands up against the dark and blinds it. Where does he get such brightness from? Why is he willing to share it with me?

Bronze-Man, I'm scratching out to you on parch 'cause you have the answer. You are more bright than even me and my Teagan lit together. Now, the fire in my hideaway only pretends to be like you. Soon, I grasp, you will light things in a bigger way and the pic will become even brighter for us both.

Strange, we have not touched, not in the old ways, woman-to-man, and back. But I feel it—the wanting of it. Mom-dame would say it was a "body thing", made by stirrings of hidden parts inside of me. She would speak out that the wanting is best controlled and fought, not given in to.

"Do not wish for what was," she would say. "Stay with your own kind and your own kind only; the tribe is your survival."

All good for her to say, but this one, my Teagan, I cannot wish away my wanting of him. It is not a body thing…only. It is a crayon story. I hear his voice in my head and I want more of it. This night, all I can do is scratch it. My same mom-dame, the one who taught me how to use a pen, had said from her big Law House that no one is to read or write. For her and the other dames, it is a not-good thing—it makes our minds fight with one another. I ponder her ordering and wonder, *is mind-fighting always a not-good thing?* To make a fire, don't we have to spark a flint to a rock? Is that not a fight of sorts, and is not the result of that fight the beginning of light? That is why I hunted out paper and snuck it from the pig plant; to scratch pen to parch. That is how you who read my scratching hear and crayon me into your minds now.

Few other folks seek this new *life-sharing-life* idea. They, most all of them, hunger for old food and old cloth. Paper is not a need for them. I admit, scratching has not seemed a natural thing for me either. Sure, I have been doing it, but I read my scratching and grasp it to be only "so-so". I have watched Teagan do it, and for him it is like a breathing thing. I am needy…no, *wanty*, that's better wording…of his writing. I feel invisible when I am next to him, as I watch the pen in his hand, and he lays down his beautiful letters. So, I hunger to try it more, too. Maybe I can learn from it why it is so good-right to him. Maybe, Bronze-Man, in my own scratching, I can learn not just to want light, but to be light.

Teagan:

I remember when Portunus finally revealed Truth to me.

We were collecting ants to be planted for defense of the dens. I was focused on the technique he had shown me of carefully excavating the nest without disturbing the business of the workers, and in doing so capturing the queen. The work was tedious but would reap the best benefits for transplanting the mound.

"What do you think the ants believe of you?" Asked the robed man.

I knew that a lesson of some sort was in the making and so tried to focus on his voice as I meticulously searched out the core of the nest. When Portunus determined that I was properly multi-tasking, he continued.

"Those critters have their own perception of what is right. It is to serve their egg-layer as they have instinctively done their whole lives. Their reasoning does not allow for anything but. Then you come along with a new plan; to take them as your own, not to destroy or change their course, but to alter its result, thus adding...blessing...their existence with a higher cause, one they do not perceive in their current condition."

I sensed the lesson was to be more profound, so I nodded my head, pretending I understood my mentor's meaning, and waited. He rewarded my patience by unwrapping far more of his wisdom.

"Let's say those ants, especially the queen, do have a sense that you are involved in their activities, and some, hopefully many of them sense that you mean them no harm.

"Some of them, however, see you as a threat, an unwelcome presence. They will surely strike or flee to protect what they believe to be their plan... their will. And, by the way, other diggers—let's call them armadillos—may have also tried, are trying, to serve their own purpose; not for benefit, but for destruction or some other selfish desire."

Now Portunus had my attention. He was describing not ants, but us. The question in my mind was, *Whom or what is digging up our nest and to what purpose? I'd want to know that before agreeing to the plan!*

"Their grasping the full extent of your plan to uproot them, change their location and your desire to help them and others by this action, is moot. Your purpose; altering their course by your desire, is greater, regardless of their want.

"On the other hand, what if the ants were somehow let in on the secret, even having a simple version of the plan shared with them, in hopes that they would join willingly in the cause, with hopes that they would cooperate toward, not away from the Higher relationship?"

"Wouldn't they all have to cooperate for that to work? Even if one ant rebelled, it would result in a battle of wills...chaos within the mound." I couldn't believe that I had just opened my mouth in argument. Now I was the one being resistant.

But in return for my rebuttal, Portunus rewarded me with an amused smile and replied, "Yes, that would be the struggle. But if even one ant, specifically the queen let's say, were to agree to the broader plan, even at the risk that most of the worker ants might forsake their ruler's purpose; then what might happen?"

"Others might follow the leader's example and... the greater purpose would be served." I knew and blurted out the answer, but in the back of my mind, another question started shouting for attention. *How? Who or What is the Higher Power that is doing the bigger work?*

Portunus could somehow hear my question too and responded to it, "What do you think happened to all the people who disappeared in the Blanking? Do you really believe they just vanished into thin air, by some sort of uncontrolled mechanics or random luck? Do you really think the universe runs itself without origin, without design or plan?"

My mind knew the answer, but I could not speak it out loud. *No, something...Someone had to cause and maintain it!*

The monk spoke my thoughts, as if his own, into the open. "And if you were one who yet did not accept...believe in that reality...then how would you rationalize our current misfortunes? By what cause...or entity would such things happen? To what purpose...if any at all?

But let's say you began to discern some outside presence at work. What if you started questioning what kind of entity would do such a thing and toward what purpose? Wouldn't you want to seek that answer with all your heart? Wouldn't you search out the meaning of the relationship you might have with the Greater?"

Yes, my mind screamed. I had stopped my work on the nest but remained crouched by the center of the mound. The critters around me became aware of my presence and started crawling over me. Yet, in my stillness, not one stung. Portunus turned back to the nearby mound he had been working with but spoke words of encouragement to me over his shoulder, "Keep digging."

By any standards, the Ant Analogy provided by Portunus was basic and not entirely complete. But it's subliminal meaning struck me hard. Others may laugh at my naivety—my accepting and absorbing the idea that there is not only greater truth and purpose outside of any I might make up, but that a *Greatest Truth* exists, a High Truth that defines all truths, all Purpose, all love.

Verse IX

It is not always the song that awakens the spirit, but more often the cry.

—Ga'al

Ilona:

LAVA, AND LOTS OF IT! Somewhere in the middle of the night an explosion wakes us and we run to the mouth of the cave to see lightning and flaming clouds pluming into the distant sky above and beyond the river cliffs. I can't tell how far away the eruption is, but the noise is shattering in my ears. The heat of it is everywhere around us so, it is close enough, which was too close—life ending close.

And then I see it, the bright red and orange glow of liquid so hot, it melts the lip of a rock ledge just in sight over the river bend. As the molten soup drips down into the water below, hissing steam and the smell of sulfur fill the air. I choke when trying to take even a sip of a breath.

Now what, now where? My brain races to find answers. If we stay, we will either suffocate or boil. If we run…where to? We are in a canyon with few exits and our cave will soon become an oven to cook us quickly into cinders. There is really only one choice and it is not a good one. I grab my Teagan's hand and pull hard, running fast to the river's edge to dive in, hoping the lava's heat upstream has not yet risen its temperature too high to tolerate.

I immediately regret the choice. My skin is pricked by a thousand stinging needles and the burning is beyond any fire I have ever come near. Even though the sky is alive, the roiling rapids are dark and I am thrown into boulder after boulder afore I can anticipate and dodge them. Somehow I'm able to stay afloat, but I have lost my grasp and sight of my Teagan. I have no choice of course—the water bouncing me in every direction—as if it is alive and trying to wear me down; to swallow me as a meal.

The only hope left is that, as I am carried away, the heat of the volcanic flood starts to diminish. I seem to have passed beyond the rockiest part of the river and into its wider portion. Still the current is fast and I have to struggle to work toward the shore. That's when I realize, there is no shore, only straight and sheer cliff walls with no outcroppings to grab for.

How long can I endure this? Where is my Teagan? Bronze-Man will you save us? They are my last conscious questions as some object comes from behind and strikes me in the head.

It was a dream. Thank you Bronze-Man, for you waked me from it with strange, whispered words, "Peace be with you." I rise quietly from my pallet as to not disturb my Teagan, who does not seem troubled in his sleep, and I go to rekindle a small fire. By its light, I pick up the Good News book and turn to a passage written by a friend of yours named John. He wrote that you died by way of a living nightmare, and God brought you back to life from that terrible ending. You showed up in a room where your friends were hiding in fear for their lives. —Your first words to them? "Peace be with you."

Peace, after that nightmare, after my dark dream? Yes! Even as I finally now remember the last image of the terrible memory—a face of some wreck, the one who had chased after me in an earlier violent vision. All I could see was his face, way too close to my own. He had smiled as if holding some secret, some weapon he plans to use to separate my new treasure from me.

But you hold a bigger secret weapon, Bronze-Man. You hold me and my Teagan…forever, no matter what happens. How do I know the words in the book are right? Because I hear your loving voice in them—each and every one of them. How do I hear your actual voice, know it to be yours? Only you have the answer to that and I don't need the answer, I'm just hungry to listen. Whatever is coming, lava or surly wrecks or both or more, your words are making us ready for it.

Afore, I had tried to grasp how mom-dame's speaking out that she-dames and wrecks being different in their bodies was not important; that in their work and living, they were exactly the same in every way; in doing everything.

It has been one moon-cycle's time since I found and brought my Teagan to live with me. I can scratch for certain that he is different from me in lots of ways. And I'm different from him too. Sure, I'm a better hunter and he's a better parcher, but there are man and woman body parts that are different too. There are—I don't know how else to tell it—man ways he does things, and man thoughts he speaks out, and man habits he does as natural as the ways I ponder and do as a woman. I am more of a *toucher* than he is, wanting to feel the sensation of my body close to his. And I seem to get happier and sadder than he does 'bout things. He is more 'bout fixing things than me—not just broken stuff we find by the river, not just our outer body wounds, but also he wants to fix our mind wounds too.

I don't grasp that I always want all those things fixed and he is good-right 'bout not pushing the fixing. He doesn't always want to talk out loud (like blabbering me!) and so I am grasping how to watch how his body tells of what is going on in his mind during his silent times. Then I try to share it with him, and he is a good listener to me.

We are different, like I remember Mom-dame and Dad-wreck being different. I grasp that different body ways and brain ways and feeling ways are good-right and even better-right when a man and woman share the differences, speak out 'bout them so that they do not become a battle between the two.

I am looking towards the time when we will also share a deeper body-to-body time. We both have pondered it out-loud, one to the other, but there is something holding us back from the doing. It is a…waiting thing. We ponder together it will be a thing that you, Bronze-Man, will speak out about to the two of us.

My Teagan tried to use my way of wording things when he spoke out one night, "Together, we are crayons of music."

Those were sweet words—pretty as flowers—and he was almost right. But you, Bronze-Man, had me speak—glue—my words out loud in a way that completed his. "Somebody had to make the crayons first afore we could ever color our song together."

So now, we're doing a very new thing together. Our Good News Book is telling us 'bout it; The thing is called *praying*—kind of speaking out to you, Bronze-Man…Jesus. The speaking out may just be inside us—what we're thinking—or it may be an out loud—speaking to share with each other. We pray and wait for you to tell us with your light-answers, what you're wanting of us.

Afore our man and woman body sharing, we want it to be a big praying thing for us. It's a something we both want to be good-right and hopefully soon, if that is good-right with you.

I can't grasp this. It is more downside-up than the finding of my Teagan and almost as bright as meeting you, Bronze-Man.

Remember the Good News book we had found? My Teagan was reading it to me by the candles we had made using armadillo poo. Funniest stuff, it doesn't stink and smells like chocolate—or what I remember chocolate smelling like.

So, by the choco-dillo-light, My Teagan spoke out 'bout a profit-wreck named Isaiah telling the wrong-pondering folks of his time:

> "—They will hide in caves in the rocky hills or dig holes
> in the ground to try to escape from the LORD's anger and
> to hide from his power and glory!
>
> "A day is coming when human pride will be ended, and
> human arrogance destroyed. Then the LORD alone will
> be exalted."

To me, this sounded like lofty high-talk, but I grasped what he was saying: We are all messed up, no matter what we ponder and do, and we had better grasp fast that you, Bronze-Man, are the best-right one whose ways are good-right to follow, afore even worse stuff starts going on.

My Teagan said that a friend from his old clan had spoken out to him another Isaiah saying:

"Nobody is good-right, nobody."

That's how I remember it spoken. Maybe the words were different, but that's how I grasped it best-right.

It was side-ways to me, that some wreck from My Teagan's clan was Bible-smart and I asked him who it was.

"It was me, but I'm not at all smart, just ready to learn more," said a strange, robed wreck who had quietly showed up at the cave mouth.

"Portunus!" said my Teagan.

"Who?" I shouted: "That's my dad-wreck!"

My Teagan's looked real puzzled and spoke out, "Your what?"

Teagan

I was flabbergasted. I wanted to run to my mentor and hug him, but there was way too much information flooding my brain and too many epiphanies to assimilate. Instead of running, I hyperventilated in the spot where I stood and then collapsed in a faint.

Two of the most important faces of all time filled my vision when I awoke. Beautiful Ilona was chattering in a way I had never heard her before. She wasn't talking to me but to Portunus. He was smiling and responding in a way that suggested they were not only familiar with one another but had been for years. They were both talking so fast, in between hugs, laughter, and tears that it was difficult to keep up.

"You are not ended!"

"No, who told you that I was...Oh, Jessica, I am so sorry."

"Ilona, call me Ilona...you are not ended!"

"How did Teagan find you?"

"He did not, I found him. I blew."

"You b...? Ahh, the shofar."

"You are not ended!"

"Nor are you, praise Jesus!" Is he, okay?

"Jesus?"

"No, Teagan!"

"He was afore you showed up."

They both turned from their banter to stare at me. I must have looked as if I was in shock, which I was, and they both reached to touch my forehead.

"He's fine, my Teagan is just fine. He'll come to his senses soon."

"—Your Teagan?"

"Sure, he is, Bronze-Man pointed me to him and gave him to me."

After our reunion, I could barely contain myself. I was maybe a little jealous of this new discovery; about Portunus being the father of beautiful Ilona. *Why had he never shared with me about his family?*

I wanted to join in their celebration, but felt like I was an outsider, peeking through a curtain at a very private and personal reconciliation. As their discussion deepened, I excused myself and went outside to consider the ramification of this family gathering.

If Portunus was her father, then that also meant…Oh sweet Bronzeman, *that means that Aella and Portunus are…*

"—I'm sorry for the delay in getting to you." I jumped as Portunus came up quietly from behind me, interrupting my newest bombshell realization in mid-stride. "I'm sure you understand."

I *don't understand at all!* My brain silently shouted at him.

The man smiled and sat down on a boulder next to me. I could tell by his approach that another important sharing was in the mix. I couldn't fathom what could be any more revealing than what I was just contemplating.

"You realize, don't you, that you and Jessica…Ilona are not the only ones that Jesus has been revealing himself to in this apocryphal season?"

Well, I guess I was wrong…he has again found a way to command my complete attention.

"There is so much I need to impart to the both of you in so little time," says my mentor. "I suspect you have many questions and concerns of your own that you want to discuss."

—*You think?*

Portunus pauses for just a moment and then states, "I'm going to ask that you trust me a little while longer and I think the answers to many things will be explained."

I had learned to never try to predict my mentor's ways or intent, but I had also never been disappointed by his timing or his results. I nodded and he offered his warmest smile to me in return. Then he reached into his pack which he had brought with him and pulled out one item. Seeing it caused me to literally "whoop" with excitement. It was my pack full of paper and journals that I had hidden in my den. Then I realized, I also had been keeping secrets from my friend and well deserved any dressing down he was about to give me.

"I want you to know that I was not the one to uncover these," he said, handing me the closed-up pack. By the mentioning of "these", it was evident he had perused the contents. "Honestly, I don't know who had rifled through your den, I have my suspicions but I'm not going to make accusations without proof. That said, I entered your room to protect your keepsakes. The Spirit led me to gather them and return them to you.

"You knew I was alive?" These were the first words I had spoken out loud since he had sat down beside me. He knew I was trying to be patient but that I could not contain myself from interrupting. He smiled and continued the explanation of his discovery.

"When I entered your den, the contents of your pack were strewn all over the floor. I'm pretty sure whoever did the damage also took the liberty of treating themselves to the reading of your personal history, beliefs, and feelings."

"Then we are both in danger," I warned.

"We have always both been in danger," he chuckled.

Then Portunus reached into his pack once again, retrieving two more items that he handed me as his second surprise. The first was my flute. This item stunned me into grief, for whoever had ransacked my quarters had also deliberately stomped and crushed the workings of my cherished instrument. I tenderly fingered the remains and could not focus on my mentor's words. He recognized my mourning and waited until my tears cleared and I nodded for him to continue.

The next item was the most astounding gift. It was his ram's horn…the shofar he had used to signal our clan on numerous occasions. He noticed more tears now welling up in my eyes. I wanted to tell him this was too great a treasure to pass over, but he put up his hand to interrupt my protest, and then he spoke, also struggling with his emotions.

"I know this will not replace your flute. And I might tell you that this is for you to use for heralding our clan, but it, and you, have taken on a far more important role. This horn is an exact match to the one that J…Ilona keeps. The two should serve as a shared calling over the both of you—the bonding that your Bronzeman has invited you into. I am no longer her or your keeper. He wants you to hear his love for the both of you as one with him."

I absorbed in serious silence what he had just shared. Then standing up, I invited him to follow me back to the cave. "I believe there is something Ilona and I want to ask you to do for us."

Aella:

Do they realize the danger coming at them? I think not. As I wind my way through the canyons, trying to track my prey, my thoughts criss and cross as well. Earlier, I had successfully fought off the strange visions that have been plaguing me and now am focused on one thing only.

How will I exact my revenge?

That's when the blow hits me. I am knocked to the ground, tumble and turn to identify my adversary. It is a dame!

Teagan:

Portunus and I had just entered the home-cave and I had immediately gone to Ilona and hugged her intensely. I whispered to her, describing the moments her father and I had just shared outside. I showed her the shofar he had just given me, and she then lifted her teary eyes toward her father. I then took her head in my hand gently and brought my face close to kiss her, then whispered one more thing in her ear. I had barely finished the request and she began nodding eagerly.

"Yes, oh yes!" She was crying openly now.

He looked at us in a way I would not have expected. Portunus stared intensely without a smile or frown into, first Ilona's eyes, then mine, then back to hers, then to me again, repeatedly. I became uncomfortable as the examination drew out over many minutes of silence. There was no indication as to his thinking, only that he was processing what was before him...long and hard. And then only one question came from him. "What would you have me do?"

Ilona spoke to her father before I could open my mouth to share our request. It didn't matter, her words were mine as well.

"Will you make us married?"

The stoic face of her "dad-wreck", as she had always defined him to me, held firm for only a moment. It's crumbling started in the smallest way-a single tear escaped from his right eye. Then he shocked us with his answer.

"No."

Ilona:

The water was less noisy this day, so my dad-wreck took us to stand by the river edge. My Teagan held my hand. I remember the simpleness of it all. There was no bird-song in the air, no other fidgeting people, no pomp, or practiced things.

It felt like all time and no time at all that the man in the robe stared at us. He looked then around the whole place and closed his eyes, took in a breath, and let it out slowly. I had done that lots of times as a good-right thing afore I was going to scratch pen to parch, or when I wanted to get all my brain pondering something big. I grabbed that this was a big time, a big thing we were all doing, so I closed my eyes too, took in deep air, held it tight and then let it loose in slow time. Next to me I heard the slow time air coming out of my Teagan and pondered that he too was getting ready for the big thing.

"I first want to confess feeling like an interloper in this scenario," my dad-wreck started telling. "In the first such covenant union between a man and woman, there were only two people and their Creator in attendance. I can't tell you when the first officiator in history, such as me, showed up to patch together some special words to bless the event. What I can share is that I am also receiving a profound benefit in the moment. And so, I give thanks to the Designer of the moment."

Aella:

My reactions are thankfully quick. *This one will be ended just as all others who have tried to subdue me.* Holding her off with one arm, as best I can, I reach with my other hand for my knife, but cannot find it! *Alright, hand-to-hand it is.*

"This is not a struggle of arms, you fool. It is one of wills."

She speaks! And the voice is so familiar, but from where do I know her? I make a kick that rolls us over and down an embankment. Now I am on top and try to expose her face, but like me, she is masked to avoid the Rippers and I can't make out her face. "Who are you?" I shout at her.

With another roll she is on top and screams back, "—Your worst enemy."

I punch out and am able to escape her grasp. Jumping up I search for an advantage and see to my astonishment, a pool of clear water to the left of where we have landed. I run to it and hear footsteps in closing pursuit behind me. At the last possible moment, I jump and turn in the air to grab her and pull her into the pond with me. *If I am to die, so will we both!* I ready myself for the ending struggle.

We sink into these strange waters, weighted down by our suits, and I wonder why we have not yet hit bottom? I open my to eyes to again strike out and de-mask her. Now I am beside myself... literally.

It is me I stare at. I am not drowning, no longer sinking, no longer suited, but nude and floating in the water.

A bright golden man floats by me and speaks in the most familiar voice of all. "Give me a drink of water."

What? Who are you that would ask me for such a thing?

"If you only knew who was asking, you would ask me for life-giving water."

I laugh. *Where would you get such a thing? Why is this water different from any other?*

"All who drink the water of the world will thirst again, but whoever drinks the water I give will never be thirsty again."

Who are you!

"You know the answer, you just need to drink."

Lord!

I awake by the pool and cannot at first remember. I can't remember how I arrived here, what I am doing here...who I am, what I feel...why I am...new.

And then I remember the water. I am...separated...from myself; my will is gone. I am no longer in my suit, but only garbed in my tunic. I stand and look around for evidence of the attack, the battle, the other... me...and I search most, for Him. He is not here, yet...He is. I recall how He replied after I called out His name.

"You are now mine, Ga'al; that is your white stone name, as you have overcome your rebellion against me and against my bride."

I remember my past, but my name from then seems unimportant. He has renamed, restored me and I am no longer hateful of life. I do not thirst but still the water calls to me. I try to stand to walk to its edge but discover that my right hip must have been displaced in my wrestling. So, I crawl over to peer into its depths- and I am blue!

His will is done.

Teagan:

"—Now let me explain why I told you 'No' when you asked if I would marry the two of you," said my mentor. "The answer is simple. I am not qualified to do so. There is no person on this planet who has that singular authority."

Portunus, in his monkish way, is leading us to some important new understanding.

"Here, there are only two people who meet at a crossroads and only they can choose to end their solo adventures."

"Sounds like a terrible idea, right—to give up one's individual identity to become some sort of gelled collective?"

How does he do that? He just identified a secret concern I hadn't even known I was harboring!

"The Designer's plan was never to extinguish or sacrifice the individual in a marriage, but to create a bolder way of relating; thinking alike, wanting alike, working together voluntarily—not by forced means—to seek agreement based on shared desire."

And now Portunus throws in the curve ball.

"Honestly, my being here is unnecessary; it is the three of you who are committing to the covenant.

"Wait, did I just say, 'the three of you?' But just previously I said this was a joining of two!"

Yes, you did.

I believe that One; a supernatural partner, consecrates—makes holy... separates-out and distinguishes the uniqueness of two...male and female.

He is also the one who joins them in body, mind, and spirit through a very special arrangement in which he is the crucial third participant.

"It takes all the partners, all three to make it work. It is the most beautiful of covenants because it is modeled after the very first covenant. Don't trivialize that, don't forget it.

Ilona:

"—So, can it be messed up?, my dad asks us. "You bet. Right from the beginning and through to the end. Both of you can mess it up badly. That's where the third partner comes into play. The third partner wants your union to work as much as, and more than you do. So, another piece of advice…

"—Trust your third partner. Don't get in the way. Seek the help and fellowship of the third partner in all you do, together and apart. And then, no matter how hard you try to mess it up, it will be made more beautiful, more full of love and care than anything you might imagine.

"I'll be quiet soon, I promise, but there is one more purpose as to why I told you 'no' when you asked me to participate with you here. Look, I'm standing here with you, I must have been lying to you when I said, 'no', right? Well, that depends on you. You have the power to change my 'no' to, 'yes'. I share with you now that your third partner is actually present with us. He is ready, He is waiting. He is the One who will join you perfectly and completely.

"But if you enter into your life together, without Him, then…well, remember my earlier comment about messing up at the beginning? I had messed up and have suffered more deeply than I can confess. I have deeply hurt those I deeply love most because of my selfish un-unified way of thinking."

NO MORE, I speak into myself as I listen to my dad. I am free to choose the new way, new life, with my Savior, my Bronze-Man! And so,

I live, newborn and One in Him. Now I'm ready to stand together with my Teagan.

"If you choose another way, so be it. I will not judge you, but I will also not walk with you. Choose now your God, whether it be the gods of your fathers, or of the world, but as for me and my family…"

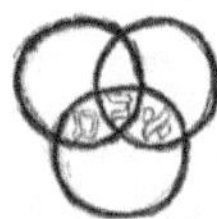

Teagan:

"—I can't speak for other people's perception of God, but I think I have a pretty good feel for God's perception of them, and of me." Portunus is wrong about one thing. He can and is speaking for me, and into me. Each word jolts the fibers of my soul.

"The problem comes in trying to share my faith with another who may have little to no regard for scripture or spiritual comparisons. Some say there's no proof of God and won't consider your personal encounter with God in testimony to His existence. Others will begrudgingly give license to the idea of a Supreme being, but don't offer him any true level of subservience that is deserved of one who is supreme. If he is God, why don't we treat Him as God? They probably can't grasp the idea that the Ruler of the universe would actually bother to take the time to pursue, or desire a personal relationship 24/7 with humanity, much less one individual human.

"Either way, when someone who has come to experience that depth of love offered by their Savior, it is challenging at best to relay it to someone who hasn't encountered the truest, deepest love. So, God offers His Spirit through His son to invite and engage. Complex? You bet, but it can happen, to anyone, at any time; if they are open to the invitation."

Here, Portunus smiles tearfully at us and says, "Such a deep, rare love, not humanly conceived, can even be shared by two people, by a man and woman… if they are open to the invitation…if they ask their God to join them.

"I am a witness to it and that gives me the special honor of bragging about it. Shouting about it to the world and to the universe. I want to warn you-this is powerful stuff, a greater and higher thing you are involved in.

"Why would I warn you of the greater thing? Because greater things are not to be taken lightly. Greater things are to be taken most seriously. After all, to be greater, such things need to be made greater, by greater partners participating in greater ways."

The man stoops and reaches behind him to pick up the matching set of ram's horns that lay there for this moment. He hands them to us and asks, "Are you prepared to invite your Lord to this joining? If so, now is the time to let him know in demonstration of your shared faith."

My beautiful bride and I put our lips to our instruments and in that perfect moment trumpet in harmony, our baptismal song to our Bridegroom and King.

Ilona:

A look down at my glowing blue hand that holds my horn and the sight of it tells it all. Not even my dad's giant tears are able to put out our blue flames. He seems to be having trouble finding more words to say, so in silence we all just…flicker.

Then he finally finds his voice, saying, "I am so honored to be here to start this walk with you, but your God, Yahweh who began the good work in you, in each of us, will be the one to bring it to completion on the returning day of Yeshua HaMashiach. What God has joined together, let no-one separate."

My dad is done; my Teagan and I are one.

Ga'al:

I am married! Not as before, but anew. My bridegroom has come for me by surprise and now he asks me to join the others with whom he has and will wed.

This is my new sight, my new hearing, my new thinking and doing.

In the distance, I hear two horns echoing through the canyons. I can't discern from what direction they blow for the canyon echoes play tricks on my ears.

But he knows, and he will guide. I am slowed by my impairment, but not stopped. If anything, it tells me I am still able to battle, only my objective and ways of combat have changed. He has caused me to overcome my past and so a puny limp is nothing to stop my walk with him.

Verse X

"There are two kinds of seekers in the world, those seeking proof and those seeking disproof.

PS We are all seekers."

—Mark A. Cornelius

Ga'al:

"I had forgotten how bright light could be 'till Bronze-Man showed up and plopped my Teagan in the sand for me to find."

That is how she introduced his presence in her life, "Plopped". I had to laugh at the word use. But the ongoing discovery is far from amusing…

"—He is new. I can't tell it right. Like the smell of sunrise when all is made awake. When we stare at each other, I hear his speaking without a word coming out. When we do speak, it seems the same voice. When he touches me, I forget all that Mom-dame put in my head. When we stare at…"

I absorb the words on the page, scratched-written by a dame encountering love in its first moments, and gasp. Suddenly, I'm looking at the wonder of that moment in the present. It has its own life, breathed into existence from separate ones. But I am not freed by her experience. I can't move, why? His heft continues to press on my body, his excitement and sweat rain on my flesh.

It is my old wound, surfacing to remind me of who I once was, who I must not become again. The pain of the memory is beyond my coping. I shriek out loud to my healer; praying not to wake the injured in the cave, but to help me once and for all escape my tortured past.

Ilona:

That was not like I supposed it to be. I thought joining would be just a pleasurable thing, a feel-good thing. But it was so much more of a thing. My Teagan snoozes next to me and I watch him closely. I can almost breathe his breath as my breath, grasp his thoughts as my thoughts. I feel newly alive…combined in the joining of him and me. We are *us*.

In a funny way, Mom-dame had it right when she spoke out 'bout she-dames needing to be *alike* in their brains, what she named, *one-minded*. I wonder if she conceived that idea first when she and my dad joined?

—Or maybe she didn't grasp the oneness then and that is why she grew to be so angry and alone? Bronze-Man, I have to tell you of a sadness. I feel my darkness trying to creep back in when I ponder 'bout my mom-dame not being here to see me joy-filled. I'm down 'cause I want to share my grasping of oneness with my Teagan, with her. You have spoken out to me in your Good News book that you will answer our praying. Can you tell me if I will ever be able to share with Mom-dame of this best-right day when my Teagan and I became *us*?

Somehow, I grasp that she would like to know that, and that no matter how hard it tries, there is no darkness that can hurt *us* now; inside or out. We can both wake up safe, no matter what dreams try to attack!

My Teagan still slept, and to give him the gift of that pleasure for a while more, I snuck out from our cave for a walk.

"Do you know what all animals and growing things have in common?" I jumped at the voice and then made sense of it. It was my dad-wreck, no more a wreck, really. He was sitting on a boulder, legs crossed in the dim light before day.

It stirred another brain pic, a memory of seeing him do this in the mornings on the porch of our home. He would sit there, his legs crossed tight, somehow cocked together and he would be facing the sky where the sun would soon peek up. I would always come sit by him and he taught me the crossing and cocking of my legs, the quiet breathing, the clearing of my fear before the light of day. Afore my Teagan, those were my best times of living.

I had forgotten the clearing way; or at least I had stopped their practicing when my...Dad had left. I could not find clearness without him. Mom-dame did not know the way to do it. Now, seeing him here, I crossed my legs next to him on the rock and we sat in quiet. This was a new best time too; a fresh and clear moment nearly as good-right as the being with my Teagan and feeling so peaceful after our joining in the night.

The familiar smell of my dad made me happy-sad. He was here now, but I somehow grasped his closeness would not last for long. He reached out and took my hand in his, tenderly, gently, then released it. He continued looking forward toward where the light of the sun would show, and finally he answered his question for me.

"Everything sleeps. Animals, insects, bacteria, even plants enjoy a circadian rhythm of rest. They and we stop for a time, to receive new strength, even new growth, new...awareness of life, in the down-time."

I didn't always grasp my dad's lessons right away, but this one was good-right in this moment. I wanted to tell him 'bout my dark brain pic, but I pondered that he already saw it on my face. He smiled and spoke out more.

"Sometimes the sleeping shakes things up a bit, making us afraid of what is, or what might be. But it's what we do with the shaking when we do what all other life does; when we wake up to the next new moment."

"What should I do?" I wanted to ask, but figured he must also have just had a bad brain pic and so it seemed good-right just to sit cross-legged together in our mind-clearing and silent praying.

My dad took my hand again and squeezed it, not too tight, not too long.

"Sweet Jaybird, I can't tell you how you should awaken, it's different for every creature and every person. But I can tell you how it begins. You have to choose between light and darkness."

Jaybird! My nickname from when I was a little-folk—how could I have forgotten that? My dad was doing a strange thing now. He was crying and speaking out at the same time.

"For me, when I made that choice", he shared, "I became aware of how important it was...is, to confess. To admit not just to myself, but to those I love most, that I have made great mistakes in my life.

"The other trait I've learned that is common to all nature is wakefulness. I've had that conversation with Teagan but have not taught him about rest. Instead of me blabbing on so much, I suggest the two of you share your discoveries with one another.

"So, after confessing, comes repenting—acting in the wakefulness of the light, turning to face its...His direction, away from the dark."

My dad was making mostly good-right sense, but I was not sure who the "He" was whose direction I should be facing to. Was he speaking out about Bronze-Man? His sharing about resting and waking caused me to wonder in my mind, *Am I trying to turn off the light by holding on to my darkness still? Do I want to close my eyes to the light, trying somehow to shut it…Him…out 'cause I'm afraid of what not being fearful and sad might look like?*

Dad shared more. "I knew, once I admitted my wrong ways, that I was immediately forgiven by the One, my Savior, who I had confessed to. I had not been honest with him and so I had to change that. I had to find healing, seeking out new people to love, and sharing relationship with them, as I have with Teagan.

I also had to intentionally search for those I had abandoned, and those with whom I had not been honest: Your mother, you, myself. I had walked away from lovingly confronting our differences. I had rationalized that your mother had wanted me to leave (and that was true) but just as much, I had wanted an excuse to be gone. I had even justified that you would be better off under her influence alone. I was wrong and cowardly about all of this.

"Amazingly, I experienced something unexpected from my confession. Forgiveness. My Lord and Savior loved me more, not for what I had done or planned to do; He loved me for my desire to change, my wanting to love Him as much as He loves me.

"And that's when I realized that I would be incomplete until I loved others as He had loved me, by forgiving them for what I thought they had done to me. The hardest part of that was to accept that the ones I was forgiving may never recognize their need to be forgiven—and that was okay. The act of forgiving was not for their benefit (although it might alco become a blessing they eventually come to appreciate). The act of forgiving another person, was for my benefit, to cleanse me of my resentment and my assumed injuries.

"So, Jaybird, I hope you understand now, or come to understand this most important thing I will tell you here and now…I forgive you."

He was good-right. I didn't know I needed forgiving, until this very time. His speaking it out made a most colorful pic in my mind of our hands held together as if they had never been nor ever would be apart again.

Teagan:

The morning is as perfect as I ever remember one. The air smells almost a as clean as in the days...before. I turn on my side. My bride—*My bride, what a beautiful thought, a sweet song within me brought to life*—must have gone outside sometime after the passion of our joining in the night. I imagine you, Jesus, are walking with her, healing her soul, your words touching her lovingly within. I might be jealous of your intimacy, were you not whispering to me in the same manner.

Portunus had given us privacy in the night, his sensitive kindness showing itself even in this small thing. Before his leaving, I remember him turning back for a moment. He had smiled and then headed out for his own conversational reflections with his Creator. Since I do not hear him, I suspect he has not yet returned. I move from the pallet and begin to pen my thoughts.

Something Portunus had said in yesterday's ceremony came back to me. "I am no longer your keeper."

So, what are you then to me, to us? I ask the absent Monk.

He has been a sustaining and guiding force in my life and a renewed inspiration for his daughter. Certainly, those qualities will not vanish. Will he take on some new purpose now? Portunus had told me he thought his purpose would evolve, but he hadn't been clear in what it was.

And what of Ilona's and my purpose? Do we stay in this place, in hiding? Do we set off on a new venture? Where to? How? My beautiful bride shared with me the map given to her by her friends, Ramon, and Maria. It made no sense—head toward what used to be the southwestern United States, and then to Mexico? My love explained that she had spoken to the couple, who had come from there, and they revealed that the whole region had been torn apart. It is now fragmented islands in a much bigger ocean. How would we know our way—was the map actually presented from you, Lord, and with enough detail to navigate properly?

Trust, you of little faith, is your response to me. Through those words, I somehow perceive a loving smile.

I am reluctant to write more details of my reservations, it serves no purpose in the moment until I am given…Higher counsel. Until then, paper is a precious thing to spend without proper vision or purpose.

My thoughts circle back to my mentor. Being familiar with his daily routine as I am, I can see him in my mind's eye, taking in the early air, saying a personal prayer, then moving to the water to wash and prepare for the day. I hear strange noises and try to tie them to his normal activity. I cannot. When the clanging of two auger-spears splits the air, I know danger is near our door.

Suddenly, another voice erupts outside.

"So, you thought you could hide them from me!"

I know the timbre all too well and shudder at the presence of Zeke, back in my life.

Ga'al:

"—So, you thought you could hide them from me!"

With these words revealed on parch, the picture comes into harsh focus. Teagan writes of the one they call Zeke who has come for battle. I am chilled with the writer as he reveals the grisly details…

> —I hear more shouting echoing loudly through the canyon
> walls, so that even the rapids did not completely dilute the
> words. "Die, blue freak cur!"

Instantly, I'm up, grabbing my leggings and crashing into things making my way out of the cave. Running out, rather than peering to see what awaits, is my biggest mistake. Before me, a futile battle is already in progress.

I watch as Ilona whips a stone into her sling, twirling and releasing it with amazing speed. The stone hits Zeke in the shoulder just as he is in his windup to throw his weapon her way. Her hit was just enough to affect his aim. I watch in slow motion horror as the projectile hits Ilona in her side, causing her to crumple to the ground.

The beaten and bloodied body of Portunus has also fallen awkwardly at the warrior's feet so now only Zeke remains standing. When the warrior sees me, a noxious grin crosses his face, and he does not bother to finish his work on Ilona. Instead, he brings the battle toward me, advancing. I know I have scant seconds to react. I hastily pick up and throw a large rock, but he anticipates my action and dances easily out of the way at the last minute.

"So, Fluter, you are not yet ended. Let's fix that, shall we? There is much more fleshing to be done!"

He stops his charge, walks almost casually back to Ilona's wounded body, and in a single fluid motion, plucks his weapon from her side, flinging it my direction. I might have actually caught the weapon as it comes close to impaling me. Instead, I too dodge. The weapon grazes my side as it sails past. Turning instantly in a new direction, away from the cave, I run.

The good news is that Zeke now ignores my bride's still body and pursues in my direction. *Now what?* I think. Do I try to run around him to grab more rocks? Will that allow him too much time to catch up to me?

"You're making this easy, Fluter. I can hear your path just as I tracked you from your stupid horn blowing!"

So that's how he found us! Please, I pray, *Let him follow me and not return to finish his other kills.*

And he does follow! I am no match for Zeke in battle, but in a race, I am more fleet and nimble.

"Coward! Running won't save you either!"

I get out ahead enough to dodge between boulders into the nearby canyon trail leading away from the river, so that I am not in his line of site.

"You pathetic perverted freak. Painting yourself and your whore blue, and pretending to be some kind of monk-wanna-bes? Do you see where that got him?"

I have to be careful because I do not want him to give up his chase, but then again, I certainly don't want to be caught. I make sure to be noisy, kicking stones as I sprint, and I hear the pursuit continue behind me.

"It's one-thing to raid the dame-camp; but to live with one? Are you daft?" Zeke challenges me.

Good, he wants my hide most. I have barely enough time. While fleeing him, I reach into my tunic pocket for the pouch filled with the special jelly I always carry with me. Best as I can, I take repeated finger-fills of the substance and rub it over my body and clothing.

"Can you, stupid teso? Can you possibly explain it...your attraction to the she-bitch tribal leader's daughter?"

Just another turn, through the canyon trail, and I'll be at my goal.

"Did I tell you I found your writings? Your precious memories and hallucinations of your magic light-friend?"

No, he hadn't told me and now I know what his vengeance is really all about.

"You idiot. There is no spiritual voodoo in this rotten place to save any of us; especially you."

I make the corner and there it is. The open space seems safe enough to run through, but I know better and make a wide circle to avoid the center sand. It's a risk because Zeke might follow my example. Instead, when he rounds the corner, he sees the "shortcut opportunity" and takes it. As he tries to close the distance between us, I abruptly reverse course, causing him to stutter and turn back. I'm nimble enough to then make back and forth strides while Zeke dances in the middle ground trying to forecast my direction.

What he fails to predict in the back-and-forth play is the new participants in our scrimmage. Underneath him they mass, swarming and gushing from within the ground, the fire ants wrap his legs, then his lower torso with alarming speed. In his fury, the military clansman has ignored the ground and only now realizes his folly.

After I had been rescued by Ilona, I knew there might be a chance of pursuit; I thought then, by the she-dames. Instead, it is my own clansman who now struggles in my trap.

And in the moment is the answer to my question, *who is my enemy?* The answer comes not from me, but from my

Savior's voice within me. I was becoming more and more familiar with.

"And how will you know my enemy?" Asked Bronzeman.

"Damn you, and your bitch, and your stupid god." shouts the ants' new meal from the middle of the insect sea.

"O LORD, how I hate those who hate you! How I despise those who rebel against you! I hate them with a total hatred; I regard them as my enemies."

I had read it to Ilona from Psalm 139 just two days before. It is not my enemy at all that I should be concerned with. It is your enemy, God, who I must stand against.

Trying to react in time, Zeke makes a mighty effort to escape the waves of his crawling consumers, fiercely brushing and stomping the attackers away. It's too late. The ants have found their way beneath his sting-suit. They pierce his skin with their own ferocity and their prey is instantly paralyzed from the waist down. He drops to his knees, his screams of pain announcing his soon-coming end, to the uncaring wilderness. I detect with each peal, a slight, then steady fading in his voice.

Zeke melts from his kneeling position to lay face down in the sand, the army quickly carpets the man's whimpering, writhing body. And it is over. The red mound, that had been Zeke the mighty military Overseer, takes on a new purpose, bubbling and wriggling in busyness as nature's work is efficiently done.

I ran to my love, Ilona, who lay still on the battle ground, oozing blood from her side and her head. Though unconscious, her breathing was steady. I tore off pieces of my tunic to use as bandages and wrapped the wounds to stem her bleeding as best I could. I carefully searched for broken bones and found none, so I gently lifted and carried her back to the cave.

Laying her gently on our pallet next to the fire, I made sure she was still properly bandaged, and that her pulse and breathing were still constant. Then I made another round back to the battleground and a frightening sight. Portunus' still body remained inert on the ground. I ran to him and searched desperately for the pulse of life. "Lord, please!" I begged of you, Bronzeman, and you heard. There it was. My fingers felt the very faint fight of a valiant heart within.

Best as I could, I plugged the leaking holes with dirt as he had taught me. He was much heavier a burden than Ilona, so I had to drag my mentor back into the cave. I pushed and kicked away objects as I struggled with him, finally pulling him onto the pallet by the fire alongside my injured bride.

Grabbing Portunus' pack and our own stash of medicinals, I searched and found a precious flask of iodine along with several other treasures: rubbing alcohol, a syringe, and several other vials he had kept secret even from me. Penicillin! *How had he protected those?*

I quickly washed his wounds and poured the alcohol directly in. The body reacted with jerks—a hopeful sign for the moment—and I turned to assess Ilona's condition.

Her breathing was very shallow. The wound to the side of her head was ugly but it was her torso lesion that demanded attention. I dressed the gouge and searched her body for other injuries—there were no others; thank you, Bronzeman, her protector.

Rapidly searching our stores, I found the healing herbs and balms that daughter and father had taught me to use. Carefully washing the damaged flesh of both, I then applied the cures and sutured the worst gashes. As I kneeled between the inert ones, I knew there was only one other thing to do:

>*—Jesus, son of the Most High God, man of bronze, helper, and healer of the weak. I have done what I can. I have laid hands and poured oil. It is your strength and power that we now depend on. Please, Protector, whatever your will is in these coming moments, give Ilona and Portunus recovering strength, even if you must sap it from me, I give it all freely, that their living, however long or short, may be to your purpose and glory. In the name of you, my Savior, I pray to you with our Father above.*

Amen.

Ilona:

She doesn't know I am woke. It's good-right I'm using squinted eyes to peep her 'cause, well, I don't know why she's here. Is she my healer or ender? Mom-dame parches by the fire and by my right, my dad lays still as death. Then, he rasps a rugged breath, and she looks to him, dipping a cloth in water and placing it on his forehead with that thing I can hardly remember seeing from her—tenderness.

Tears wash my face and blur my peeping. I want to brush them away, but I'm too weak for the work. I want to cry out, "Momma," like a babe, but my voice hides inside me. It might be best, I still don't grasp if this action of her's is a game.

Worst is my next pondering, *Where is my Teagan!* Has he been ended by the other clansman, or by Mom-dame?

Noise from the outside grabs my attention. Through my squinty-teary eyes, I see it has caught Mom-dame's attention too and she pulls her knife. I peep through the blur as best I can at the cave mouth. Is it the attacker-wreck again? *What can we do?* Mom-dame turns using her animal-moves, fluid, silent, ready to pounce. But now she freezes, dillo-style.

At the cave mouth, framed by the outside light, my Teagen stands…

Ga'al:

Where is he now? I remember thinking that as I tended to my daughter's injuries. It has been two days since I discovered their cave. Has he abandoned his cause or was he ended in the same skirmish that imperiled Ilona and John?

There was no evidence of his return. If he was still alive and he discovered me in the very cave where he had also lived and cared for this tender one…what would be his reaction to me?

I had just turned my focus back on my patients when the one whom I had tortured, the one who had brought life back to my dead body by the river, beyond my understanding of his act, appeared at the cave mouth. In the time we stared at one another, the entire text and history I had just consumed, replayed in my mind.

This time the face fit the man. This time I grasped the quality of him whose life I had meant to extinguish. He too glowed with the mysterious blue essence, and I realize that all in this room have shared something spiritually profound.

I couldn't fathom his thoughts in the moment. He was one of the writers of the journals. He certainly would have concluded now who I was, what I was capable of. His senses must all be on high alert, reacting automatically to my presence and the threat I posed. Would he flee in the moment, abandoning those he had protected? Or would he face his foe, standing his ground to protect his claim? I saw no weapon, but did he carry a hidden blade? Might he fling it toward where I sat before I could evade it's sting? Any and all of these actions were his options.

I had only one advantage over him. It was an unusual bit of *high-ground*. I had read the accounts exposing the struggle and the overcoming love he had shared on parch. Would he understand my next intentions? Would he finally submit to what he should have done when he had the chance? I rose from the bedside of my beloved daughter and husband and walked purposely to the man my daughter called, "my Teagan". I opened my arms wide to show I carried no weapons, and my mind prepared for his just and merciful act of blood-sacrificing me.

Instead, when I came close, he started to drop to the ground, and I had to rush to catch his limp body.

We met in an odd embrace.

Ilona:

—or leans, is a better parch-picting of it. My Teagan looks to Momma, then to my still-dad and then finds me with his eye's. He moves one leg toward my direction, wobbles, then crumples. Now my voice comes out, "my Love!"

Momma had already gone to catch him and cocks her head back my way when I cry. The look of her is of shock, then more—her tears match mine. She quickly pulls my Teagan to the straw by the fire, lays him carefully there, and then her move to me is a quick one.

Momma crouches to stroke my hot head, meets my eyes and sees me look to my Teagan, then back to her. She offers more tears and then a nod of her head. Stroking me one more time, she moves to crumpled-Teagan and tends to him.

Ga'al:

Is he aware of me? If so, what will happen in these next moments? I remember the words from his last entry and know that my coming close to him puts me in mortal danger:

> "O LORD, how I hate those who hate you… I regard them
> as my enemies."

When he comes to, will he still see me as his enemy? Will my presence in his sanctuary, where his new family lay tragically injured, threaten him to the point of reacting in defense?

There is no time to waste, I see where he too, has lost much blood and I must save him, regardless of the risk to me.

Teagan:

—Maybe I am dead. There is a big problem in what I'm seeing before me. It's the face of Aella, the she-dame who had tortured me and whom Bronzeman had helped me heal by the river. My thoughts are, as Ilona would say, "sideways," meaning I am totally confused by what my eyes tell me. *How did she get here? Where is Ilona and Portunus? How am I back in the cave?* There is no sense to my senses nor answers to my questions.

Then I do remember one thing. I had been grazed by Zeke's spear before running toward the ant trap. I had thought the slice was superficial and didn't even consider it after my antagonist had been dispatched. I became engrossed in caring for my bride and my mentor and that is when you, Bronzeman, gave the strangest command.

"Scribe it. Right now."

Scribe it? The attack? Why?

"Now."

I had learned never to question you twice, so I detailed as much of Zeke's invasion and demise as possible.

"Well done, good and faithful servant," you encouraged. Then I checked on my patients and realized their wounds needed more cleansing, so I made my way out to the river for fresh water. It was only after I had filled two leather sacs that I looked down to see a trickle of red mixing into the current and realized, it was my own blood leaking away.

I had to make it back to the cave fast or else…

—I guess the 'or else' happened because I don't remember anything else until my eyes opened in the cave. I must have made it to the door and collapsed, or maybe Aella found me and dragged me back to our shelter.

The second scenario seems unlikely, I'm sure she would have simply pushed my limp body into the rapids to let me sink to oblivion.

Which brings up one more crazy query. With the dame warrior hovering above me, how am I still breathing?

Her eye's meet mine. She is smiling at me, and her voice forces its way through the dizziness of my dementia, "I am not your enemy."

I realize there is another more bizarre change to her appearance, besides the warmth of her smile. She is blue.

Yup, I must be dead.

Ilona:

As my real momma cradles my head in her lap and feeds some kind of good smelling broth to me using her old spoon, a Good News story Teagan had read to me, comes back to my memory. I crayon it out in my mind, imagining the tale as if I were in the pic as well:

I see the wreck named Paul, who had hated Bronze-Man followers and tried to blood-sacrifice or punish bunches of them. He was laying down 'cause he had been dazed by the same light I had been dazed by—bronze light. Bronze-Man spoke out to the hater, Paul, "What's your problem with me?"

My Savior, in a flash, turned into crazy Paul's Savior, too. Paul's eyes were blanked for a short time and you, Bronze-Man, spoke in to him that he needed to see in a new way, and to tell others all 'bout what he was seeing new.

I'm grasping that you, Bronze-Man, have some waking up words for Momma like you did for Paul and me. I'm starting to grasp more of how you are changing her. And suddenly, you start also working more on me in a hard way, speaking inside of me…

"—There is one more thing,"

I'm not wanting to hear your details of the one-more-thing, 'cause I already know what it is. I've been hiding it deep inside me for a good-long time and now you say, "No more hiding".

It has to do with my ponderings during the time when I was just passed the age of being a little-folk. I had begun to grasp that I had to make a choice. I grasp now that it was you, Bronze-Man, telling me to choose. But just 'cause you told me I needed to choose didn't mean you were going to force me to make the best choice. You wanted me to walk in my own way and You left the choosing up to me.

I watched my folks closely, being their way-different selves, doing their own way-different kinds of walking. Momma seemed so strong-minded, where Dad was more quiet and waiting, as if he was listening for some kind of help from somewhere. Momma hurried. She didn't wait at all. And Dad never walked as if he grasped that you, Bronze-Man, were waiting for him, for Momma too; waiting for each of them, and for me, just like you waited for Paul: to choose.

When Momma lied, speaking out that Dad had died, it made my choosing easy. Your bronze light was just in my head, no more than that. There was no outside-anybody or any light that would bring my dad back. From then on I had to just walk alone on my own, or not walk at all.

I grasp now, Bronze-Man, that there is outside help, but in that afore-time, I became so dark inside that I gave up trying to find the help. That was how I was pondering when the Blanking took my little brother, Caiden, plus all the others, and that's when I turned into a Shorter.

'Course, that wasn't all there was to my darkness, and you, Bronze-Man, are now asking a tough thing…

"—Crayon it in your mind, it needs to be freed. I'll Love you through it…"

It will not be easy, but you are not about easy. You are about right.

Ga'al:

Finally, we are at the juncture. There had been before, no right time to explain, in any rational, practical way, what had brought me to be who I portrayed as dame-mother. And now, my daughter is figuring out the truth for herself. I can see her mind working through what I know to be the condemning facts of my ghastly past...

> —I had finished my red-sacrificing of Ramon. The exhilaration of the slaughter was a tingle that coursed my entire being. I shouted out my accomplishment as a war-cry that was joined by the cries of all the dames in the Law House. All but two that is.
>
> Ramon's partner, Maria, could not stop her shrieking from the seat she had been forced to watch from. She broke loose from the dames holding her down and ran to cover her mate with her sad sobbing body. I hated her in that moment, not just for her grief over the loss of a wreck, but for her example that I could see was infecting the one person I was trying most to influence by my new ways...Jessica.

Ilona:

—It was too much for my now-not-mom-dame to swallow. When she saw the great love of a dame for a wreck, even with the wreck being ended. She turned stopped her war-cry and 'stead, joined in with the widow's shrieking, rose her club and then brought it down upon the mourner so many times that it totally mixed the two, Mama Maria y Papa Ramon, into one pulp.

I watched with my eyes but could not grasp the pic in my mind. My once-mom-dame had ended my mama y papa for all time, and with them she ended for me, any true life; even though my ears told me that my heart still pumped loud and fast within. I was ended in all other ways, no Mom, no Dad, no care....

—So, if I was dead and dark, how was I able to still walk and speak out and secretly parch and finally leave that hell-full place of dames? Only you, Bronze-Man, knew what I needed. Only you, Man-of-The-Father's-Light, could show me to my home-cave; could lead me to almost dead Teagan; and bring my dad back to hand-hold and share our wedding-moment. Only you, Saver of the dead-me, would give words through the husband and dad you brought to me as gifts. And by their love, only you could teach me the one and hardest thing to do.

You did all these things to ready me for something I still can't grasp as right but ponder it to be the most beautiful gift ever. You gave it to me by words, but your speaking out of it to me was just the beginning. Now I live the words—there's no other way to scratch it's meaning—and I grasp that I need to give it to others too. It's my turn. I want to give my re-found momma, your deep and true words that throb in my newly alive heart.

Bronze-Man, I pray that you make me strong enough to speak out to my momma what you have spoken into me from your throbbing heart. I'm gonna need as much of your love as you can possibly feed me to do it.

Ga'al:

They all are sleeping as they heal. It's a good sign, a hopeful thing, a…I suppose *miracle* is a word, and a holy action, I'll admit to recognizing here. The resting of the invalids gives me more time to absorb the outpourings of the journals. My glance goes to the steel canister in which they had been secretly and lovingly guarded and something my daughter wrote…scratched earlier inspires me. My trembling hand reaches within the box once more and at its inner base I discover a false bottom. Wedging my knife into one corner, I'm able to work the compartment free. Another parchment, this one folded and tied by another rarity; wrapping ribbon for gift packages, comes free.

I remember the colorful trimming from my own stock! I play my fingernails over the textured ridges of the strips, igniting vivid memories of my childhood holidays. Family times of gift sharing that I had buried into the deepest crevices of my soul. I thought the emotions of those days to be safely repressed, until this moment. Now more memories surface and flood out through my eyes. More recent and painfully wonderful times with John, Caiden, and Jessica gathered on the floor under a decorated tree. The scent of forest pine somehow teases my nose and the crinkling sound of wrapping paper being torn in eagerness comes to my ears. I want to attack the senses that allow such things to resurface.

But a new battle claws its way into my awareness. It refuses to let me force the past images back into that closet of those beautiful, better times so long ago. I am terrified of them and yet starved for them. It's no use; I give in to their power, letting them wash my wounded soul, and I unashamedly sob.

Ilona, then Jessica, had obviously borrowed some of my ribbon and more recently has used it to bind the precious parch contents she had hidden within the canister. On the outside of the paper is scribed in perfect cursive writing:

Mama y Papa

I unfold the document and turn its colored side to discover a map, vast in territory and meticulous in detail. Through the center of it is a river, leading ever on to an ocean. On the parchment, typography of canyons and mountains, even instructions of places to avoid, dot and fracture the landscape. It is all meant for another journey to be taken; the best path marked by green crayon while red crayon warns of dangers along the way.

Unravelling this new mystery will not be a quick thing. Outside, lightning flashes and I know I am in the safest of places for that task. Another piece of wood on the fire better illuminates the atlas and my navigational study begins. As I study, my mind works out other hidden pathways that I must navigate. I am reluctant to travel the paths of my conscience, but my newfound spiritual relationship insists.

Is there anything I have done right? I think back and forth between then and now. I can point to my suffering and the injustices heaped upon me. I can blame others, easily. I can tout all I have done to vanquish my sisters and my cause. But am I the victor, or as much the fault?

The three others in this place can be restored to me, but I realize it will not be by my hands, not by my plan. I think back to something strange my love, John shared. At the time, I don't think even he believed the reality of the words, but I suspect now they live deep within him.

"I am dead, it is Christ Jesus who lives within me."

At that time, the words he spoke in my hearing made no sense, but now I hear a new voice within me. I see in my mind's eye, the face that is not mine, yet is mine to possess. I sense the Spiritual, so close, and yet am I worth what you have done for me, Jesus? Is there anything I can do to deserve what you have done to reclaim me?

Even before I ask the question, you have answered me.

"Believe."

I do believe, please help me with my unbelief.

I hear stirring behind me and turn my head to see Ilona standing behind me. She studies me studying the map and then without a word, comes and sits by me. We sit together, protecting our individual thoughts from one another for what seems like hours, but I'm sure is only minutes.

And then my daughter announces, "It is time for me to speak out to you."

Teagan:

I open my eyes to see that I have somehow been transported to the straw pallet by the fire in our cave. I lay on my sick bed and watch through the smokey haze of a well stoked fire. It's really all I'm capable of in my weakened state.

Ilona:

I had hidden the worst of what I had seen inside the darkest part of me—scared that letting it out would crumble me into nothingness. Now the darkest things have been let out of the box and I trust that you, Bronze-Man, will heal me even better than my dad could heal.

So, it is time to speak out. I reach deep within for strength and speak daughter-to-momma, dame to dame...

Teagan:

"Seek,"

The word is lit up in my mind and directs my still groggy eyes to widen and scan the surroundings. To my left, in my lying position, I see Portunus also stretched out. To my right, I peer at two more distant figures. Sleepy goo from a long slumber slowly clears from my vision and I make out the forms to be Ilona and Ga'al. Their backs are to me, and they sit in silence, both staring straight—not toward one another—at something beyond. What I see must be a vision, because no words are being spoken, yet I can understand every thought of the two—mother and daughter. Just as the aroma of the burning wood invades my nostrils, so the spiritual interplay of Aella (who apparently has renamed herself, Ga'al) and Ilona now somehow are sneaking into my soul-space.

First, I see the body-language and the facial expressions of Ga'al shift between great sadness and what looks to be urgent concern. It is as if she harbors a tragic message from a distant land that must be shared, but which she knows will deeply maim those who receive it.

Then I look to my beloved and behold a rollercoaster processing of "ponderings"—as she calls them—working through her expressions. At once: She is innocent and eager to welcome, as a child might receive a long lost relative; also she is rebellious, like a teenager who has tasted the freedom of thought and experimentation in those years and does not want to let go of her newfound liberty. She displays a posture of penitence, wanting desperately to cleanse herself of her past struggles.

How can I know these things based on nothing more than the staring contest unfolding before me? I can't explain it. It is what I have come to call a *Bronzeman moment*—where his spirit seems to electrify my senses. I know it to be his interaction because every time I have sensed in this way, my accuracy of discernment has been uncanny.

What he is revealing is the passionate tussling of family, trying to earnestly understand in this titanic reunion, how together, they might stitch and mend the emotional and mental gashes inflicted by each to the other.

"Ask,"

I am rocked by the urgency and compassion in the voice that speaks into me. It is not me, nor the other occupants, but purely a spiritual imperative that now broadcasts through the air. Ilona's hands reached over and gently take the hands of her mother's.

"Knock," the imperative vibrates within my soul.

I remain prayerfully silent and watch to see the response unfold. My beautiful bride turns her head to the other woman while continuing to hold her hands and speaks out softly...

"—As much as I want to be different from you, I grab we are too much the same. Angry, hating, hurting. It is not good-right for either of us. I am being changed. Now I am learning one way to know others—even you, who lied to me and tricked to make me into you. My new way is called Love. It is not the ugly love you tried to teach me. My Love gives me a different way. I can Love both enemy and friend, even when they try to hurt the deep part of me. My Love can choose to trust, or not trust them through its working..."

Ilona:

—Looking Mom-dame squarely in the eyes, and using language and words she will understand, I tell her,

"At this moment you are neither friend nor enemy to me. You will have to show me the difference, the change that has happened in you, afore I will choose which to call you. But one thing will remain the same either way; the same simple words spoken by my Savior, Bronze-Man Jesus, to me, I now speak out to you...

—I love you, Momma, and I forgive you."

Ga'al:

—*Forgiveness?* She has stabbed me with a weapon of which I am totally unfamiliar and unable to defend against; weapons that fix, not destroy.

How could this have all happened? It seems like a marked map with a beginning and a destination drawn by an unseen, but very real connecting line. I imagine a "You are here" statement written very close to the ending of the trip. It is beyond coincidence. It feels…planned.

Impossible…isn't it? How could my daughter…forgive me for what I have done? Even for the things I thought had been noble but now admit as the tasks of a vengeful assassin?

Yet she has. She loves me even after the pain…the murder I have inflicted on her.

Love poured out for someone so unlovable? What is she saying? The words make no sense. Why would someone offer that? And just because she forgives; does that actually change me in some way?

Then, bridegroom Jesus, you remind me that your sacrifice made no sense either, nor did your pursuit of me when I did not even realize I needed your sacrifice, or my daughter's forgiveness. I am learning...relearning as I emerge from the cocoon of death from my past life, that the only sense that can be made of it is centered in another word: It is the word she had used earlier to define her new life; it is the word John had clung to so long ago and tried to share with me; it is the word that was more than a word and more than the passion, and more than the care that people share with one another.

It is the only word and action of total surrender:

Love.

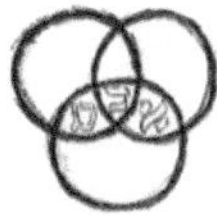

John stirs on the bed, and I re-soak a cloth with cold water to bathe his feverish forehead. A strange sensation takes hold of all of my being. It's power over me is old, one I had tried to forget and never allow to invade me again. It is fear.

I'm not afraid of him, my trepidation comes from what he reminds me of—without him I am not...one. That is why I was so resentful, that is why I could not let my emotions surface. I feared they would overwhelm me. Our sweet son is gone, our daughter has changed. My...John is fading before me, and the truth is that I am the one who has been moving away purposefully, intentionally, fearfully. And then the strangest of all thoughts confronts me: Is it the same with you, God? Have I been purposefully hating the idea of you in order to hide from the truth of you?

Dammit, listen to the futility of my questioning—asking for an answer that I already know. I am the idiot, I should have fought harder for my family, for my soul, for my God.

John's eyes open and he takes bearing of his surroundings. His glance meets that of Jessica-now-Ilona, then Teagan's and now he centers on me. A smile, then his eyes close again and he releases a deep sigh.

A new fear rises in me. *Is that the end? Is he gone? I have things to say!*

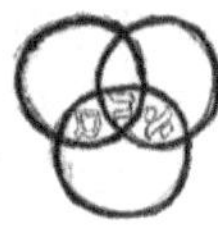

Ilona:

They are together, my momma and dad! Thank you, Bronze-Man, for lighting their lives.

Ga'al:

It is an eternal minute or so before his body responds with a full intake of breath and John's eyes open once more. The smile reappears, and he weakly rasps, "I knew you were there. Why didn't you end me?"

He knew? Was he speaking about the other cave at the park in Tucson? Of course, that's what he meant. And why hadn't I ended him? There was reason enough, I had been maddened and violated enough. Why indeed?

"Because I love you." They are the strangest and most freeing words I have ever spoken.

I continue to bathe his face and swollen body with water. I want so badly to help, but the *want* is not always the *do*. I am tired and sleep calls loudly. Another closing of his eyes. Mine jar open. He sighs, then a cough—the fight of life is still in him, even if for a brief time, and so I will fight with him. I will not fail him; I will not abandon him in this moment…

Ilona:

—My Teagan sleeps in my arms. I never want to let go. Then an out-loud wheeze from my dad wakes up my love and we both crawl over to the body in Momma's care. The three of us wash his face and swollen body with wet rags. Then Dad's weak life reappears. He searches for Momma's face, reaches with a shaking hand for hers, and whispers, "Bring the children close..."

Ga'al:

I think he is delirious. Our children? One is grown and changed, no longer a child. Sweet Caiden certainly remains a child; but is gone blissfully and permanently from this hell. Then I realize by his stare that he is speaking of Ilona and Teagan. "Bring them close," he whispers.

I don't need to do anything. Teagan and Ilona together pull themselves closer to join me. John looks for me as in a fog, finds my face and smiles. He says softly. "Please forgive me."

"Oh God, yes, I do, YES!" I'm sobbing again and he reaches feebly reaches for Teagan's hand, pulls it toward mine and says to me, "Here is your son." Then he looks to the younger man and rasps, "Here is your mother."

My mind screams, *Where have I heard those words before?* Once more, a raging flood begins its escape from my eyes.

"Jessica," the dying man's eyes are having trouble finding his daughter, but she squeezes closer and helps him find her through her own sobbing voice.

"I'm here, Daddy, right here."

"He makes all things new. He has given you all things…" Another cough and a struggle for breath. He finds his daughter's eyes again and smiles, "He is wiping away all your sorrows, all your tears."

Then one last sigh, and the escape of all breath. Peace glazes his face, and the blue of his skin rises into the sky like a brilliant cloud, finally disappearing from view…

Ilona:

My daddy is gone to meet you, Bronze-Man, he is gone to share his story with you, Caiden, and Mama Maria y Papa Ramon. He is gone and is waiting for us to meet you too, someday soon, not just in Spirit, or in the clouds, but when you return to your earthly kingdom.

Chorus

"Hope is hearing the music of the future.

Faith is dancing to it."

—William Carl Frey

Ga'al:

I have buried many companions throughout my blood-soaked path. But John's internment struck me in a far different way. For the first time, the exertion of digging deep into the hard soil caused me to consider in full: humanity's and my personal struggles.

We were more than complicit in our reckless social experimentation. We invented nuances and histories that honored one culture above another, when in truth, we had all fallen short. We assumed full control of our marginalizing ways, abandoning well tested principles, relationships, and family structure. We abandoned gender and natural order as if we were the designers of our origins. We attacked, dismissed, and shunned others who disagreed with our individually proclaimed lifestyles, rather than listening to one another's stories to seek commonality.

Who was I back then? And why does that question plague me now? Was I not the same as I am? Am I the same as I was, only grown more? How pompous of me to think I have matured into anything of value. The only thing I have grown to become is the foremost of miscreants.

Worst of all, we, I, being the foremost (just like Paul, the ancient letter writer), abandoned God. Instead, I embraced my selfish opinions and desires rather than seeking the embrace of my Creator.

This is the ugliest confession that I make, but I have been taught by John, Ilona, her...Teagan, and most painfully, most mercifully by you, Jesus, my God, my Lord, my Savior, that only by confessing and turning to journey in a radical new direction, can I be freed from my past.

I consider the two as they mend in their deep sleep, and I wonder if there is any chance that I too can be healed from such deep and tragic wounds.

So, I have made my decision. My Ilona and *our* Teagan, as I now call them, are healing. Our prayers and discussions about a "next step" continue. I have never been the best one at peering into the future. I hadn't considered a hopeful outcome for my life for a very long time, and I am having to relearn how to look to other sources to understand my destiny.

Reading through the Bible found by Ilona, I imagine a very complex future. A future that actually includes me; calls for my participation. But the road to that outcome seems fraught with peril. A journey to a totally reshaped Mexico? Following a map that seems miraculous in its content? I have never before trusted in the visions of others and so this is literally new territory for me. Bridegroom Jesus, I'm in desperate need of your encouragement and wisdom for this endeavor.

When we begin our travels, we will most certainly be slow moving targets, especially because of the permanent injury to my hip. Suddenly I feel I am old baggage of no value for any significant journey. My family, and my God, however, view me differently. Can I become better by them, by you, my beloved new Bridegroom?

We have constructed a rude cart to help haul our supplies and possessions. While traveling through what I perceive will be hostile terrain, we will certainly be scouted and found. Whether our discovery is by friend or foe, I will not be the best in determining which is which. My history has been to consider any who are not of my tribe as enemies—then to strike first, asking questions after. But you, Lord, are showing me a new way: Love my enemies and pray for those who persecute me? That path will be difficult, as with John, I suspect that somewhere along the way, I will be ended. It is the way of things in this wounded world. Yet with you, all things are possible—the healing of my family, and the healing of me.

So, I dare to hope.

By your Grace only will I survive, as best I can. That is perhaps a miracle too. I'll have to consider the significance of that admission, along the path.

Whether or not I survive to the Mexicos, I hope and pray a better life for Teagan, Ilona, and my soon-coming grandchild. They don't even know of it yet, I've not let on, but at least I have the ability to discern the signs and future of that miracle!

Protector above all, I plead for your hand of blessing to cover the three of them. And if it is your will, at least let me become a...good-right, not a sour, legend in their history.

Teagan:

Seek and you will find, ask and it will be given, knock and the door will be open. I realize the words have been breathed into me with a longer-term meaning and mission in mind. I am now the one to be a servant protector for both Ilona and Ga'al. Months ago, it would have been an improbable mantle to assume, but with you, Lord Jesus, all things truly have become possible.

I have you, and through you, John Portunus, to thank for the honor of it. Amazing that such an overwhelming task as walking almost two thousand miles through more dangerous and desolate land than we have ever encountered, seems right, seems to be your…calling.

I am as prepared as I can be for the responsibility, not because of any distinctive qualifications, but because I am available. It was Portunus who taught me the great lesson:

> "Remember, you have only the choice of 'Yes', or 'No', but your answer will not always fit. You may desire an outcome, one way or another. You may want life or death or light, or dark, but what you receive may be something altogether different. Maybe it will be completely opposite of your wanting. The important thing to remember is that your choice is still your choice, regardless of what answer another person imposes on you.

> "So, what, you might ask? If I choose life and someone more powerful than me chooses for me, death, what's the point? Maybe the answer is in adapting the question a bit. What if someone more powerful than me offers a new option I had not considered before, but I don't accept the terms? What if I refuse to answer, thinking there is no need; to answer is pointless because of the futility of it? And even if I choose to answer, what if the result of the

answer is actually impossible to see clearly, because I don't
have all the information? What if instead of fully knowing
the outcome; based on my relationship with the more
powerful One, I'm asked to "trust" the outcome? Can I
trust in that—awaken to that—even though everything
and everyone around me shouts for me not too?"

I have come to realize that the question is a *what-if* proposition. The *no-answering* option allows for easy escape from realistically and honestly confronting the locomotive headlamp that may be warning me of impending doom. But is an elusive option actually an option at all? Is the train still on course regardless of my refusal to face reality? What if the poser of the question, or the consequences of my 'no' or 'no-answer', care not of my opinion? What should I do with that reality? What if there is not only another opinion, but a more enlightened one, even a superior one? What if there is One that is more powerful than all of us and my choice is contradictory to His?

All these arduous thoughts could consume my attention. Instead, I'm learning to be encouraged, inspired to simply answer…"Yes." Yes, to your bidding, Lord, regardless of the peril.

Throughout my life, I haven't been good at trusting, or at having faith in you. I admit it. My god was government, my church was the halls of human legislation.

Even when I was nearly sodomized by Zeke, still I did not seek you out. But you sought me. You corrected my course, you were, and are faithful to me where I had faltered, where I continued to hesitate. You have blessed me beyond and in spite of my penchant of saying, "No," to you, and I struggle now to find some way of thanking you.

Yet you inspire and I will try in my small ways, struggling to thank and obey. First, I will protect, with your guidance and wisdom, the family and new relations you have given me.

Second? Well, Lord, I still can't not write. It is the way you made me, and so it is the way I will express my gratitude. The words are yours; I submit myself only as your humble scribe:

> There is hope, hear its song in the rush of rising tide
> Compassion tames the chaos with an everlasting light
> You've fed my heart's desire, now we beat within its rhyme
> The question finds its answer, you have loved me back…

—to life.

Ilona:

We are packed and ready—mostly. Afore leaving our cave though, there are two more important *do's*. I ask Momma and my Teagan to sit inside one final time. Then I search out Mama y Papa Dillo and feed them two Rippers that I had managed to carefully catch. The dillos busy themselves with their snack and I grasp that they deserve a bunch more treats in reward for protecting us. I pray that you, Bronze-Man, will make sure they'll be happy hunters long after our parting.

Next, I reach down to my special travel case which I had left in the cave for this moment. Inside it is a treat for Momma, my Teagan and me. I reach in and pull from it, the most special of my pics. It is a crayoning of my dad's circles that he had burned into his skin as a sign of his love for you, Bronze-Man.

Dad is with you now, but we remain. The memory of him, his love, and his teaching were important, so I want us to share as he shared. I show the pic to Momma and my Teagan, and they grasp fast what I want.

"Yes," they both say, and so we help one another fire-scratch Dad's sharing-symbol onto our skin in the same way; for all other folk to see.

Ga'al:

Before we set out for the Mexicos, Teagan makes a remarkable suggestion. I can't begin to fathom the outcome of the undertaking. It is even more bold, more risky, more…you, Lord, than the perilous journey the map will lead us on.

Ilona's beloved insists we must return to the wreck dens and the dame tribe camp. Ours will be the visible testimony of reconciliation. He says that you hunger for a communal mending. Sexual warfare and personal rebellion have nearly killed us off; I will be your example to all that even the worst can be redeemed. I had never thought to offer myself in such a way; it took the courageous vision of my son-in-law to see the possibility.

And so, our first hike is a fording across the river to the Barrens. This is no small task considering the burden of porting our supplies, but miraculously, there is another strong earthquake and for a period, the river ceases to flow! We cross and then the tumult rushes back in. I am learning just how important your timing is when choosing to follow your call.

All my senses tingle as we near the dens. Teagan assures me that, without Zeke's influence, his clan will be far more willing to receive us. I think him naïve. Then again, you have inspired him deeply, so I remain guardedly hopeful but fully alert in anticipation that he may be mistaken.

We arrive at dusk and the early evening fires of their camp help guide us to our objective. When nearly there, Teagan halts our progress with a silent motion of his hand.

He whispers, "Stay here," and he jogs off to scout and access what I assume is the only safe passage inside.

The sun continues to set, and a brilliant clear night sky emerges. There is a new moon tonight, and the darkness accentuates the massive star blanket still known as the Milky Way, illuminating the sky in a spectacular way. Interrupting its flow above the eastern horizon, rises the notorious V4641 Singularity. I now understand it not to be an omen of death or reprisal, but instead, your work in the heavens. It heralds a new age, which has begun in turbulence, but proclaims your return to complete your creation. I absorb the blessing as a sign of good favor from your hand, Jesus.

To my reckoning it is about an hour's time before we hear footsteps. I know the cadence; it is Teagan finally returning. When he is close enough to see, a completely unpredicted expression is on his face. He looks as if he has just beheld a comedy show or maybe some magician's performance. He seems to be having trouble in shaping words to describe his recent experience.

"You are not going to believe what you are about to see."

He is right, but there is a component to the coming moments, of whose effect even he cannot have foretold.

Teagan leads us to a rock outcropping and whistles a code which I assume would either allow us in or signal the time for arrows to rain down on us. Praise and thank you, our God, it is the former.

When we walk into the camp and toward the fire, I am first astounded to see a dame running toward me, screaming with joy and arms open wide. It is a second before I recognize her. It is Ellen! Behind her follow Abigail, JeongHyun, and three others. They consume Ilona and I in passionate hugs and laughter.

"We thought you were dead!" one exclaims.

"I can't believe you came for us," another wonders with a chuckle and a kiss to my cheek.

We chat excitedly while the dames lead us ever closer toward the fires where many wrecks and more dames cheer and clap. It is as we draw near to the main fire that the greatest of all shocks greets me…

"Father?"

My daughter confirms my confused recognition, "Grandpop?"

And to ours is added Teagan's bewilderment, "What? No, that is Matada, the Head Clansman I told you about."

Now it is the tall black man who runs out and falls to his knees before us. Even in this position, he is almost at our height, and he throws his arms about us, bringing us to our knees with him.

"How can this be?" He cries. "How can this be!"

Ilona:

Momma had told me long afore that she figured Grandmom and Grandpop had either been blanked or had died as had my dad. At that time, I had no reason to doubt her. But now I see by her shock that she truly did not believe they had survived.

I'm shaking all over, I'm so excited. I look to my Teagan. His face looks all puzzled: No words come from his mouth and stopping up his words; that's a hard thing to do!

"Mother…?" My momma asks of her father who shakes his head and shrugs his shoulders. He speaks out that Grandmom was by his side and then was simply gone. Momma nods her head and responds, "She always had a beautiful belief in Jesus." Those words from Momma spoke out all of it—Grandmom had been blanked and is joy-filled now with you, Bronze-Man!

We celebrate beneath the bright night stars, and almost everybody shares their stories around the fire. I hear their tales and it helps me grasp how you, Bronze-Man, had planned this new gang's coming together.

I and my Teagan and Momma learn, through everyone's recounting:

After Momma and my Teagan fell along with the tree, down into the Rushmore, the warring pretty much stopped. Zeke tried to keep the blood-sacrifice going, but nobody's heart was in it. He yelled lots and even ended a few of his wrecks who refused to restart their battling ways.

Soon enough, Grandpop, in his big voice, shouted at him, "Enough,". Zeke seemed ready to battle him too. He had stared angrily at Grandpop for long moments. Then he turned away and took off toward the Barrens.

That's the last they saw of Zeke and it began his hunting for Dad, Mom, my Teagan, and me.

After Zeke had left the fighting-field, the she-dames and the wrecks stood for a long while, all staring at the many still bodies on the ground. And something started to change. Grandpop had walked over to a mound of dame bodies and started singing, sadly, an old song over them:

> Swing low, sweet chariot,
> Comin' for to carry me home
> Swing low, sweet chariot,
> Comin' for to carry me home

As he sang, he tenderly bent down, gathered up into his arms one of the ended dames, and hugged her close to himself. He gently laid the body by an ended wreck warrior's carcass, and while still singing, went to pick up another and place it also by the two.

Ellen, the one Momma had made lieutenant, softly started singing the same tune with Grandpop and she too started bringing bodies to the pile. Soon enough, all the wrecks and dames were singing and brining. There were too many to bury—no shovels anyway and the ground was rock—so, that night, there was a fire kindled to the great pile. Dames and wrecks, all, had held hands and spoke out the stories of the ended ones whose bodies lit the night sky.

That was the *night of new-life,* as they now call it. And they have been together since. Momma, my Teagan, and I share our stories too, the gladdest and saddest being Dad's; when he helped wed my Teagan and me and when Zeke ended him. There is a great crying from all, for him. Maybe mine is the loudest crying of all.

From this night on, we are neither tribe nor clan, but by your doing, Bronze-Man, we have become all one, Kin.

Teagan:

Our great fire-sharing carried us through the night, just as Matada had begun the carrying of bodies that terrible day. We had also died with the others here, now we are trying to come to grips with, understand "new-life" as the group called it.

I continue to wrangle with emotions and thoughts I do not fully understand. *How can I heal from the memory of this tragedy, how will we survive together and avoid another separation? How am I supposed to go on without the help and encouragement of my lost friends and family?*

And you, Spirit of my life, speak more light into my soul:

"They are not yet Blue."

Of course, you would remind me! I had almost fallen back into my old ways, my self-pitying, self-defeating way of thinking. You mean for me to do more and so I once more must trust your voice and speak your words out loud.

"There is a reason for all of this, a greater thing is about to happen."

My words stopped everyone in their tracks. I could see puzzled looks on almost everyone's faces, and then I caught a glance from Ga'al who nodded to show she, too, was hearing your voice. My beautiful bride standing beside me, took my hand with her three fingered hand, squeezing gently to encourage me on. *On to what? I have no idea where to go with this! But then, you do, Bronzeman. Lead me wisely:*

> "I'm sure you have all noticed that the three of us, myself, my…Ilona and Ga'al each share an unusual characteristic with the wonderful man who guided us. You, clansmen, called him Monk, and for good reason. He was a strange and amazing counselor to us. But his "blueness" was never fully explained, except to we three. That is about to change."

Every eye is opened for you, every ear is tuned to hear your revelation. I sense your prompting me from within, to continue. Your presence in the moment is confirmed by the rapt attention focused on me by those around the fire:

"The coming apart of our planet, the sadness known as the Blanking and the division of each individual soul was no accident. These are no coincidences, and in fact, all that has happened and is happening to us is connected by two truths:

> "We live in a fallen world, fallen by our own rebellion; no one else's.

> "There was before our time a creation, spoken out by a Creator, who now invites one last opportunity for relationship.

"We three have met this Supreme Creator in our hearts and know Him to be God. He allowed us very broken creatures, to reconcile with Him through an inconceivable set of actions: God became human; dwelt with us; was blood-sacrificed because of us; and rose from the dead to lead us.

"I ask myself every day, why the ruler of the universe would do this for me? I'm reminded by Him, every day, that the *why of it* is not ours to know. It is the *what of it* that he shares now:

> "…God loved the world so much that he let his only Son
> be blood-sacrificed, so that everyone who believes in him
> may not die but have eternal life.

"We three are about to embark on the boldest of journeys. But before we could commit to its demands, we each had to admit our failings and spiritually bow before our Savior, wedding our lives together with him as our…Bridegroom, believing in him as our only hope and our eternal Companion.

"Each of you has the same choice as we. 'Yes, He is God and I will serve him only,' or 'No, I do not believe what you claim.' With those of you who say 'Yes,' we will celebrate in even more amazing ways than we are experiencing tonight. To you who choose no, please understand we will still pray for you and love you, but from this point on, our walk together will be separate from one another."

I had no more words to spend. I did not know how you would convict each heart, but I knew it was yours to do, not mine. My beautiful bride however added the perfect end-cap to the invitation.

"It's simple to grasp. Any more speaking out is just blabbing."

Beyond the crackling of the fire and evening birdsong, there was silence. I pleaded with you in my heart of hearts for some sign that our sharing had been pleasing to you and would at least be a seed planted in the barren-broken-hearts of each of them.

I could not make out from exactly where and with whom it started, but a glow, a faint but beautiful azure aura began to glaze its light throughout the body of the camp. Soon there were no gaps, just one complete brilliance that shimmered more intensely than even the fire's blazing.

Matada, standing tallest in his new blue light, grabbed the hands of Ilona and his daughter on his other side and began to dance in place. It seems that he is full of motion and singing history, for he began another tune:

> "It's getting near dawn
> When lights close their tired eyes
> I'll soon be with you my love

> Give you my dawn surprise
>
> I'll be with you darling soon
> I'll be with you when the stars start falling
>
> I've been waiting so long
> To be where I'm going
> In the sunshine of your love."

Most of the others knew the words and soon, with coaching, everyone was gathered in the sharing of their individual rhythms and voices. We continued through the night and finally greeted the dawn, with the sunshine of your love, Bronzeman.

Ilona:

The moment of Zeke's ending had affected my Teagan greatly, especially the pain caused by the hate of one toward another. You spoke out to me 'bout that too, Bronze-Man. When we hiked to the dens and I rekindled with Grandpop (what a gift that was!), it helped me remember who I had been 'cause of him.

He had shared afore that Grandmom and he had lived out bad times caused by other folk. And it was for the strangest reason; Grandpop and Grandmom were colored differently—one from the other. Grandpop was dark, dark. I don't have a crayon that pics him good-right, he is all glossy and shiny. Grandmom was also hard to pic; she was white with a sprinkling of pink, all mixed together. She was even named Lilly for a milky flower from the country of Japan where she had been born.

Why some folks don't like the mixing of colors, I don't grasp. Stirring things together happens in life a whole lot more than…well there is no such thing as unstirring that I can ponder.

I do grasp that the ones who try to stop the stirring, most often end up getting in the way of your work, Bronze-Man. My momma has finally grasped that, while Zeke for sure did not.

I also grasp that I'm for sure not gonna stop stirring. My Teagan and I will be a good-right mix and our new little-folk will be her own special crayon color 'cause of us.

There it is, scratched out, my first mention of what is now happening in my body. I am both excited and fearful, but I'm told by Momma and others that those two emotions are natural for a mom-to-be.

How do I know our baby is gonna be a her? A new momma can usually tell. But if I have that grasping wrong, I ask your forgiveness, Jesus. You know best, what is, and what will be. I'm only asking that you help my Teagan and me teach our *her* or *him* 'bout your Love; the Love you have taught to us.

—And forgiveness; the thing you call grace? Help us teach that too, as a living thing in us; no matter what the stirring of our color.

Ga'al:

In just a few short days, it will be time. All of our new…kin, have chosen to follow with us on the adventure. My father—father, yes, I'm still reeling from your gift of our reunion; thank you!—has become a beacon of your light. He shared with me that mother was always hopeful, most always patient in her encouragement for him to divine your presence, Jesus. My father was always stubbornly resistant, convinced that humankind would rise on their own accord to a higher plain.

As I peer through the mirror of past times, dimly lit, you, Bridegroom, shine new light on their relationship, and how their divisions, divided me.

When my mother was blanked, and when the remaining people of the world showed their true colors, father became embittered and even more determined to reinvent society rather than turn to see your hand in it all.

That is why he gathered his clan. That is why he chose this isolated place to hone his men into his own new creation.

The parallels to my own venture are too blatant to be ignored. Before, I might have been divided, but I became my father's daughter. And now?

—I was asked by John, long ago. "What if I am wrong?"

Teagan had shared that his mentor had even expanded on that question, asking, "What if we are each, what if we are all, wrong?"

The consideration has bothered me all along this new walk of ours:

If we are all wrong, then what is the point of trying?

Now being rejoined with my father, I see what I was oblivious to for so long. That a father can be wrong, but so can a mother. I see that we each and all are fallible, but more importantly that we can also help one another, not by planting seeds of doubt or prideful ideas, but by helping, through example, the turning of our soul's attention toward the light of a Supreme Father's eyes; a Father who also has the Spiritual essence of a Mother, who knows His Creation through the eyes of a child, a son, a daughter, and who patiently, yet desperately desires to share His vision with us as a perfect family.

I bow to You now, my Father, and recognize Your Love. I thank You for the second, third and continued chances You have provided to bond with my daughter and her Teagan, with my earthly father and with all those who you have given us as kin. I know Your mercy for those wandering this planet blindly, is finite. But your grace is eternal. Help me now to be a miraculous example of what You do best: Loving an enemy into becoming a friend.

Just this morning, words from my previous life, inspired by you and spoken out by me in confusion, returned to my consciousness:

I must find you too John, and the boy, to tell you…something… something about forgiveness. What is it I must tell you? Will I remember it when I wake up?

You have opened my eyes, Lord, along with my heart. I realize, it was not only to John, not only to Teagan and Ilona and our kin, or my heavenly Father that I have to tell. There is another pain that has to be reconciled, one more healing. I have avoided it, even when bathed and baptized in my newfound love for you, Jesus.

As you, and my family have forgiven and love me, now it is myself I must forgive. Only then can I be completely reconciled.

On this trek, we have sought safe evening shelter, solace from storms and earthquakes, attacks, and injuries. Many of these come from outside forces, but some have come from within. You have been with us, with me, through it all and tomorrow we will begin the march to our next reunion.

More caves, more fires to stoke, and my thoughts take a new course, beginning with a question:

Where will your path lead me?

A powerful urge overcomes me. I can't explain it because it argues with everything I had come to believe. I had forbidden its practice, believing it to be the very evil that led us to our destruction. But now, just as you sternly, but Lovingly corrected your servant Paul long ago, so you, Spirit, are revealing a corrected Truth to me. It is breathed into me as a difficult, but wonderful phrase, a personal gift from you to me.

"Do not try, but instead follow and obey."

I realize now that it is not my seeking You that is most important. Of all the religions and belief systems I have dissected and dismissed, there is one spiritual reality that cannot be ignored. The truth is that You, Father God, pursue us, not the other way around, and it is up to us to receive rather than reject Your ways and Your embrace; serving You and sharing Your reality with others as You request, not as we invent our purpose to be.

And so, my trembling hand reaches out in defiance of my past beliefs. I take a piece of parch and with my other hand reach for the pen before me. I have not touched these tools in many years. Yet they feel a part of me, as if the implements had been rendered unusable by some diabolical force, and by you, are now redeemed. They beg to be used again. Stiffly I begin, scratching, made more alive with the flow of ink. The thoughts that have been swirling deep within my darkness, pulse onto the parch.

As if on cue, the sun in the sky, tears a rare break in the dust-clouded sky outside the cave. Its rays warm this place, and me within. I'm suddenly, encouraged to let all the memories, experiences, pain, and conflicts fly out. As my scripting quickens, I find drops of water hitting the page and realize they are my drops, raining nourishment for new growth onto a long droughted landscape.

It is time to blend my own story into theirs and release us all from burdens we no longer need carry. Lord. Let my words and my heart be acceptable to You, my God, and my Redeemer:

> —The smoke that shrouds the cave entrance invites only
> the brave to breach its mysteries. I once considered myself
> courageous and strong enough. But now, I am finally who
> I once fought never to be…

Outro

Why am I so sad? Why am I so troubled? I will put my hope in God, and once again I will praise him, my Savior, and my God.

—Psalm 43:5

Ilona:

HELP ME, BRONZE-MAN! I was warned that there would be no joy without pain, no new-life without suffering, but…Help me!

Teagan:

I can't focus—too many things at once: Strobing orbs of flame that singe us as they plummet from the night sky, earth-shattering explosions around us, deluging death vaporizing friends close by; and closer, louder, more blinding still, the repeated screams of my beloved, "Help me!"

We have endured so many unspeakable calamities throughout our wilderness journey: Attacks by animals and humans alike. Blistering heat and killing cold. Poisonous air and miles of wasteland void of water. Somehow our kin have all overcome, together, until now.

In the night, a groaning next to me invaded my sleep. There is no cave or cove for shelter in this place, and so we had all bed-down on the open ground, exhausted from a long-day's travel.

The groaning came from my bride, Ilona, and I was instantly awake to the realization that it is "her time". Our child comes. Now something else is fighting for my attention, a sound like I once heard coming from a jet aircraft flying at low altitude, a sound of supersonic power, scraping friction in the sky above. Meteors.

They have come down before, the havoc they wreak is well understood, but this is different…terribly more. The rocks above us avalanche in countless numbers. There is nowhere to hide as they choose their helpless targets below. And Ilona, on the ground, her legs bent and cramped close, stares beyond the fire-filled atmosphere, pleading to the heavens for sanctuary from a greater pain.

I am helpless before her on my knees, not knowing how to help. A rocketing boulder explodes on the ground only yards away and I'm tossed like a pebble, almost landing full force on the laboring mother. My extended arms catch my fall just in time, but a snap and agonizing sting signal that my right arm has been broken. Somehow I stay hovering as a poor tent over my convulsing bride, protecting her from flying debris caused by the nearby strike. Dirt, rocks, and body parts slap at me, trying to attack the treasure below that I cover.

"Move!" Its Ga'al, who unapologetically pushes me to the side and herself assuming the role of guardian. I wonder at why until I feel the dripping from my head and realize I have been badly gashed on my head.

There is no time for my own injuries. Ilona begs for a work of mercy. I crawl to a position at her feet and by the light of the phosphorus inferno raining down, I'm able to see between her legs, a glossy protrusion, the crown of a tiny head, pulsing and expanding, trying with the mother's help to escape from darkness into brilliant life; into a world that might kill us all at any moment.

Ga'al knows the moment well, sensing and seeing the struggle of the dame beneath her. "Push!" she yells inches away from the face of her screeching daughter.

And Ilona obeys. I can't see her face; her mother protects her from the barrage pelting us from above. Steam from tiny flaming pellets hitting The amazon's back, and that I know must be striking me too, tinge the air with a sulfuric odor, choking our lungs and voices. Still, I find enough breath to join the command, "push!"

And the head of our child fully emerges, with my wife's last scream in contraction. With difficulty, I am able to receive the gift delivered. My good arm slides beneath the tiny naked life and I pull it to my belly, bending over to protect her from the surrounding calamity.

Two trembling hands appear. They reach from nearby to the infant, extending to touch and massage the youngling I nestle. Quickly, a squalling cry comes from my daughter's mouth. I am transfixed as I watch the little one fight as her mother fought, as her grandmother fought for survival. I do not look away from her but recognize the additional hands that have come in to be those of Ga'al. They now have produced a familiar blade which expertly cuts the life cord connecting mother to child. The new life is freed to battle on her own.

I sense the storm above is moving away. The air quiets and we are left for a moment in a smoldering darkness. A warm breeze brushes my face and I hear the soft gasps of my beautiful bride asking, "Please, let me hold her."

I struggle not to stumble as I lift and pass our baby gingerly into the arms of her greatest earthly provider. I marvel for a moment as mother cradles her new love, and then I notice the umbilical is still stringing from her uterus.

"One more good push please." It is Ga'al beside me who whispers and then helps me extract the final birth-mass from Ilona's sweating and fatigued body.

I turn to the gallant amazon and am about to thank her, when I see her slump to the side and down onto the still smoking ground by her daughter and granddaughter.

"Momma?" Ilona whimpers into the darkness.

At that moment, the wind carries away enough of the clouds and dust to reveal by moon's light, that one life has been traded for another.

This is another of those memories that will forever burn in the present tense of what remains of my life.

Ilona:

Bronze-Man Jesus, you crayon for me a deeper grasping of how our trek was all planned out afore. You inspired Papa Ramon y Mama Maria to offer The Way Back Home map, humbly and lovingly to me. I wonder if, at the time, they realized the sacrifice it would require of them, and now of us.

But you didn't stop your afore-planning there. Making our way through the hateful landscape toward the Mexicos, we merged with other small bands of travelers—all of them, incredibly, blue—to become one roving wave of a clan-tribe. Any other group seeing our approach would be nerve-wracked by our shared glowing and the blasting notes from the ram's horns my Teagan and I played along the way. Marching along with our clan and blowing, I ponder us to look like the Israelites of old, on their exodus trek. Just like our Good News book tells 'bout them, I grasp for sure that we too don't look like a tasty treat for attackers: And for that, we all give good-right thanks.

We have lost and buried many loves along the way, not the least being my momma. Each of their blue was strong, but this world has shown it no longer stomachs-well that particular coloring. Our fallen kin are terribly missed. We grasp by the watching of their auras rising to the heavens when they pass, that we too will rise and gather with them once more, soon enough.

I must, we must, not forget 'afore-times', to avoid their hurtful replaying. So, not only do I scratch more and more, but also I read the parch to remember it good-right. My Tegan and I are collecting and grouping together our parch-ponderings, along with those of my amazing mom-dame. As I re-read our separate stories, I see a new tale coming alive. Where we were so separate, now You have color-mixed us all together good-right, readying us for some new adventure full-known only to you, Abba God.

Our sharings remind me too, that we had not started as simple servants, all ready to say, "yes" to you without question. We are a *walking-work* of your making, Bronze-Man—learning all along the way what "yes" really means to you.

One thing I know for sure, Abba God; You put inside of me, a warrior's heart. I am fearfully and wonderfully made. But what I have learned, by my ponderings, is that your wanting for me is not to fight against you; but to battle for you, in the way you want my battling to be.

Can I teach others to full-trust Your plan when I still rock-hard resist? Can any of us win our self-war that way? Can we learn the new way altogether; readying ourselves to accept the battles and sacrificing necessary? I'm trying, Bronze-Man; trying beyond the loss of my momma, my dad, Caiden, and the others. I'm trying to grasp the perfectness of your Love. Your desire is now deep-rooted in me; more and more I am depending on you, not on myself or any other.

So, we trust your commanding. My Teagan and I risk our flank by sharing the deepest hurts and happiness of our parched stories with all our kin. They deserve to know…the "all" of it. I ponder that someday, our daughter Chaya, and her soon-to-be brother or sister, will be struck most by our scratch and crayoning. My story, all our stories, are only partly known. That has been for a purpose; to protect her and all of us. Now I see that we have protected too much. Understanding our struggles and your saving-healing ways in those times, Bronze-Man, will not damage, but 'stead, it will sing of your redeeming-war; your Love song, your battling to seek still more of your lost ones.

And Abba God, we, your found-ones, your family, will journey on, battling together as You have taught me through Bronze-Man Jesus. I will fight for them, and them for me, holding one another closely, patiently soothing, sharing our grief, our tears, and laughter, and Your saving; just as I imagine it will be when You hold us close.

Help me by Your Love, by the Grace of Your Son and by fellowshipping with Your matron Spirit, to be a good-right warrior-mother and bride. Help me share Your tenderness with my Teagan, my children, my grandchild, and with all our…Your kin.

Teagan:

Savior, I'm grateful you do not reveal in advance, the full extent of struggle and agony each new step of our travels will entail. It might convinced me to abort the undertaking, against your purpose. Not only the deadly meteor shower, but a lack of drinking water, near starvation, superheated lava pits, hurricane force winds, more earthquakes and other violence have not abated. Through those and more, we have lost loved ones, but too have gained some. The "new blue" as I call them, have somehow persevered as we have; all miraculously being joined by your hand according to your cosmic timing throughout our exodus.

There is always celebration when they join us, not only for their spiritual contribution to our body, but also because of their knowledge of that particular region which we are negotiating. Every time I start doubting the accuracy of our "map of hope", you provide a contingent who verify our location, point us to water and whatever scant resources might be available. They contribute to our story with their own accounts of loss, survival, and revelation.

Ilona and I try to mingle with our growing kin as best we can under the circumstances. Each has similar dreams, visions and voices that are leading them to our mysterious rendezvous. All contribute to our common biography. Every evening we strive to keep kindled, weather permitting, the tradition of the fire-sharings. By the embers of those gatherings, the two of us work to compile what is quickly becoming a book of histories for some future sharing which we do not yet understand.

Along our way, Father Matada has become a great champion, assigning duties to individuals, ordering our plans, listening intently to the needs of the masses, and doing his best to find ways of distributing our meager provisions in a way that will see us through to our destination.

That destination? The Mexicos still remain elusive to us. Ramon and Maria's Way Back Home map is well drawn but does not offer a scale or measure of distances. All we know is that each feature it presents is eventually come upon. That gives us hope as we walk out the next steps of the mystery atlas.

Ilona:

It has been a long trek for sure. By the old counting, near seven years. I'm not just measuring the trek from the clan-dens toward the Mexicos. I'm telling the time of our whole story, from the Blanking to right-now. Bronze-Man Jesus, now after all that time, I have a confession. You know it already, but I want to scratch it and speak it out all the same. Things I thought would be better after my marriage to my Teagan, after your work in me, after the birth of sweet Chaya, still seem downside-up in ways.

Afore, there was plenty of sadness buzzing around inside of me, trying to poke and sting me like the Rippers tried to do. But when you gave and took back Momma and Dad; when you gave me back my grandpop and my Teagen, and most special for the two of us, Chaya, I thought the sad would be finally done.

When we are all finished with this rough trek, I had pondered that the only leftover rough stuff might be my next birthing (Please Bronze-Man let that time be less crazy than the last!). Now I grasp that my low-low days will likely stay on inside me; that it is natural for me to be gloomy. Days will still show up when moving is hard. Those days, the doing will still be harder, and wanting to be happy will be work—hard work. Sure, my dark will not be like afore—you are already helping to lighten it—but it will still return. For letting it still happen, I think somedays I'm mad at you. Why not just end it altogether?

There's a story of yours in our Good News book telling that you will, "…wipe away all tears." And it also says. "…no more grief or crying or pain."

When does that come? I only ponder its time, but you grasp the time for sure. Can you speak it out to me more clearly? I'm grasping that your Good News words spoke it out long ago and that I am just not yet skilled with the grasping of it. So, I need your help with finding the truth of it. I grasp now (please tell me if mine is a good-right pondering), that you still let me have gloominess and to be near-to-dark; so that I can help others who don't know what light looks like; so that I can help them see your light?

I grasp that my helping them, my scratching life and crayoning life and living life with you as my light, no matter how close to dark life seems, is your good-right purpose for me. Bronze-Man, unless you tell me different, that's what will be my joy.

Anyone reading this scratch or hearing me speak it out might blab, "These are not the words of Ilona, they are too soft—she shows herself on the outside to be tough and hard." Have you not been hearing? I have down times, just as all folk have down times. Remember my momma's *mom-dame story*; remember my story. I chose to trek away from my old dark ways, but it will always try to catch up.

I once pondered my tale to be a private thing. But maybe there are other folks lots like me who need to hear it for sewing back together their own hearts? If so, simple enough; here it is:

> Your healing, Bronze-Man, through the telling of my story, your light, making my light turn on; is being scratched and crayoned for any others who want to see, and light up their own dark. I don't grasp yet if there is more purpose than that, 'cept to help me, and maybe others, feel and live good-right, together.

I want my words to speak out good-right. These are my keeps; this is my new way, your way, Bronze-Man. I don't grasp if any other folk aside from my close-kin will ever read the scratch or see the crayoning you are giving me to do. I know it is scratched and colored way different from the fancy way my Teagan tells and Momma told it. It's the tale of my heart's tearing apart and of your sewing it back together.

Bronze-Man, one big thing I have grasped by the light you give for helping me see past my dark living, is that your plan is brighter than all light and dark.

Brighter light is Your will for us.

Teagan:

A full year of passage through the treacherous deserts and volcanic lakes of the vast badlands has finally come to an end. Miles off, the shifting of the wind and the smell of salt air, promised unmistakably that we were nearing the ocean. What we did not know was what awaited us at its shores. It was decided that a small group of us would scout the area before exposing our entire complement to any risk of hostility. I, Father Matada, and Ellen volunteered to recon ahead. I remember intensely, our first sighting of the ragtag armada docked in the bay waters.

We had hiked a ways from our kin and came to a small rise consisting of dunes which took some trudging to negotiate. There at the crest we first spied the makeshift harbor. At encountering the sight, the three of us fell to our knees. Like the waves cascading over the rocks surrounding the inlet before us, the swirl of our emotions in that moment are still not easily described.

Ellen and I cried silently, while Matada shared his wailing sobs. Each of us were struck by the realization that the prophetic map of hope that had guided us here, was indeed the product of your divine providence, Lord Jesus.

When we finally stood at the gangplank leading up to what appeared to be the largest ship, a sole figure emerged from a hatch in the vessel and approached us. His name was Jason, and he had the most archaic of southern American accents I ever remember. Yet his powerful compassion and easygoing personality immediately washed away any fears we may have held.

As we climbed the walkway together to enter the ship, I was reminded of what we had gone through, apart and together to arrive at this place. It was not spoken, but I knew we each wanted John, Ga'al, and all those we had lost along the way, to have experienced this ecstatic moment with us.

At the hatch, we stopped briefly. Matada ran his fingers across the rusty hull. I could almost hear his thoughts as my own...*will this bucket carry us or sink us?*

"Your will, Father," we both spoke out at the same time and at that, we shared a loud, very special laugh.

We were brought before an unusual council. It was headed by Jason who seemed a natural servant-leader. Another man, not much more than a boy, stood by him. He had a slate tablet with paper clipped to it and he busied himself with writing. His actions reminded me of the court reporters I frequently observed in congress, scribing history as it happened. I liked this young man, Küllo, most, without yet knowing him in depth; seeing much of my younger self in his focused character.

To Jason's other side was a beautiful woman of native American decent whom I recognized immediately. She was the daughter of the once United States President, Blueroad. Ayita sadly shared that her father had died in an incident involving the nefarious Darius Mede in the land of New Israel.

Another spectacular specimen, a man simply introduced by the others as Black Jackson stood silently behind them. Every time I glanced at him; a peace I cannot describe washed over me. Oddly, he carried what I thought to be a child in a harness strapped to his chest. Upon more careful observation (no, her voice actually entered my thoughts!) she corrected me and jokingly explained that she was the *big cheese* for this operation. Big is not how I would have described Ki until I learned the size of her heart.

Next to those two stood another woman they called Roxanne. She was introduced but did not immediately offer up her story, remaining a mystery for the moment.

Speaking of stories—in rapid fire we are caught up on an overwhelming number of world events that have been affecting the Earth and its remaining inhabitants during our isolation.

Apparently, Darius Mede the infamous climate advocate and scientist had created a substance called Flexsteel that has enabled some of the world's population to protect themselves from the ravaging elements that plague the entire planet.

Although Mede's design has found great purpose in this moment, his other actions have been deplorable beyond the pale. Not only has he raised up an army of cloned beings to do his bidding, but now he is in attack mode against all believers in you, Bronzeman. His close associate, Johnathan Trible continually tries to misrepresent and distort your purpose through his media distribution. Thankfully, we are told, Küllo, along with a distant helper named Han Ko, have found a means of sharing the spiritual victories you have been accomplishing through your people. Each day, reports through Ki's visions, announce the growing numbers of Blue. And that reminded me. I am so used to it now, I almost forgot to share that all on this ship, and all on the other ships are Blue!

Ga'al had once shared her assessment of Mede's character with us, but I don't believe even she would now comprehend how profoundly he has abused his great talents. We are all aghast when Jason also shares that the two witnesses, described in Biblical prophecy, had also appeared and it was Mede's forces who caused their final demise. The Southerner testified that the blue of the two, Moses Folzman and Fitzgerald Elijah Hindeland, rose most brightly.

More of the God-work is ultimately unveiled by Roxanne who finally shared a significant portion of her history. She reveals that she encountered a young scientist by the name of Danny Adamson who began experiencing strong visions about the impending cataclysm soon to be unleashed on the planet. He and a small number of others, tried to warn world leaders, including Darius Mede of the impending doom. But it was to no avail. During this period, just as the micro-quasar, V4641 made its approach, Bronzeman revealed himself to the skeptic, Danny. He ultimately discovered his faith and, in that moment was changed. Danny became physiologically and spiritually connected with Bronzeman beyond what any others before had experienced. He was the first to become *Blue*—the perfect reflected essence of Jesus' eternal light.

Another astounding mystery is given light. We are taken out on the deck of the ship to examine its bow. Like the fronts of all ships anchored here, it sports an engraved emblem. It is the three interlocking circles of the triune God!

Jason says they were spiritually led to inscribe the logo. All had sensed there should be more to the emblazing, but no-one had been able to agree on what that would be. At that moment, the three of us pulled up the sleeves of our tunics to reveal the three circles with John Portunus' Hebrew icons etched within. It was the turn of all those we had just met to drop to the deck and weep.

I wish Ilona had been there to witness that reaction. It was at her beckoning that her mother and I joined with her in the branding of the symbol on our upper arms. When her grandfather had seen the work displayed, he too insisted on receiving the mark, as did every other member of what my bride refers to as our clan-tribe.

And so, we returned to Ilona and the others, who had waited patiently for us just beyond the dunes. We shared with them, our great encounter and revealed another discovery laid out by Jason and Küllo. We now have a new destination! By your plan, Lord, we are headed for, of all places, New Israel! There, we are told, we will meet another amazing individual named Ilbani the Keeper. I have no idea as of yet about his importance. The time is come for our sailing adventure and all are ready to cast off.

As we file up the gangway for the last time, I turn to my beloved and share with her that I feel like a passenger entering Noah's ark. She looks at me, puzzled, and I'm struck that she does not yet know the story. I share an abbreviated version and she smiles. Then she replies, "Bronzeman too is our ark." Ilona has always possessed the ability to simply convey the deeper things you desire for us to share, Bronzeman. Praise you for her touch to my life.

We have found a different kind of haven in which to rest; not a cave, not dug in and cowering beneath mounds of dirt waiting out a storm, but deep within the hold of a sailing vessel. This place is still foreign to Ilona and me. Here, men and women have stood side by side, hand in hand throughout the turbulent times. What my beautiful bride and I had to once keep in hiding, here is openly shared. But how can we adequately share with our new kin, our struggles of old. Is it even important? Haven't we all suffered unique individual trials?

We have met privately with Küllo after sharing our journals and histories—our…parch-scratch—with the Tartulian. He believes our stories to be so significant that he has asked permission to meld the War of the Lost Song, as he has titled our history, with the histories of all those he has encountered in his travels. The young reporter tells us that his and our documentaries will be kept protected in another location for a greater revealing later.

Küllo also shares a significant unveiling. It seems that the reason these ships and missionaries even exist is by your calling, Bronzeman, to gather the remaining remnant of the 144,000, mentioned in the book of Revelation. He and the other leaders of this quest believe that we, in this region of the world, are that remnant. Our return to your Promised Land, as a part of this group, is an overwhelming honor. None of us feel worthy. All of us are reminded that our struggles have strengthened us for some future work in your soon-coming Kingdom…

—The Blanking, our suffering and self-persecution, all of it, is overcome by you. A new age is begun, heralded by the raising of our ships' anchors. Our eyes have been opened and our purpose unfolds!

Ilona:

Today is a good-right day. We stand on the decks of our boats ready to launch. I look across the bay and can't grasp the coming together of it all. I catch site of one of the other larger boats and see it's deck filled with passengers garbed like plains-people. Maybe all or a part are the digies who had disappeared from the Barrens, that my Teagan described. He hopes to connect with them soon to find out. I am joy-filled to see them, and so many other crayon-colors of folks sailing besides us.

I hold Chaya in my arms, so that she too can see the many boats, and whisper to her that our ships will carry us to a very different land. I know she and all our spiritual kin; those who have been ended, those who live, and those who are still to come, will all call it home. We are told that New Israel has been re-made too, and that you, Bronze-Man, are soon to be our King—not just as a visiting spirit, but as flesh and blood. I can hardly ponder how beauty-filled it will be to meet you face-to-face.

I have learned here in this place that you are known as *Jesu,* and in our soon-to-be new home, you are called *Yeshua.* But when we all come together, when we bow in our Love for you, will you give us all one name to know you by? Our Good News book says that's going to be the way of it. I grasp that the day I hear and speak that name out, my dark will disappear and my living will be forever lit.

A Mexico Islander, a broad-shouldered wreck, climbs one of the masts of our vessel. At its peak, he mounts what my Teagan calls a crow's nest.

The Islander faces down to us on the deck and then looks out to the other boats. With a smile he waves in great sweeping strokes to everyone and yells out, "Unidos! Unidos!"

Every voice on every boat erupts in response, "En Jesu Unidos", En Jesu Unidos!" The Islander leans down and motions for my Teagan and me to join him on the high place. I pass Chaya into the arms of her great-grandpop and begin the climb. Our second child is not yet swelled in my belly so going up is not much work. We have a purpose in our climb which we have been practicing for. "En Jesu Unidos," goes on, and when we reach the nest, the chant transitions into a song. It is new, a tune that my Teagan and I also birthed together. You, Bronze-Man Jesus sung its notes into our matched hearts, much like you sung new notes into my dad's and momma's hearts; much as you have sung into the heart of each Blue on these boats, and beyond.

Ours is a good-right sonnet-song, Lord, scribed by our pens. We have taught it to our kin in the wilds, with all its shouts and whispers. It is your teaching—The story of your miracle made alive in each of us, all of us.

We sang out our song as we climbed over the dunes, and as one, up the gangplank to meet our sisters and brothers; who had waited so long for our arriving.

My Teagan and I sing with all of them now. Then, bringing our shofars to our lips, we both blow together, one long clear beauty-filled blast. It is our clarion call, taught to both of us by my dad. It sings out over the waters and beyond, that we are coming to be with our King.

The two of us then play in practiced cadence, the wholeness of our living song. We are joined in it by all our kin; each in their distinctive harmonies, language, and experiences. My Teagan looks toward me, and one tear is blown from his cheek by the wind. It flies away, seeking to blend with the chop of the sea below, joining with the flying tears of all those sailing with us. Our memories, our past sorrows, along with our present joy, overflow to help float us on our way, buoyed with new hope. This is our time of joining, our time of shared worship of you, Bronze-Man.

Will they be our last tears? I don't grasp the answer: what is Your will, Abba God? What is Your timing for our future?. You are still crayoning Your pic. I find hope that each of us, all of us, can come to grasp the beauty of the symphony of reconciliation You sing with us. Our together-song is found; no longer lost; and is shared by all the voices and stories surrounding us:

Burning war rages 'round me, I'm blinded by its flames
Alone, in desperation; healer hidden, without name.
My wounds bleed into darkness, sinking down, my body cries
I am no-one, in the ashes, seeking something I can't find

Others wander with me on this dark and barren plain
Yet silently we travel, never sharing, seems in-sane
Still, I wonder, like me, are there any in the crowd
Who seek the question's answer that we cannot speak a-loud?

Is there hope, or has our anger, snuffed out that ember's glow?
Is there peace or has chaos crushed the power of its hold?
Why bother with the dreams of a long-forgotten time?
Can the question find its answer, to bring me back…?

Are we hunted, hiding lay, to e-scape the arrow's flight?
Are we hunters after prey, hunger screaming deep inside?
Are we both, inside confusion, just wrestling to survive?
Is there another wanting someone from the ashes to revive?

Is there someone with desire to heal, to redeem?
Can I find another's heart to fill this hole inside of me?
Is there anyone who cares, any searching same as I?
To bring breath to the passion that will bring me back…

As I lay in desperation, comes a voice from far outside
Bringing beauty with a touch, the impossible to find
I am raptured in a moment, caught up by loving-kind
Tender-mercy quench the flames and bring me back…

There is hope, hear its song in the rush of rising tide
Compassion tames the chaos with an everlasting light

You've fed my heart's desire, now we beat within its rhyme
The question finds its answer, you have loved me back…
to life.

The question finds its answer, you have loved us back…
to life.

As our praise floats out over the waters, I grasp that, to find our true Love, a war must be fought inside each of us. And through that battling, each, and any of us, can learn the song of that Love, first sung by you, Bronze-Man.

He brought me to his banquet hall and raised the banner of love over me.

—Song of Solomon 2:4

AUTHOR
MARK A. CORNELIUS

MARK A. CORNELIUS has authored numerous books, video productions, a journal ministry, musicals, and several podcast series.

His works include *RUT Management—Discovering Adventure in the Routine of Life, Believement—Breaking Through the Belief Barrier, Welfare Christianity, Thunder Buffalo Goes Home, Tomorrow's Bread, Marginalized, UnMeasuring—What if we are ALL Wrong?* and the popular fiction series The Ruach Saga (*including The Singularity, The Book of Seconds, Bronzeman, and War of the Lost Song*).

His books can be purchased at https://quantumdiscovery.net/shop/, and at www.RUTmanagement.com.

Amos 3:6-8, The Bible

Mark has authored other insights and blogs, all of which can be obtained on his website. You can experience Mark's passion for writing at **www.MarkCornelius.me**.

Catch Mark's podcasts at:

Watchmen podcast:
https://www.youtube.com/channel/UC3fA03AhXRh RZNhNyrEhgA

Mark My Words (Critical Thinking) podcast:
https://www.youtube.com/channel/UCR8Csunh9mJMOZHjT97NUZg

Travel with Mark at his blog: **www.DeepEndFaith.blogspot.com**, and dive into discussion on **E-mail: Markcwrites@gmail.com**, or **Facebook: https://www.facebook.com/Mark-My-Words-103741988034911**.

Join Mark in asking his ongoing journey question…

"WHAT IF?"

Looking forward to our journey together!

ILLUSTRATOR - Shay Cavender was born in Nashville, Tennessee. She began her drawing career at a young age doodling and writing short comic strips. Her unique style specializes in animals both real and fantastical. Currently she is a student at the University of Tennessee at Martin as a Graphic Design major. She plays Trombone in the UTM Marching Skyhawk Band and aims to continue playing her instrument later in life despite her art-oriented career direction. Drawing and illustrating are her passions along with her love of animals including dogs and reindeer. In the future, Shay hopes to secure a profession that will utilize her distinctive talents.